"ANOTHER WINNER"
—*Atlantic Monthly*

"One of the English language's best living mystery writers!" —*St. Louis Post-Dispatch*

"Spellbinding . . . marvelous . . . devastating . . . a Gold Medal winner for certain" —*Publishers Weekly*

"An exceedingly taut tale . . . literate, witty, sophisticated" —*Boston Globe*

"Ingenious . . . excellent . . . suspense as taut as the last seconds of a race" —*Chicago Tribune Book World*

Books by Dick Francis

Blood Sport
Bonecrack
Dead Cert
Enquiry
Flying Finish
For Kicks
Forfeit
High Stakes
In the Frame
Knockdown
Nerve
Odds Against
Rat Race
Risk
Slayride
Smokescreen
Trial Run
Whip Hand

Published by POCKET BOOKS

Dick Francis

TRIAL RUN

PUBLISHED BY POCKET BOOKS NEW YORK

POCKET BOOKS, a Simon & Schuster division of
GULF & WESTERN CORPORATION
1230 Avenue of the Americas, New York, N.Y. 10020

Copyright © 1978 by Dick Francis

Published by arrangement with Harper & Row, Publishers
Library of Congress Catalog Card Number: 78-20204

ISBN: 0-671-83186-0

First Pocket Books printing August, 1980

10 9 8 7 6 5 4 3

POCKET and colophon are trademarks of Simon & Schuster.

Printed in the U.S.A.

Thanks

to

Andrew and Andrew

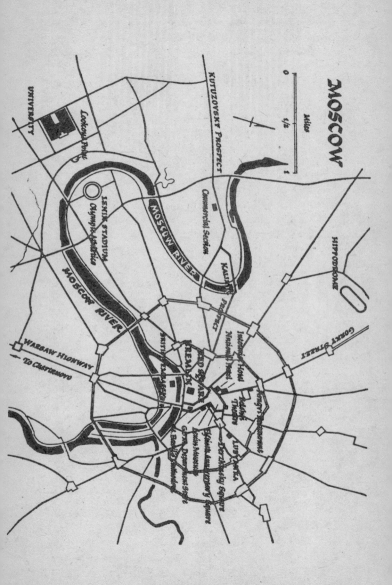

MOSCOW

Miles
0   1/2   1

KUTUZOVSKY PROSPECT

UNIVERSITY

Lookout Point

LENIN STADIUM
Olympic Arena

MOSCOW RIVER

Commercial Section

MOSCOW RIVER

Kalinin Prospect

HIPPODROME

GORKY STREET

WARSAW HIGHWAY

To Chazemovo

St. Elizabeth

KREMLIN

Red Square

Intourist Hotel
National Hotel

Bolshoi
Theatre
Sverdlov Square

Lenin Museum
GUM Dept. Store
Dzerzhinsky Square

Metropole Hotel
Marx Square

1

I could think of three good reasons for not going to Moscow, one of which was twenty-six, blond, and upstairs unpacking her suitcase.

"I can't speak Russian," I said.

"Of course not."

My visitor took a genteel sip of pink gin, sighing slightly over my obtuseness. His voice was condescending.

"No one would expect you to speak Russian."

He had come by appointment, introduced on the telephone by a friend of a friend. He said his name was Rudolph Hughes-Beckett; that it was a matter of some—ah—delicacy. That he would be glad of my help, if I could spare him half an hour.

The word "mandarin" had drifted into my mind when I opened the front door to his ring, and every gesture, every intonation since then had deepened the impression. A man of about fifty, tall and spare, with uncreased clothes and quiet shoes. An aura of unflappable civilized composure. A cultivated voice speak-

1

ing without much lip movement, as if a muscular tight-
ening round the mouth area could in itself prevent the
issue of incautious words. There was control, too, in
every movement of his hands and even in the way he
used his eyes, rationing their forays into small courteous glances at my background between longer disciplined concentrations on my face, the backs of his
own hands, or the glass holding his drink.

I had met many men of his type, and liked many,
too, but to Rudolph Hughes-Beckett I felt an antipa-
thy I couldn't pin down. Its effect, however, was all
too plain: I wished to say no to his proposals.

"It would not take a great deal of your time," he
said patiently. "A week . . . two weeks, we calculate,
at a maximum."

I mustered a careful politeness to match his own.
"Why don't you go yourself?" I said. "You would
have better access than I."

The faintest hint of impatience twitched in his eyes.
"It is thought better to send someone who is intimate
with—ah—horses."

Ribald replies got no further than a laugh in the
mind. Rudolph Hughes-Beckett would not have been
amused. I perceived also, from the disapproving way
he said "horses," that he was as unenthusiastic about
his present errand as I was. It did nothing to warm me
toward him, but at least it explained why I instinctively disliked him. He had done his well-trained best,
but hadn't in that one word been able to disguise his
inner feeling of superciliousness—and I had met that
stance far too often to mistake it.

"No cavaliers in the Foreign Office?" I said flippantly.

"I beg your pardon?"

"Why me?" I said, and heard in the question all the
despair of the unwillingly chosen. Why *me?* I don't
want it. Take it away. Pick someone else. Leave me
alone.

"I gather it was felt you should be approached because you have—ah—status," he said, and smiled faintly as if deprecating such an extravagant statement. "And of course," he added, "the time."

A right kick in the guts, I thought; and kept my face flat and still. I took off my glasses and squinted at them against the light, as if trying to see if they were clean, and then put them back on again. It was a delaying tactic I had used all my life, most often unconsciously, to give myself a space for thought—a habit that had started when I was about six and a schoolmaster asked me in an arithmetic lesson what I had done with the multiplicand.

I had pulled off my owllike silver rims and stared at his suddenly fuzzy outline while I thought wild panicky thoughts. What on earth was a multiplicand?

"I haven't seen it, sir. It wasn't me, sir."

His sardonic laugh had stayed with me down the years. I had exchanged the silver rims for gold, and then for plastic, and finally for tortoise shell, but I still took them off when I couldn't answer.

"I've got a cough," I said. "And it is November."

The frivolousness of this excuse was measured by a deepening silence and a gradual reverential bowing of the Hughes-Beckett head over the crystal tumbler.

"I'm afraid that the answer is no," I said.

He raised his head and gave me a calm, civil inspection. "There will be some disappointment," he said. "I might almost go as far as to say—ah—dismay."

"Flatter someone else," I said.

"It was felt that *you* . . ." He left the words unfinished, hanging in the air.

"Who felt?" I asked. "Who, exactly, felt?"

He shook his head gently, put down the emptied glass, and rose to his feet.

"I will convey your reply."

"And regrets," I said.

"Very well, Mr. Drew."

"I wouldn't have been successful," I said. "I'm not an investigator. I'm a farmer."

He gave me a sort of sideways down-the-nose look where a less inhibited man would have said, "Come off it."

I walked with him into the hall, helped him on with his coat, opened the front door, and watched him walk bareheaded through the icy dark to his waiting chauffeur-driven Daimler. He gave me, by way of farewell, merely a five-second full frontal view of his bland expression through the window. Then the big car crunched away on the gravel toward the gate, and I coughed in the cold air and went back inside.

Emma was walking down the oval sweep of Regency staircase in her Friday-evening come-for-the-weekend clothes: jeans, cotton check shirt, baggy sweater and cowboy boots. I wondered fleetingly whether, if the house stood for as long again, the girls of the twenty-second century would look as incongruous against those gracefully curving walls.

"Fish fingers and the telly, then?" she said.

"More or less."

"You've got bronchitis again."

"It isn't catching."

She reached the bottom of the stairs and made without pause toward the kitchen. It always took a while with her for the brittle stresses of the week to drop away, and I was used to the jerky arrivals and the spiky brush-offs of the first few hours. I no longer tried to greet her with warmth. She wouldn't be kissed much before ten, nor loved before midnight, and she wouldn't relax until Saturday teatime. Sunday we would slop around in easy contentment, and at six on Monday morning she would be gone.

Lady Emma Louders-Allen-Croft, daughter, sister, and aunt of dukes, was "into," as she would say, "the working-girl ethos." She was employed full time, no favors, in a bustling London department store, where, despite her search for social abasement, she had recently been promoted to bed linen buyer on the second floor. Emma, blessed with organizational skills above the average, was troubled about her rise, a screw-up one could trace back directly to her own schooling, where she, in an expensive boarding school for high-born young ladies, had been taught in fierily left-wing sociology lessons that brains were elitist and that manual work was the noble path to heaven.

Her search for immolation, which had led to exhausting years of serving at tables in cafés as well as behind the counters in shops, seemed to be as strong as ever. She would in no way have starved without employment, but might quite likely have gone to drink or pot.

I believed, and she knew I did, that someone with her abilities and restless drive should have taken a proper training, or at least gone to university, and contributed more than a pair of hands; but I had learned not to talk about it, as it was one of the many no man's lands which led to shrieks and sulks.

"Why the hell do you bother with that mixed-up kook?" my stepbrother frequently asked. Because, as I never told him, a shot of undiluted life force every couple of weekends was better for the heart than his monotonous daily jogging.

Emma was looking into the refrigerator, the light shining out of it onto her fine-boned face and thick platinum hair. Her eyebrows were so pale as to be invisible without pencil, and her lashes the same without mascara. Sometimes she made up her eyes like sunbursts; sometimes, like that evening, she let nature take its course. It depended on the tide of ideas.

"Haven't you any yogurt?" she demanded.

I sighed. A flood of health foods was not my favorite. "Nor wheat germ either," I said.

"Kelp," she said firmly.

"What?"

"Seaweed. Compressed into tablets. Very good for you."

"I'm sure."

"Apple cider vinegar. Honey. Organically grown vegetables."

"Are we off avocados and hearts of palm?"

She pulled out a chunk of Dutch cheese and scowled at it. "They're imported. We should limit imports. We need a siege economy."

"No more caviar?"

"Caviar is immoral."

"Would it be immoral if it was plentiful and cheap?"

"Stop arguing. What did your visitor want? Are these cream caramels for supper?"

"Yes, they are," I said. "He wanted me to go to Moscow."

She straightened up and glared at me. "That's not very funny."

"A month ago you said cream caramels were food for angels."

"Don't be stupid."

"He said he wanted me to go to Moscow. On an errand, not to embrace the Marxist-Leninist philosophy."

She slowly shut the refrigerator door.

"What sort of errand?"

"He wanted me to look for somebody. But I'm not going."

"Who?"

"He didn't say." I turned away from her. "Come and have a drink in the sitting room. There's a fire in there."

She followed me back through the hall and folded herself into a large armchair with a glass of white wine.

"How are the pigs, geese, and mangold-wurzels?"

"Coming along nicely," I said.

I had no pigs, geese, or, indeed, mangold-wurzels. I had a lot of beef cattle, three square miles of War-wickshire, and all the modern problems of the food producer. I had grown used to measuring yield in tons per hectare, but was still unconvinced by government policies which paid me sometimes *not* to grow certain crops and threatened to prosecute me if I did.

"And the horses?" Emma said.

"Ah, well . . ."

I stretched out lazily in my chair and watched the light from the table lamp fall on her silvery head, and decided it was really high time I stopped wincing over the thought that I would be riding in no more races.

"I suppose I'll sell the horses," I said.

"There's still hunting."

"It's not the same. And those are not hunters. They're race horses. They should be on a track."

"You've trained them all these years. . . . Why don't you just get someone else o ride them?"

"I only trained them because I was riding them. I don't want to do it for anyone else."

She frowned. "I can't imagine you without horses."

"Well," I said. "Nor can I."

"It's a bloody shame."

"I thought you subscribed to the 'we know what's best for you and you'll damn well put up with it' school of thought."

"People have to be protected from themselves," she said.

"Why?"

She stared. "Of course they do."

"Safety precautions are a growth industry," I said with some bitterness. "Masses of restrictive legislation to stop people taking everyday risks . . . and accidents go right on happening, and we have terrorists besides."

"You're still in a right tizz, aren't you?"

"Yes."

"I thought you'd got over it."

"The first fury may have worn off," I said. "The resentment will last forever."

I had been lucky in my racing, lucky in my horses,

and steeplechasing had taken me, as it had so many others, to soul-filling heights and depths of passion and fear and triumphant exaltation. Left to myself, I would in that autumn have been busily racing at every opportunity and fixing my sights as usual on the big amateur events in the spring; for while I hadn't the world's toughest physique when it came to chest infections, to which I was maddeningly as prone as cars to rust, I was still, at thirty-two, as muscularly strong as I would ever be. But someone, somewhere, had recently dreamed up the nannying concept that people should no longer be allowed to ride in jump races *wearing glasses*.

Of course, a lot of people thought it daft for anyone to race in glasses anyway, and I daresay they were right; but although I'd broken a few frames and suffered a few superficial cuts from them, I'd never damaged my actual eyes. And they were *my eyes*, goddammit.

Contact lenses, though restricted, were not totally banned, but although I had tried and persevered to the point of perpetual inflammation, my eyes and contacts remained incompatible. So if I couldn't wear contacts, I could no longer race. So goodbye to twelve years' fun. Goodbye to endeavor, to speed, to mind-blowing exhilaration. Too bad, too bad about your misery— it's all for your own good.

The weekend drifted along on its normal course. A drive round the farm on Saturday morning, visit to the local Stratford-upon-Avon races in the afternoon, dinner with friends in the evening. Sunday morning, getting up late, we sprawled in the sitting room with logs on the fire, newspapers around like snow, and the prospect of toasted ham sandwiches for lunch. Two satisfactory nights had been passed, with another, one hoped, ahead. Emma was at her softest, and we were as near to a married state as we were ever likely to get.

Into this domestic calm drove Hughes-Beckett in his Daimler. The wheels crunched on the gravel: I stood up to see who had arrived, and Emma also. We watched the chauffeur and a man sitting beside him get out of the car and open the two rear doors. From one stepped Hughes-Beckett, looking apprehensively up at the façade of the house, and from the other . . .

Emma's eyes widened. "My God! Isn't that . . .?"

"Yes, it is."

She swept a wild look round the cozy untidy room. "You can't bring them in here."

"No. The drawing room."

"But . . . did you know they were coming?"

"Of course not."

"Good heavens."

We watched the two visitors stroll the few steps toward the front door. Talk about not taking no for an answer, I thought. This was wheeling up the big guns with a vengeance.

"Well, go on," said Emma. "See what they want."

"I know what they want. You sit here by the fire and do the crossword while I think of ways of telling them they can't have it."

I went to the front door and opened it.

"Randall," said the Prince, holding out his hand to be shaken. "Well, at least you're at home. Can we come in?"

"Of course, sir."

Hughes-Beckett followed him over the threshold with an expression compounded of humiliation and triumph. He might not have been able to persuade me himself, but he was going to take joy in seeing me capitulate to someone else.

I led them into the blue and gold formal drawing room, where at least the radiators were functioning even if there was no welcoming fire.

"Now, Randall," said the Prince. "Please go to Moscow."

"Can I offer Your Royal Highness a drink?" I said.

"No, you can't. Now, Randall, sit down and listen, and stop beating about the bush."

The cousin of the monarch parked his backside firmly on a silk-covered Regency sofa and waved Hughes-Beckett and me toward adjoining chairs. He was of my generation, though a year or two older, and we had met countless times over the years because of our common pleasure in horses. His taste had taken him more to hounds and to polo than racing, although we had galloped alongside in several point-to-points. He was strong-minded and direct, and could be bracing to the point of bossiness, but I had also seen his tears over the broken-necked body of his favorite hunter.

We had met from time to time on indoor social occasions, but we were not close personal friends, and before that day he had not been to my house, nor I to his.

"My wife's brother," he said, "Johnny Farringford—you know him, don't you?"

"We've met," I said. "I don't really know him."

"He wants to ride in the next Olympics. In Moscow."

"Yes, sir. So Mr. Hughes-Beckett said."

"In the three-day event."

"Yes."

"Well, Randall, there's this problem . . . what you might call a *question mark*. We can't let him go to Russia unless it's cleared up. We simply can't—or at least I simply *won't*—have him going there if the whole thing is going to blow up in our faces. I am not, positively not, going to let him go if there is any chance of an . . . *incident* which would be in any way embarrassing to—er—other members of my family. Or to the British nation as a whole." He cleared his throat. "Now, I know Johnny is not in line to the throne or anything like that, but he is after all an earl and my brother-in-law, and so far as the press of the world is concerned, that's fair game."

"But, sir," I said, protesting mildly, "the Olympics are still some way off. I know Lord Farringford is good, but he might not be selected, and then there would be no problem at all."

The Prince shook his head. "If the problem isn't dealt with, however good Johnny is, even if he's the best we've got, he will not be selected."

I looked at him speculatively. "You would prevent it?"

"Yes, I should." His voice was positive. "It would no doubt cause a great deal of friction in my own home, as both Johnny and my wife have set their hearts on his getting a place in the team. He has a real chance, too, I admit. He won several events during the summer and he's been working hard at improving his dressage to international standards. I don't want to stand in his way. . . . In fact, that's why I'm here, asking you to be a good chap and find out what, if anything, there is to make it risky for him to go to Russia."

"Sir," I said. "Why me? Why not the diplomats?"

"They've passed the buck. They think, and I must say I agree, that a private individual is the best bet. If there is . . . anything, we don't want it in official records."

I said nothing, but my disinclination must have been obvious.

"Look," the Prince said. "We've known each other a long time. You've twice the brains I have, and I trust you. I'm damned sorry about your eyesight, and all that, but you've got a lot of empty time to fill now, and if your agent can run your estate like clockwork while you chunter round Cheltenham and Aintree, he can do it while you go to Moscow."

I said, "I suppose you didn't get the no-glasses rule passed just so that I'd have time to go on your errand?"

He listened to the bitterness in my voice, and chuckled in his throat. "Most likely it was all the other amateurs, who wanted you out of their daylight.''

"A couple have already sworn it wasn't.''

"Will you go, then?'' he said.

I looked at my hands and bit my fingernails and took my glasses off and put them on again.

"I know you don't want to,'' he said. "But I don't know who else to ask.''

"Sir . . . well . . . can we leave it until the spring? I mean, you might think of someone better.''

"It's got to be now, Randall. Right this minute, in fact. We've got the chance of buying one of the top young German horses, a real cracker, for Johnny. We—that is, his trustees . . . I suppose I should explain. His money is in the trust until he is twenty-five, which is still three years ahead, and although of course he has a generous living allowance, a big item like an Olympic-type horse needs to come out of the capital. Anyway, we will be happy to buy this horse, and we have an option on it, but they are pressing for a reply. We must say yes or no by Christmas. It is too expensive except for an all-out attempt at the Olympics, and we are damned lucky to have been given the few weeks' option. They've got other buyers practically queuing for it.''

I stood up restlessly, went to the window, and looked out at the cold November sky. Winter in Moscow, chasing someone's possible indiscretion, maybe digging up a lot of private dirt, was an absolutely revolting prospect.

"Please, Randall,'' said the Prince. "Please go. Just give it a try.''

Emma was standing by the sitting room window watching the Daimler roll away down the drive. She glanced assessingly at my face.

"I see he suckered you,'' she said.

"I'm still fighting a rear-guard action.''

"You haven't a chance.''

She walked across the paneled room and sat on the

long stool in front of the fire, stretching out her hands to the warmth. "It's too ingrained in you. Service to the sovereign, and all that. Grandfather an equerry, aunt a lady-in-waiting. Stacks like them in your family for generations back. What hope have you got? When a prince says jump, all your ancestors' genes spring to attention and salute."

2

The Prince lived in a modest house only a shade larger than my own, but a hundred years older, and he opened his door to me himself, although he did have living-in staff, which I did not. But then he also had a wife, three children, and, apparently, six dogs. A Dalmatian and a whippet oozed between his legs and the doorposts and bowled over to give me a good sniffing as I climbed out of my Mercedes, with a yapping collection of terriers cantering along in their wake.

"Kick 'em out of your way," advised the Prince loudly, waiting on his doorstep. "Get *down*, Fingers, you spotted oaf."

The Dalmatian paid little attention, but I reached the door unchewed. Shook the Prince's hand. Made the small bow. Followed him across the rugs of his pillared hall into an ample sort of study. Leather-bound books in tidy rows lined two of the walls, with windows, doors, portraits, and fireplace leaving small surrounds of pale-green emulsion on the others. On his big cluttered desk stood ranks of photographs in silver frames, and in one corner a huge white cyclamen in a copper bowl drooped its pale heads in the grayish light.

I knew, and the Prince knew I knew, that his act in opening his door to me himself was a very unusual token of appreciation. He really must have been quite extraordinarily relieved, I thought, that I had agreed to take even the partial step I had; and I wondered a bit uneasily about the size of the pitfalls which he knew would lie ahead.

"Good of you, Randall," he said, waving me to a black leather armchair. "Did you have a good drive? We'll rustle up some coffee in a minute. . . ."

He sat in a comfortable swivel beside his desk and kept up the flow of courteous chatter. Johnny Farringford, he said, had promised to be there by ten-thirty. He took a quick look at his watch and no doubt found it was roughly fifteen minutes after that already. It was good of me to come, he said again. It was probably better, he said, that I shouldn't be tied in too closely with Johnny at this stage, so it was perhaps wiser we should meet at the Prince's house, and not at Johnny's, if I saw what he meant.

He was strongly built, fairly tall, brown-haired, blue-eyed, with the easy good looks of youth beginning to firm into the settled character of coming middle age. The eyebrows were bushier than five years earlier, the nose more pronounced, and the neck a little thicker. Time was turning him from an athlete into a figurehead, and giving me unwanted insights into mortality on a Monday morning.

Another quick look at his watch, this time accompanied by a frown. I thought hopefully that perhaps the precious Johnny wouldn't turn up at all, and I could go contentedly back home and forget the whole thing.

The two tall windows of the study looked out to the

sweep of drive in front of the house, in the same way as those of my own sitting room. Perhaps the Prince, too, found it useful to have early warning of people calling: time to dodge, if he wanted.

My Mercedes was clearly in view on the wide expanse of raked gravel, standing alone, bluish-gray and quiet. While I idly watched, a white Rover suddenly traveled like an arrow across the uncluttered area, making straight for my car's back. As if in horror-struck inevitable slow motion, I waited helplessly for the crash.

There was a noise like the emptying of ten metal dustbins into a pulverizing plant, followed by the un-interrupted blowing of the horn, as the unconscious driver of the Rover slumped over the steering wheel.

"Christ!" said the Prince, appalled and leaping to his feet. "Johnny!"

"My car!" I said, involuntarily betraying my re-grettable priorities.

The Prince was fortunately already on his way to the study door, and I followed on his heels across the hall, bursting into the fresh air after him at a run.

The reverberating crunch and the wailing horn had brought an assortment of horrified faces to the win-dows and to the fringe of the scene, but it was the Prince and I who reached the tangle first.

The front of the Rover had half mounted the back of my car in a sort of monstrous mechanical mating, so that the Rover's wheels were slightly off the ground. The whole arrangement looked most precar-ious, and an assaulting smell of petrol brought one face to face with possibilities.

"Get him out," said the Prince urgently, tugging at the handle of the driver's door. "God!"

The door had buckled under the impact, and was wedged shut. I raced round to the far side, and tried the passenger door. Same thing. If he'd tried, Johnny Farringford couldn't have hit my Mercedes any straighter.

The rear doors were locked. The hatchback also. The horn blew on, urgent and disturbing.

"Jesus," shouted the Prince frantically. "Get him out."

I climbed up onto the concertinaed mess between the two vehicles and slithered through the space where the windshield had been, carrying with me a shower of crumbling glass. Knelt on the passenger seat, and hauled the unconscious man off the horn button. The sudden quiet was a blessing, but there was nothing reassuring about Johnny Farringford's face.

I didn't wait to look beneath the blood. I stretched across behind him, supporting his lolling head, and pulled up the locking catch on the offside rear door. The Prince worked at it feverishly from the outside, but it took a contortionist maneuver from me and a fierce stamp from my heel to spring it open. The thought of sparks from the scraping metal was a vivid horror, as I could now hear as well as scarcely breathe from the flood of escaping petrol.

It didn't make it any better that it was the petrol from my own car, or that I'd filled the capacious tank that very morning.

The Prince put his head and shoulders into the Rover and thrust his wrists under his brother-in-law's armpits. I squirmed back into the buckled front space and disengaged the flopping feet from the clutter of clutch, brake, and accelerator pedals. The Prince heaved with his considerable strength and I lifted the lower part of the inert body as best I could, and between us we shifted him over the back of his seat and out through the rear door. I let go of his legs as the Prince tugged him backward, and he flopped out free onto the gravel like a calf from a cow.

God help him, I thought, if we've made any broken bones worse by our rough handling, but anything on the whole was better than incineration. I scrambled along Johnny Farringford's escape route with no signs of calm, unhurried nonchalance.

Assistance had arrived in a houseman's coat and in gardening clothes, and the victim was carried more carefully from then on.

"Take him away from the car," the Prince was saying to them, while turning back toward me. "The petrol . . . Randall, get out, man."

Superfluous advice. I'd never felt so slow, so awkward, so overequipped with knees and elbows and ankle joints.

Whether the balance of one vehicle on the other was in any case unstable, or whether my far from delicate movements rocked it over the brink, the effect was the same: the Rover began to move while I was still inside it.

I could hear the Prince's voice, rising with apprehension, *"Randall . . ."*

I got one foot out free, began to put my weight on it, and the Rover shifted further. I stumbled, hung on to the doorframe, and pulled myself out by force of arms. Landed sideways on hip and elbow, sprawling and ungainly.

I rolled and put my feet where they ought to be, with my hands on the ground like a runner, to get a bit of purchase. Behind me the Rover's heavy weight crunched backward and tore itself off my Mercedes with metal screeching violently on metal, but I daresay it was some form of electrical shortcircuiting which let go with a shower of sparks like a hundred cigarette lighters in chorus.

The explosion threw the two cars apart and left both of them burning like mini infernos. There was a hissing noise in the air as the expanding vapor flashed into a second's flame, and a positive roaring gust of hot wind, which helped me onward.

"Your hair's on fire," observed the Prince, as I reached him.

I rubbed a hand over it, and so it was. Rubbed with both hands rather wildly, and put the conflagration out.

"Thanks," I said.

"Not at all."

He grinned at me in an unprincely and most human fashion. "And your glasses, I see, haven't shifted an inch."

A doctor and a private ambulance arrived in due course for Johnny Farringford, but long before that he had woken up and looked around him in bewilderment. He was lying, by that time, on the long comfortable sofa in the family sitting room, attended by the Princess, his sister, who was taking things matter-of-factly and mopping his wounds with impressive efficiency.

"What happened?" Farringford said, opening dazed eyes.

Bit by bit they told him: he had driven his car across a space as big as a tennis court, straight into the back of my Mercedes. Nothing else in sight.

"Randall Drew," added the Prince, making the introduction.

"Oh."

"Damn silly thing to do," said the Princess disparagingly, but in her concerned face I read the lifelong protectiveness of older sister to little brother.

"I don't . . . remember."

He looked at the red stains on the swabs which were piling up on a tray beside him, at the blood dripping from a cut on one finger, and appeared to be going to be sick.

"He used to pass out at the sight of blood," said his sister. "A good job he's grown out of it."

Johnny Farringford's injuries had resolved themselves into numerous cuts to the face but no obviously broken bones. However, he winced every time he moved, pressing his arm across his waist as if to hold himself together, which spoke to me rather reminiscently of cracked ribs.

He was a willowy fairly tall young man with a great

deal of crinkly reddish hair extending into tufty bits of beard down the outer sides of his jaw. His nose looked thin and sharp, and an out-of-door tan sat oddly on his skin over the pallor of shock.

"Creeping . . . shit," he said suddenly.

"It could have been worse," said the Prince dubiously.

"No . . ." Farringford said. "They hit me."

"Who did?" The Prince mopped a bleeding cut and clearly thought the remark was the rambling of concussion.

"Those men. I . . ." He broke off and focused his dazed eyes with great deliberation on the Prince's face, as if the act of keeping his glance steady was also helping to reorganize his thoughts.

"I drove here . . . after. I felt . . . I was sweating. I remember turning in through the gates . . . and seeing the house."

"Which men?" said the Prince.

"The ones you sent . . . about the horse."

"I didn't send any men."

Farringford blinked slowly and reestablished the concentrating stare.

"They came . . . to the stable. Just when I was thinking . . . time to come here, see this fellow . . . someone you want me to . . ."

The Prince nodded. "That's right. Randall Drew, here."

"Yeah . . . well, Higgins had got my car out . . . the Rover. Said I wanted the Porsche, but something about new tires . . . so I just went into the yard to see if Groucho's legs O.K., which Lakeland said they were, but wanted to look myself, you know. . . . So there they were, saying could they have a word . . . you'd sent them. I said I was in a hurry . . . got into the Rover. They just crowded in after me . . . punched me. One of them drove down the road, past the village . . . then they stopped, and the sods knocked me about. Gave them as good as I got . . . but two to one. No good, you know."

"They robbed you?" the Prince said. "We'll have to consider the police." He looked worried. Police meant publicity, and unfavorable publicity was anathema to the Prince.

"No." Farringford closed his eyes. "They said . . . to keep away . . . from Alyosha."

"They *what?*" The Prince jerked as if he, too, had been hit.

"That's right. Knew you wouldn't like it."

"What else did they say?"

"Nothing. Bloody ironic," said Farringford rather faintly. "It's you . . . who wants Alyosha . . . found. Far as I'm concerned . . . whole thing can stay . . . buried."

"Just rest," said the Princess anxiously, wiping red oozing drops from his grazed forehead. "Don't talk any more, Johnny, there's a lamb." She looked up at the two of us, standing at the sofa's foot. "What will you do about the cars?"

The Prince stared morosely at the two burned-out wrecks and at five empty extinguishers which lay around like scarlet torpedoes. An acrid smell in the November air was all that was left of the thick column of smoke and flame that had risen higher than the rooftops. The firemen, still in the shape of houseman and gardener, stood in the background, looking smugly at their handiwork and waiting for the next gripping installment.

"Do you suppose he fainted?" said the Prince.

"It sounds like it, sir," I said. "He said he was sweating. Not much fun being beaten up like that."

"And he never could stand the sight of blood."

The Prince traced with his eye the path the Rover would have taken with an unconscious driver had not my car been parked slap in the way.

"He'd've crashed into one of those beeches," said the Prince. "And his foot was on the accelerator. . . ."

Across the lawn, a double row of stately mature trees stretched away from the house, thick with crisscrossing branches, and bare except for a last dusting of dried brown leaves. They had been planted, one would guess, as a break against the northeast winds, in an age when sculpture of the land was designed to delight the eye of future generations, and their sturdy trunks would have stopped a tank, let alone a Rover. They were lucky, I thought, to have survived where so many had fallen to drought, fungus, and gales.

"I'm glad he didn't hit the beeches," said the Prince, and left me unsure whether it was for Johnny's sake or theirs. "Sorry about your car, of course. I hope it was insured, and all that? Better just tell the insurers it was a parking accident. Keep it simple. Cars get written off so easily these days. You don't want to claim against Johnny, or anything like that, do you?"

I shook my head reassuringly. The Prince smiled faintly with relief and relaxed several notches.

"We don't want the place crawling with press, do you see? Telephoto lenses . . . Any sniff of this and they'd be down here in droves."

"But too late for the action," I said.

He looked at me in alarm. "You won't say anything about us hauling Johnny out, will you? Not to anyone. I don't want the press getting hold of a story like that. It really doesn't do."

"Would you mind people knowing you would take a slight risk to rescue your wife's brother, sir?"

"Yes, I should," he said positively. "Don't you say a word, there's a good chap." He cast a glance at my singed hair. "And not so much of the 'slight,' come to that." He put his head on one side. "We could say you did it yourself, if you like."

"No, sir, I don't like."

"Didn't think you would. You wouldn't want them crawling all over you with their notebooks any more than I should."

He turned away and with a movement of his hand that was more a suggestion than a command, he called over the hovering gardener.

"What do we do about all this, Bob?" he said.

The gardener was knowledgeable about tow trucks and suitable garages, and said he would fix it. His manner with the Prince was comfortable and spoke of long-term mutual respect, which would have irritated the antiroyalists no end.

"Don't know what I'd do without Bob," confirmed the Prince as we walked back toward the house. "If I ring up shops or garages and say who I am, they either don't believe it and say yes, they're the Queen of Sheba, or else they're so fussed they don't listen properly and get everything wrong. Bob will get those cars shifted without any trouble, but if I tried to arrange it myself, the first people to arrive would be the reporters."

He stopped on the doorstep and looked back at the skeleton of what had been my favorite vehicle.

"We'll have to fix you a car to get home in," he said. "Lend you one."

"Sir," I said, "who or what is Alyosha?"

"Ha!" he said explosively, his head turning to me sharply, his eyes suddenly shining. "That's the first bit of interest you've shown without me actually forcing you into it."

"I did say I would see what I could do."

"Meaning to do as precious little as possible."

"Well, I . . ."

"And looking as if you'd been offered rotting fish."

"Er . . ." I said. "Well . . . what about Alyosha?"

"That's just the *point*," the Prince said. "We don't

know about Alyosha. That's just what I want you to find *out*."

Johnny Farringford got himself out of hospital and back home pretty fast, and I drove over to see him three days after the accident.

"Sorry about your car," he said, looking at the Range Rover in which I had arrived. "Bit of a buggers' muddle, what?"

He was slightly nervous, and still pale. The numerous facial cuts were healing with the quick crusts of youth, and looked unlikely to leave permanent scars; and he moved as if the soreness still in his body was after all more a matter of muscle than of bone. Nothing, I thought a shade ruefully, that would stop him training hard for the Olympics.

"Come in," he said. "Coffee, and all that."

He led the way into a thatched cottage and we stepped straight into a room that deserved a magazine article on traditional country living. Stone-flagged floors, good rugs, heavy supporting beams, inglenook fireplace, exposed old bricks, and masses of sagging sofas and chairs in faded chintzy covers.

"This place isn't mine," he said, sensing my inspection. "It's rented. I'll get the coffee."

He headed toward a door at the far end, and I slowly followed. The kitchen, where he was pouring boiling water into a filter pot, was as modern as money could make it.

"Sugar? Milk?" he said. "Would you rather have tea?"

"Milk, please. Coffee's fine."

He carried the loaded tray back into the living room and put it on a low table in front of the fireplace. Logs were stacked there ready on a heap of old dead ash, but the fire, like the cottage itself, was cold. I coughed a couple of times and drank the hot liquid gratefully, warmed inside if not out.

"How are you feeling now?" I asked.

"Oh . . . all right."

"Still shaken, I should imagine."

He shivered. "I understand I'm lucky to be alive. Good of you to dig me out, and all that."

"It was your brother-in-law as much as me."

"Beyond the call of duty, one might say."

He fidgeted with the sugar bowl and his spoon, making small movements for their own sake.

"Tell me about Alyosha," I said.

He flicked a quick glance at my face and looked away, leaving me the certainty that what he mainly felt at that moment was depression.

"There's nothing to tell," he said tiredly. "Alyosha is just a name which cropped up in the summer. One of the German team died at Burghley in September, and someone said it was because of Alyosha, who came from Moscow. Of course, there were inquiries and so on, but I never heard the results, because I wasn't directly involved, do you see?"

"But . . . indirectly?" I suggested.

He gave me another quick glance and a faint smile.

"I knew him quite well. The German chap. One does, do you see? One meets all the same people everywhere, at every international event."

"Yes," I said.

"Well . . . I went out with him one evening, to a club in London. I was stupid, I admit it, but I thought it was just a gambling club. He played backgammon, as I do. I had taken him to my club a few days earlier, you know, so I thought he was just repaying my—er—hospitality."

"But it wasn't just a gambling club?" I said, prompting him as he lapsed into gloomy silence.

"No." He sighed. "It was full of—well—transvestites." His depression increased. "I didn't realize, at first. No one would have done. They all *looked* like women. Attractive. Pretty, even, some of them. We were shown to a table. It was dark. And there was this girl, in the spotlight, doing a striptease, taking off

a lot of cloudy gold scarf things. She was beautiful
Dark-skinned, but not black . . . marvelous dark eyes
. . . the most stunning little breasts. She undressed
right down to the skin and then did a sort of dance
with a bright pink feathery boa thing. It was brilliant,
really. One would see her back view totally naked,
but when she turned round there was always the boa
falling in the—er—strategic place. When it was over
and I was applauding, Hans leaned across grinning
like a monkey and said into my ear that she was a
boy." He grimaced. "I felt a complete fool. I mean
one doesn't mind seeing performances like that if one
knows. But to be taken in . . ."

"Embarrassing," I said, agreeing.

"I laughed it off," he said. "I mean, one has to,
doesn't one? And there was a sort of weird fascination, of course. Hans said he had seen the boy in a
nightclub in West Berlin, and he had thought it might
amuse me. He seemed to be enjoying my discomfiture.
Thought it was a huge joke. I had to pretend to take
it well, do you see, because he was my host, but to be
honest, I thought it a bit *off.*"

A spot of dented pride, I thought.

"The event started two days after that," he said,
"and Hans died the next day, after the cross country."

"How?" I asked. "How did he die?"

"Heart attack."

I was surprised. "Wasn't he a bit young?"

"Yes," Johnny said. "Only thirty-six. Makes one
think, doesn't it?"

"And then what happened?" I said.

"Oh . . . nothing, really. Nothing one could put
one's finger on. But there were these rumors flying
about—and I expect I was the last to hear them—that
there was something *queer* about Hans and about me
as well. That we were, in point of fact, gay, if you see
what I mean? And that a certain Alyosha from Moscow was jealous and had made a fuss with Hans, and

because of it all he had a heart attack. And there was a *message,* do you see, that if I ever went to Moscow, Alyosha would be waiting."

"What sort of message? I mean, in what form was it delivered?" I said.

He looked frustrated. "But that's just it. The message itself was only a rumor. Everyone seemed to know it. I was told it by several people. I just don't know who started it."

"Did you take it seriously?" I asked.

"No, of course I didn't. It's all rubbish. No one would have the slightest reason to be jealous of me when it came to Hans Kramer. In fact, you know, I more or less avoided him after that evening, as much as one could do without being positively boorish, do you see?"

I put my empty cup on the tray and wished I had worn a second sweater. Johnny himself seemed totally impervious to cold.

"But your brother-in-law," I said, "takes it very seriously indeed."

He made a face. "He's paranoid about the press. Haven't you noticed?"

"He certainly doesn't seem to like them."

"They *persecuted* him when he was trying to keep them off the scent of his romance with my sister. I thought it a bit of a laugh, really, but I suppose it wasn't to him. And then there was a lot of brouhaha, if you remember, because a fortnight after the engagement our mama upped and scarpered with her hairdresser."

"I'd forgotten that," I said.

"Just before I went to Eton," Johnny said. "It slightly deflated my confidence, do you see, at a point when a fellow needs all he can get." He spoke flippantly, but the echo of a desperate hurt was clearly there. "So they couldn't get married for months, and when they did, the papers raked up my mama's sex life practically every day. And any time there's any real news story about any of us, up it pops again. Which is why H.R.H. has this *thing.*"

"I can see," I said soberly, "why he wouldn't want you mixed up in a murky scandal at the Olympics, with the eyes of the gossip columns swiveling your way like searchlights. Particularly with transvestite overtones."

The Prince's alarm, indeed, seemed to me now to be entirely justified, but Johnny disagreed.

"There can't be any scandal, because there *isn't* any," he said. "The whole thing is absolutely stupid."

"I think that's what your brother-in-law wants to prove. And the Foreign Office also. Because anyone going to Russia is vulnerable, but anyone with a reputation for homosexual behavior is a positive political risk, as it is still very much against the law there. They do want you to take part in the Olympics. They're trying to get me to investigate the rumors entirely for your sake."

He compressed his mouth obstinately. "But there isn't any need."

"What about the men?" I said.

"What men?"

"The men who attacked you and warned you off Alyosha."

"Oh." He looked blank. "Well . . . I should think it's obvious that whoever Alyosha is, she doesn't want an investigation any more than I do. It will probably do her a lot of *harm.* . . . Did you think of that?"

He stood up restlessly, picked up the tray, and carried it out to the kitchen. He rattled the cups out there for a bit and when he came back showed no inclination to sit down again.

"Come out and see the horses," he said.

"Tell me about the men first," I said persuasively.

"What about them?"

He put a foot on a pile of logs beside the fire and fiddled unnecessarily with the fire tongs.

"Were they English?"

He looked up in surprise. "Well, I suppose so."

"You heard them speak. What sort of accents did they have?"

"Ordinary. I mean—well, you know—ordinary working-class accents."

"But they differ," I said. He shook his head, but all accents differed, to my mind, to an infinitely variable degree.

"Well," I said, "were they Irish? Scots? Geordies? London? Birmingham? Liverpool? West Country? All those are easy."

"London, then," he said.

"Not foreign? Not Russian, for example?"

"No." He seemed to see the point for the first time. "They had a rough, sloppy way of speaking, swallowing all the consonants. Southern England. London or the Southeast, I should think, or Berkshire."

"The accent you hear around here every day?"

"I suppose so, yes. Anyway, I didn't notice anything special about it."

"What did they look like?"

"They were both big." He arranged the fire irons finally in a tidy row and straightened to his full height. "Taller than me. They were just men. Nothing remarkable. No beards or limps or scars down the cheek. I'm awfully sorry to be so useless, but honestly I don't think I'd know them again if I passed them in the street."

"But you would," I guessed, "if they walked into this room."

"You mean I'd *feel* it was them?"

"I mean I expect you remember more than you think, and if your memory was jogged it would all come rushing back."

He looked doubtful, but he said, "If I do see them again, I'll certainly let you know."

"They might of course return with another—er—warning," I said thoughtfully. "If you can't persuade your brother-in-law to drop the whole affair."

"Christ, do you think so?" He swung his thin, beaky nose toward the door as if expecting instant attack. "You do say the most bloody comforting things, don't you?"

"The crude deterrent," I said.

"What?"

"Biff bang."

"Oh . . . yes."

"Cheap and often effective," I said.

"Yes . . . well. I mean so what?"

"So who was it meant to deter? You, me, or your brother-in-law?"

He gave me a slow look, behind which the alternatives seemed to be under inspection for the first time.

"See what you mean," he said. "But it's too subtle for me by half. Come out and see the horses. Now, those I do understand. Even if they kill you, there's no malice."

He shed a good deal of his nervousness and most of his depression as we walked the fifty yards across the country road to the stables. Horses were his natural element, and being among them obviously gave him comfort and confidence. I wondered whether his half-controlled jitters with me were simply because I was human, and not because of my errand.

The stableyard was a small quadrangle of elderly wooden boxes round an area of impacted clay and gravel. There were clipped patches of grass, a straggling tree, and empty tubs for flowers. Green paint, nearing the end of its life. A feeling that weeds would grow in the spring.

"When I inherit the lolly, I'll buy a better yard," Johnny said, uncannily picking up my thoughts again. "This is rented. Trustees, do you see."

"It's a friendly place," I said mildly.

"Unsuitable."

The trustees, however, had put the money where it mattered, which was in four legs, head and tail. Although it was then the comparative rest period of their annual cycle, the five resident horses looked well-muscled and fit. For the most part bred by thoroughbred stallions out of hunter mares, they had looks as well as performance, and Johnny told me the history of each with a decisive and far from casual pride. I saw come alive in him for the first time the single-minded driving fanaticism which had to be there—the essential fuel for Olympic fire.

Even the crinkly red hair seemed to crisp into tighter curls, though I daresay this was due to the dampness in the air. But there was nothing climatic about the zeal in the eye, the tautness of the jaw, or the intensity of his manner. Enthusiasm of that order was bound to be infectious. I found myself responding to it easily, and understood why everyone was so anxious to make his Russian journey possible.

"I've an outside chance for the British team with this fellow," he said, briskly slapping the rounded quarters of a long-backed chestnut, and reeling off the fullest list of successes. "But he's not top world class. I know that. I need something better. The German horse. I've seen him. I really covet that horse." He let out his breath abruptly and gave a small laugh, as if hearing his own obsession and wanting to disguise it. "I do go on a bit."

The self-deprecation in his voice showed nowhere in his healing face.

"I want a Gold," he said.

3

My packing for Moscow consisted, in order of priority, of an army of defenses for dicky lungs, mostly on a be-prepared-and-it-won't-happen basis; a thick wooly scarf, a spare pair of glasses, a couple of paperbacks, and a camera.

Emma surveyed my medicine box with a mixture of amusement and horror.

"You're a hypochondriac," she said.

"Stop poking around. Everything in there is tidy."

"Oh, sure. What are these?" She lifted a small plastic pill bottle and shook it.

"Ventolin tablets. Put them down."

She opened the cap instead and shook one onto her palm.

"Pink and tiny. What do they do?"

"Help one breathe."

"And these?" She picked up a small cylindrical tin and read the yellow label. "Intal spincaps?"

"Help one breathe."

"And this? And this?" She picked them out and laid them in a row. "And these?"

"Ditto, ditto, ditto."

"And a syringe, for God's sake. Why a syringe?"

"Last resort. If a shot of Adrenalin doesn't work, one sends for the undertaker."

"Are you serious?"

"No," I said; but the truth was probably yes. I had never actually found out.

"What a fuss over a little cough." She looked at the fearsome array of life-support systems with all the superiority of the naturally healthy.

"Gloomsville," I agreed. "And put them all back."

She humored me by replacing them with excessive care.

"You know," she said, "surely all these things are for asthma, not bronchitis."

"When I get bronchitis, I get asthma."

"And vice versa?"

I shook my head. "How about hopping into bed?"

"At half-past four on a Sunday afternoon with an invalid?"

"It's been done before."

"So it has," she agreed; and it was done again, with not a cough or a wheeze to be heard.

Rudolph Hughes-Beckett, in his London office the next morning, handed me an air ticket, a visa, a hotel reservation, and a sheet of names and addresses. Not enough.

"How about my answers?" I said.

"I'm afraid—ah—they are not yet available."

"Why not?"

"The inquiries are still—ah—in hand."

He was not meeting my eyes. He was finding the backs of his hands as fascinating as he had in my sitting room. He must know every freckle, I thought. Every wrinkle and every vein.

"Do you mean you haven't even started?" I said incredulously. "My letter must have reached you by last Tuesday at the lastest. Six days ago."

"With your visa photographs, yes. You must understand there are—ah—*problems* in obtaining a visa at such short notice."

I said, "What is the point of a visa if I don't have the information? And couldn't you have got both at once?"

"We thought—ah—the *telex*. At the embassy. We can send you the answers as they reach us."

"And I trot around there every five minutes to see if the carrier pigeon has fluttered into the loft?"

He smiled austerely, a minuscule movement of the severely controlled lips.

"You can telephone," he said. "The number is on that paper." He leaned back a little in his five-star office chair and looked earnestly at his hand to see if the knuckle-to-wrist scenery had changed at all in the last half minute. "We did, of course, have a word with the doctor who attended Hans Kramer."

"Well?" I prompted, as he seemed to have stopped there.

"He was the doctor in attendance at the three-day-event. He was seeing to a girl with a broken collarbone when someone came to tell him that one of the Germans had collapsed. He left the girl almost immediately, but by the time he reached him, Kramer was already dead. He tried heart massage, he says, and a suitable injection, and mouth-to-mouth resuscitation, but all to no avail. The body was—ah—cyanosed, and the cause of death was—ah—cardiac arrest."

"In other words, heart attack."

"Ah—yes. There was an autopsy, of course. Natural causes. So sad in someone so young."

None of this present caper would have been necessary, I thought moodily, if Hans Kramer had not been so inconsiderate as to drop in his tracks. There was nothing like death for spawning and perpetuating myths, and it looked certain the Alyosha crop had circulated simply because Kramer hadn't been around to deny them.

"The names and addresses of the rest of the German team?" I said.

"To follow."

"And the names and addresses of the members of the Russian team which came over for the International Horse Trials at Burghley?"

"To follow."

"And of the Russian observers?"

"To follow."

I stared at him. The most hopeful lead I'd unearthed in several telephone calls to people in the event world had been the frequent reference to "the Russian observers"—three men who in a semiofficial capacity had attended a number of horse trials during the past season, not just the international event for which their team had been entered. The reasons for their presence had been described variously as "spying," "seeing how events should be run," "nicking our best horses," and "assessing the standard they had to reach to make the West look stupid at the Olympics."

I said to Hughes-Beckett, "The Prince told me you had agreed to do some of the spadework."

"We will," he said. "But on the scene of international politics your errand is of limited importance. My office has been working this week on matters of greater urgency than—ah—horses."

The same faint undisguisable contempt colored his voice and pinched his nostrils.

"Do you expect me to succeed in this task?" I said.

He studied the back of his hand and didn't answer.

"Do you *wish* me to succeed?"

He lifted his gaze to my face as if it were a two-ton weight.

"I would be grateful if you would bear in mind that clearing the way for Lord Farringford to be able to be considered for the Olympics, always supposing that he or his horse should prove to be good enough, is not something for which we would willingly sacrifice any—ah—bargaining positions with the Soviet Union. We would in particular not wish to find ourselves in the position of having to tender an *apology*.''

"It's a wonder you asked me to go," I said.

"The Prince wished it."

"And he leaned on you?"

Hughes-Beckett folded his mouth primly. "It is not a totally unreasonable request. If we altogether disapproved of your errand, we would not have helped in any way."

"All right," I said, rising to my feet and stowing the various papers into pockets. "I take it that you would like me to go, which will prove you are not obstructive, and to ask a few harmless questions, and get some inconclusive answers, and for the Prince not to buy the German horse, and for Johnny Farringford not to be picked for the team, and for no one to make waves?"

He regarded me with all the world-weariness of a senior civil servant, saying nothing but meaning yes.

"We have reserved a room for you for two weeks," he said. "But of course you can return earlier if you wish."

"Thanks."

"And if you read that sheet of paper, you will find we have given you two—ah—contacts, who may be helpful."

I glanced at the short list, which was headed by the British Embassy, Naberezhnaya Morisa Teresa 12.

"One of those lower down is a man concerned with training the Soviet team for the Olympic three-day event."

"Well," I said, pleasantly surprised. "That's better."

He said with faint smugness, "We have not been entirely idle, as you supposed." He cleared his throat. "The last name on the list is that of a student at Moscow University. He is English, and is there on an exchange visit for one year. He speaks Russian, of course. We have written to him to tell him you will be coming. He will be helpful if you need an interpreter, but we ask that nothing you do will prejudice his—ah—continued acceptance for the rest of the academic year."

"As he is more important than horses?"

Hughes-Beckett achieved a remote and frosty smile. "Most things are," he said.

The tickets he had provided found me the next day sitting comfortably in first class on an Aeroflot flight which arrived at six in the evening, local time. Most of my fellow travelers in the privileged cabin were black. Cubans? I idly wondered. But then, in a shifting world, they could be from anywhere: today's ally, tomorrow's exterminee. They wore superbly tailored suits with white shirts and elegant ties, and were met at the doors of the airplane on landing by extra-long limousines. Those of less note went through normal immigration procedures, but without, in my case, any great delay. The customs men waved me through as if uninterested, though on the next bench they seemed to be taking apart a man of much my age. Every scrap of paper was being read, every pocket emptied, and the lining of his suitcase closely examined. The object of these attentions bore them stolidly, without expression. No protest, no indignation, nor, as far as I could see, any apprehension. As I went on my way, one of the officers picked up a pair of underpants and carefully felt his way round the waistband.

I was thinking purposefully of taxis, but it transpired that I, too, had been provided with a reception committee. A girl in a brown coat and a fawn knitted hat approached me tentatively, and said, "Mr. Drew?"

She saw from my reaction that she had the right man. She said, "My name is Natasha. I am from Intourist. We will be looking after you during your stay here. We have a car to take you to your hotel." She turned toward a slightly older woman standing a pace or two away. "This is my colleague, Anna."

"How kind of you to take so much trouble," I said politely. "How did you know me?"

Natasha glanced matter-of-factly at a paper in her hand. "Englishman, thirty-two years old, dark wavy hair, glasses with mottled brown frames, no mustache or beard, good clothes."

"The car is outside," Anna said. I thought that that wasn't totally surprising, as cars usually were, at airports.

Anna was short, stocky, and soberly clad in a gray coat with a darker gray wooly hat. There was something forbidding in her face, a stiffness which continued downward through the forward-thrusting abdomen to the functional toes of her boots. Her manner was welcoming enough, but would continue to be, I reckoned, only as long as I behaved as she thought I should.

"Do you have a hat?" Natasha said solicitously. "It is cold outside. You should have a fur hat."

I had already had a taste of the climate in the scamper from aircraft to bus, and from bus to airport door. Most of the passengers seemed to have sprouted headgear on the flight and had emerged in black fur with ear flaps, but I was huddled only into my fluffy scarf.

"You lose much body heat through the head," said Natasha seriously. "Tomorrow you must buy a hat."

"Very well," I said.

She had splendid dark eyebrows and creamy white skin, and wore smooth pale-pink lipstick. A touch of humor would have put the missing sparkle into her brown eyes, but then a touch of humor in the Soviets would have transformed the world.

"You have not been to Moscow before?"

"No," I said.

There was a group of four large men in dark overcoats standing by the exit doors. They were turned inward toward each other as if in conversation, but their eyes were directed outward, and none of them was talking. Natasha and Anna walked past them as if they were wallpaper.

"Who asked you to meet me?" I asked curiously.

"Our Intourist office," Natasha said.

"But . . . who asked *them?*"

Both women gave me a bland look and no answer, leaving me to gather that they didn't know, and that it was something they would not expect to know.

The car, which had a driver who spoke no English, traveled down straight wide empty roads toward the city, with wet snowflakes whirling thinly away in the headlights. The road surfaces were clear, but lumpy gray-white banks lined the edges. I shivered in my overcoat from aversion more than discomfort; it was warm enough in the car.

"It is not cold for the end of November," Natasha said. "Today it has been above freezing all day. Usually by now the snow has come for the winter, but instead we have had rain."

The bus stops, I saw, had been built to deal with life below zero. They were enclosed in glass, and brightly lit inside; and in a few there were groups of inward-facing men, three, not four, who might or might not be there to catch a bus.

"If you wish," Anna said, "tomorrow you can make a conducted tour of the city by coach, and the next day there is a visit to the Exhibition of Economic Achievements."

"We will do our best for tickets for the ballet and the opera," said Natasha, nodding helpfully.

"There are always many English people in your hotel visiting Moscow on package holidays," Anna said, "and it will be possible for you to join them in a conducted tour of the Kremlin or other places of interest."

I looked from one to the other and came to the conclusion that they were genuinely trying to be helpful.

"Thank you," I said, "but mostly I shall be visiting my friends."

"If you tell us where you want to go," Natasha said earnestly, "we will arrange it."

My room at the Intourist Hotel was spacious enough for one person, with a bed along one side wall and a sofa along the other, but the same size area with two beds, glimpsed through briefly opened doors, must have been pretty cramped for two. I also had a wide shelf along the whole wall under the window, with a telephone and a table lamp on it; a chair, a built-in closet, and a bathroom. Brown carpet, reddish patterned curtains, dark-green sofa, and a bedcover. An ordinary, functional, adequate hotel room which could as well have been in Sydney, Los Angeles, or Manchester, for all its national flavor.

I unpacked my sparse belongings and looked at my watch. "We have arranged your dinner for eight o'clock," Anna had said. "Please come to the restaurant then. I will be there to help you plan what you want to do tomorrow." The nursemaiding care would have to be discouraged, I thought, but as it was no part of my brief to cause immediate dismay, I decided to go along meekly. A short duty-free reviver, however, seemed a good idea.

I poured Scotch into a bathroom glass and sat on the sofa to drink it; and the telephone rang.

"Is that Mr. Randall Drew?"

"Yes," I said.

"Come to the bar of the National Hotel at nine o'clock," said the voice. "Leave your hotel, turn right, turn right at the street corner. The National Hotel will be on your right. Enter, leave your coat, climb the stairs, turn right. The bar is along the passage a short way, on the left. Nine o'clock. I'll see you, Mr. Drew.''

The line clicked dead before I could say "Who are you?"

I went on drinking the Scotch. The only way to find out was to go.

After a while I took out the paper Hughes-Beckett had given me, and because the telephone seemed to be connected directly to an outside line, I dialed the number of the English student at the Russian university. A Russian voice answered, saying I knew not what.

"Stephen Luce," I said distinctly. "Please may I speak to Stephen Luce?"

The Russian voice said an English word, "Wait," and I waited. Three minutes later, by what seemed to me a minor miracle, a fresh English voice said, "Yes? Who is it?"

"My name is Randall Drew," I said. "I—"

"Oh, yes," he interrupted. "Where are you calling from?"

"My room at the Intourist Hotel."

"What's your number? The telephone number on the dial." I read it out.

"Right," he said. "I'd better meet you tomorrow. Twelve o'clock suit you? My lunch hour. In Red Square, in front of St. Basil's Cathedral. O.K.?"

"Er . . . yes," I said.

"Fine," he said. "Have to go now. Bye." And he rang off.

It had to be catching, I thought. Something in the Moscow air. I dialed the number of the man concerned with training the Soviet team, and again a Russian voice answered. I asked in English for Mr. Kropotkin, but this time without luck. After a couple of short silences at the other end, as I repeated my request, there was a burst of agitated incomprehensible speech, followed by a sharp decisive click.

I had better fortune with the British Embassy, and found myself talking to the cultural attaché.

"Sure," he said in Etonian tones. "We know all about you. Care to come for a drink tomorrow evening? Six o'clock suit you?"

"Perfectly," I said. "I—"

"Where are you calling from?" he said.

"My room at the Intourist Hotel." I gave him the telephone number, unasked.

"Splendid," he said. "Look forward to seeing you."

Again the swift click. I finished the Scotch and considered the shape of my telephone calls. My naïveté, I reflected, must, to the old hands in the city, have been frightening.

Anna waited, hovering, in the dining room, and came forward as I appeared. Unwrapped, she wore a green wool suit with rows of bronze-colored beads, and would have fitted unremarkably into the London business scene. Her hair, with a few grays among the prevailing brown, was clean and well-shaped, and she had the poise of one accustomed to plan and advise.

"You can sit here," she said, indicating a stretch of tables beside a long row of windows. "There are some English people sitting here, on a tour."

"Thank you."

"Now," she said. "Tomorrow—"

"Tomorrow," I said pleasantly, "I thought I would walk around Red Square and the Kremlin, and perhaps GUM. I have a map and a guidebook, and I'm sure I won't get lost."

"But we can add you onto one of the guided tours," she said persuasively. "There is a special two-hour tour of the Kremlin, with a visit to the armory."

"I'd honestly rather not. I'm not a great one for museums and so on."

She looked disapproving, but after another fruitless try, she told me that my lunch would be ready at one-thirty, when the Kremlin party returned. "Then at two-thirty there is the bus tour of the city."

"Yes," I said. "That will be fine."

I saw as well as sensed the release of tension within her. Visitors who went their own way were clearly a problem, though I did not yet understand why. My semicompliance, anyway, had temporarily earned me qualified good marks, and she said as if promising sweets to a child that the tickets for the Bolshoi opera were almost a certainty.

The tables, each set for four, began to fill up. A middle-aged couple from Lancashire joined me with inquiring smiles, closely followed by the man who had been picked clean by the customs officers. We all exchanged the sort of platitudes that strangers thrust together by chance use to demonstrate nonaggression, and the Lancashire lady commented on the extent of the airport search.

"We had to wait ever such a long time on the bus before you came out," she said.

The unasked question floated in the air. The object of her curiosity, who was uniformed in jeans, jersey and longish hair, spooned sour cream into his borscht and took his time over replying.

"They took me off and searched me down to my skin," he said finally, enjoying the sensationalism.

The Lancashire lady said, "Ooh," in mock terror and was flatteringly impressed. "What were they looking for?"

He shrugged. "Don't know. There was nothing to find. I just let them get on with it, and in the end they said I could go."

His name, he said, was Frank Jones. He taught in a school in Essex and it was his third trip to Russia. A great country, he said. The Lancashire couple regarded him doubtfully, and we all shaped up to some grayish meat of undiscernible origin. The ice cream that came later was better, but one would not, I thought, have made the journey for the gastronomic delights.

Duty done, I set off to the National Hotel in over-coat and wooly scarf, with sleet stinging my face and wetting my hair and a sharp wind invading every crev-ice. Pavements and roadway glistened with a wetness that was not yet ice, but the quality of the cold was all the same piercing, and I could feel it deep down inside my lungs. All it would take to abort the whole mission, I thought, would be a conclusive bout of bronchitis, and for a tempting minute I felt like open-ing my arms to the chill; but anything on the whole was probably better than coughing and spitting and looking at hotel bedroom walls.

The bar of the National Hotel was a matter of shady opulence, like an unmodernized Edwardian pub or a small London club gone slightly to seed. There were rugs on the floor, three long tables with eight or ten chairs round each, and a few separate small tables for three or four. Most of the chairs were occupied and there was a two-deep row in front of the bar which stretched across one end of the room. The voices around me spoke English, German, French, and a lot of other tongues, but there was no one inquiring of every newcomer whether he was Randall Drew, newly arrived from England.

After an unaccosted few minutes, I turned to the bar and in due course got myself a whisky. It was by then nine-fifteen. I drank for a while standing up, and then, when one of the small tables became free, sitting down, but I drank altogether alone. At nine thirty-five I bought a second drink, and at nine-fifty I reckoned that if all my investigating was as successful, I wouldn't need bronchitis.

At two minutes to ten I looked at my watch and drained my glass, and a man detached himself from the row of drinkers at the bar and put two fresh tum-blers on the table.

"Randall Drew?" he said, pulling up an empty chair

and sitting down. "Sorry to keep you waiting, sport."

He had been there, I remembered, as long as I had; standing by the bar, exchanging words now and then with his neighbors and the barman, or looking down into his glass in the way of habitual pubbers, as if expecting to see the wisdom of the ages written in alcohol and water.

"Why did you?" I asked. "Keep me waiting?"

The only reply I got was a grunt and an expressionless look from a pair of hard gray eyes. He pushed one of the tumblers my way and said it was my tipple, he thought. He was solid and in his forties, and wore his dark double-breasted jacket open, so that it flapped about him and hung forward when he moved. He had flatly combed black hair going a little thin on top, and a neck like a vigorous tree trunk.

"You want to be careful in Moscow," he said.

"Mm," I said. "Do you have a name?"

"Herrick. Malcolm Herrick." He paused, but I'd never heard of him. "Moscow correspondent of *The Watch*."

"How do you do," I said politely, but neither of us offered a hand.

"This is no kid's playground, sport," he said. "I'm telling your for your own good."

"Kind," I murmured.

"You're here to ask damnfool questions about that four-letter Farringford."

"Why four-letter?" I asked.

"I don't like him," he said flatly. "But that's neither here nor there. I've asked all the questions there are to ask about that shit, and there's damn all to find out. And if there'd been a smell there, I'd've found it. There's no one like an old news hound, sport, if there's any dirt to be dug up about noble earls."

Even his voice gave an impression of hard muscle. I wouldn't have liked to have him knock on my door, I thought, if I was caught in a newsworthy tragedy: he would be about as compassionate as a tornado.

"How come you've been looking?" I asked. "And how did you know I was here, and on what errand, and staying at the Intourist? And how did you manage to telephone me within an hour of my arrival?"

He gave me another flat, hard, expressionless stare.

"We do want to know a lot, don't we, sport?" He took a mouthful of his drink. "Little birds round at the embassy. What else?"

"Go on," I said, as he seemed to have stopped.

"Can't reveal sources," he said automatically. "But I'll tell you, sport, this is no new story. It's weeks since I did my bloodhound bit, and the embassy staff have also put out their own feelers, and if you ask me, they even set one of their intelligence bods onto it on the quiet, on account of the queries that were popping up everywhere. It all turned out to be one big yawn. It's bloody silly sending you out here as well. Some fanatic in London doesn't seem to want to take 'no story' for an answer, and 'no story' is all the story there is."

I took off my glasses and squinted at them against the light, and after a while put them on again.

"Well," I said mildly. "It's nice of you to bother to tell me all that, but I can't really go home straightaway without *trying,* can I? I mean, they are paying my fare and expenses, and so on. But I wonder," I went on tentatively, "if perhaps you could tell me who you saw, so that I wouldn't duplicate a whole lot of wasteful legwork."

"Christ, sport," he exploded, "you really do want your hand held, don't you?" He narrowed his eyes and compressed a firm mouth, and considered it. "All right. There were three Russian observers in England last summer going round these damnfool horse trials. Officials from some minor committee set up here to arrange details of the equestrian events at the Games. I spoke to all three of them along at that vast Olympic Committee center they've got on Gorky Street, opposite the Red Army Museum. They had all seen Farringford riding at all the horse trials they had been to, but there was absolutely no link at all between Farringford and anything to do with Russia. *Niet, niet,* and *niet.* Unanimous opinion.''

''Oh, well,'' I said resignedly. ''What about the Russian team that went to the International Trials that were held at Burghley?''

''Those riders are unavailable, sport. You try interviewing a brick wall. The official reply that was given to the embassy was that the Russian team had no contact with Farringford, minimum contact with any British civilians, and in any case did not speak English.''

I thought it over. ''And did you come across anything to do with a girl called Alyosha?''

He choked over his drink at the name, but it was apparently mirth, and his laugh held a definite hint of sneer.

''Alyosha, sport, is not a girl, for a start. Alyosha is a man's name. A diminutive. Like Dickie for Richard. Alyosha is a familiar version of Alexei.''

''Oh.''

''And if you fell for all that guff about the German who died having a boyfriend from Moscow, you can forget it. Over here they still throw you in the jug for it. There are as many homosexuals here as warts on a billiard ball.''

''And the rest of the German team? Did you reach them, too, to ask questions?''

''The diplomats did. None of the Krauts knew a thing.''

''How many Alyoshas in Moscow?'' I said.

''How many Dickies in London? The two cities are roughly the same size.''

''Have another drink?'' I said.

He rose to his feet with the nearest he'd come to a smile, but the brief show of teeth raised no echoing glimmer in the eyes.

''I'll get them,'' he said. ''You give me the cash.''

I gave him a fiver, which did the trick nicely with

change to spare. Only Western foreign currency, the
barman had told me, was acceptable in that bar. Rubles and Eastern-bloc equivalents were no good. The
bar was for non-curtain visitors, who were to hand
over as big a contribution to the tourist trade as possible, all in francs, marks, dollars, and yen. The
change came back meticulously, and correctly, in the
currency which one had paid.

Malcolm Herrick loosened up a little over the second drink and told me a bit about working in Moscow.

"There used to be dozens of British correspondents
here, but most of the papers have called them back.
Only five or six of us left now, except for the news
agency guys. Reuters, and so on. The fact is, if anything big breaks in Moscow, it's the outside world that
hears about it first, and we get it fed back to us on the
world news service on the radio. We might as well not
be here, for all the inside info we get for ourselves."

"Do you yourself speak Russian?" I said.

"I do not. The Russians don't like Russian-speak-
ers working here."

"Why ever not?" I said, surprised.

He looked at me pityingly. "The system over here
is to keep foreigners away from the Russians and Russians away from foreigners. Foreigners who work here
full time have to live in compounds, with Russian
guards on the gates. All the journalists, diplomats, and
news agency people live in compounds. We even have
our offices there. No need to go out, sport. The news
comes in, courtesy of telex.

He seemed to be more cynical than bitter. I wondered what sort of stories he wrote for *The Watch*,
which was a newspaper more famous for its emotional
crusades than for its accuracy. It was also a paper I
seldom read, as its racing columnist knew more about
orchids than about good things for Ascot.

We finished the drinks and stood up to depart.

"Thank you for your help," I said. "If I think of

anything else, can I give you a ring? Are you in the phone book?"

He gave me a final flat gray stare, in which there was a quality of dour triumph. I was not going to succeed where he had failed, his manner said, so I might as well retire at once.

"There's no telephone directory in Moscow," he said.

My turn to stare.

"If you want to know a number," he said, "you have to ask Directory Inquiries. You probably have to tell them why you want the number, and if they don't approve of you knowing it, they won't give it to you."

He pulled a spiral-bound reporter's notebook out of his pocket and wrote down his number, ripping off the page and handing it to me.

"And use a public telephone, sport. Not the one in your room."

I scurried the two hundred yards back to the Intourist in heavier sleet which was turning to snow. I collected my keys, went up in the lift, and said good evening in English to the plump lady who sat at a desk from which she could keep an eye on the corridor to the bedrooms. Anyone coming from the lifts to their rooms had to pass her. She gave me a stolid inspection and said what I supposed to be 'Good night' in Russian.

My room was on the eighth floor, looking from the front of the hotel down to Gorky Street. I drew the curtains and switched on the reading lamp. There was something indefinably different in the way my belongings lay tidily around it. I pulled open a drawer or two, and felt my skin contract in a primeval ripple down my back and legs.

While I had been out, someone had searched my room.

4

I lay in bed with the lamp on and looked at the ceiling,
and wondered why I should feel so disturbed. I was
not one of those spies in or out of the cold who were
entirely at home with people ferreting through their
belongings, and who probably felt deprived if they
didn't. I had read and enjoyed all the books, and
hoisted in some of the jargon: mole, sleeper, spook,
et al. But as for that world affecting me personally—
that was as unexpected as a scorpion on the breakfast
toast.

Yet I was in Moscow to ask questions. Perhaps that
made me a legitimate target for irregular attention.
And of course, the most immediate questions remained unanswered, and so far unanswerable.

Who, exactly, had done the searching? And why?

There had been nothing of significance for anyone
to find. The paper with potentially useful names and
addresses had been in my pocket. I had concealed in
my luggage no guns, no codes, no tiny technology, no
anti-Soviet propaganda. I had been told it was illegal

to import Bibles and crucifixes into Russia, and had not done so. I had brought no forbidden books, no pornography, and no newspapers. No drugs . . .

Drugs . . .

I fairly bounded out of bed and yanked open the drawer in which I'd stored my box of assorted air freight. Heaved a considerable sigh of relief, once the lid was open, to see the pills and inhalers and syringe and Adrenalin ampules all more or less in the positions Emma had given them. I couldn't for certain tell whether or not they had been inspected, but at least nothing was missing. A hypochondriac Emma might well call me, but the sad fact remained that at certain dire times, the contents of that box were all that held off the Hereafter. The fates that had given me wealth had been niggardly on health: a silver spoon that bent easily. Even at my age, if one was prone to chest troubles, insurance premiums were loaded. If one's father and grandfather had both died young for lack of salbutamol or beclomethasone dipropionate, or sundry other later miracles, one discovered that actuaries' hearts were as hard as flint.

In between times—and to be fair, there were far more in between times than troubles—I was as bursting with health and vigor as any other poor slob living in the damp, cold, misty, bronchitic climate of the British Isles.

I shut the box and replaced it in the drawer, climbed back into bed, switched out the light, and took off my glasses, folding them neatly to hand for the morning. How soon, I wondered, could I decently make use of my return ticket?

Red Square looked grayish brown, with snowflakes blowing energetically across in a fiendish wind. I stood in front of St. Basil's Cathedral taking photographs in light dim enough to develop them by, wondering if even the intense deep red of the huge brick walls of the Kremlin would make a mark on the emulsion. The vast slush-covered expanse, where sometimes the self-aggrandizing parades beat hell out of the road surface for newsreels, was on that day trodden only by miserable-looking groups of tourists, shepherded in straggling crocodiles to and from a group of buses parked nearby.

The cathedral itself was small, a cluster of brilliantly colored and encrusted onion-shaped domes on stalks of different height, like a fantasy castle out of Disney. Snow lay on the onions now, dimming the blues and greens and golds that sparkled on the picture postcards, but I stood there wondering how a nation which had produced a building of such joyous, magnificent imagination could have come to its latter-day grayness.

"Ivan the Great commissioned that cathedral," said a voice behind my right shoulder. "When it was finished he was overwhelmed with its beauty; and he put out the eyes of his architect, so that he should not design anything more splendid for anyone else."

I turned slowly round. A shortish young man stood there, wearing a dark-blue overcoat, a black fur hat, and an unexpectant expression on a round face.

Round brown eyes full of bright intelligence, alive in a way that Russian faces were not. A person, I judged, whose still soft outlines of youth hid a mind already sharply adult. I'd had a bit of the same trouble myself at the same age, ten years or so ago.

"Are you Stephen Luce?" I said.

A smile flickered and disappeared. "That's right."

"I would rather not have known about the architect."

"Why?"

"I don' likhhhthhorror movies."

"Life is a horror movie," he said. "Do you want to see Lenin's tomb?" He half turned away and pointed an arm to the middle distance, where a queue was waiting outside a large boxlike building halfway along the Kremlin wall. "The cathedral isn't a church now, it's some sort of storehouse. You can go into the tomb, though."

"No, thank you."

He moved off, however, in that direction, and I went with him.

"Over there," he said, pointing to one side of the tomb, "is a small bust of Stalin, on a short pillar. It has recently appeared there, without any ceremony. You may think this is of no great note, but in point of fact it is very interesting. At one time Stalin was with Lenin in the tomb. Revered, and all that. Then there was a spot of revisionism, and Stalin was the ultra persona non grata, so they took him out of the tomb and put up a small statue outside instead. Then they did a spot more revisionism, and removed even the statute, leaving nothing but a curt plaque in the ground where it had been. But now we have a new statue, back on the same spot. This one is not the old proud glare of world domination, but a downward-looking, pensive, low-profile sort of thing. Fascinating, don't you think?"

"What are you reading at the universtiy?" I said.

"Russian history."

I looked from the rebirth of Stalin to the dead cathedral. "Tyrants come and go," I said. "Tyranny is constant."

"Some things are best said in the open air."

I looked at him straightly. "How much will you help me?" I asked.

"Why don't you take some photographs?" he said. "Behave like a tourist."

"No one thinks I'm a tourist, unless having one's room searched is par for the packages."

"Oh, gee," he said quaintly. "In that case, let's just walk."

At tourist pace we left Red Square and went toward the river. I huddled inside my coat and pulled my scarf up over my ears to meet the fur hat I had that morning, following Natasha's instructions, bought.

"Why don't you untie the ear flaps?" Stephen Luce said, undoing a black tape bow on top of his own head. "Much warmer." He pulled the formerly folded-up flaps down over his ears, and let the black tape tie dangle free. "Don't tie the tapes under your chin," he said, "or they'll think you're a pouf."

I pulled the flaps down and let the tapes flutter in the wind as he did.

"What do you want me to do?" he said.

"Come with me to see some men about some horses."

"When?"

"Mornings are best for horse people."

He took a minute over replying, then said doubtfully, "I suppose I could cut tomorrow's lecture, just for once."

How like Hughes-Beckett, I thought sardonically, to equip me with an interpreter whose time was measured in lunch hours and missed lectures. I glanced at the round, troubled face in its frame of black fur, and more or less decided then and there that my whole mission was impossible.

"Do you know Rudolph Hughes-Beckett?" I said.

"Never heard of him."

I sighed. "Who was it who wrote to you, asking you to help me?"

"The Foreign Office. A man called Spencer. I know *him*. They are sponsoring me, sort of, you see. Through college. The idea being that eventually I'll work for them. Though I might not, in the end. It's all a bit suffocating, that diplomatic waxworks."

We reached the approach to the bridge over the river, and Stephen threw out an arm in another of his generous gestures.

"Over there is the British Embassy," he said, pointing.

I couldn't see much for snow. I took off my glasses, dried them as best I could on a handkerchief, and enjoyed for a minute or two a clearer look at the world.

"Turn off right at the far side of the bridge," Stephen said. "Go down the steps to that other road running beneath it, along beside the river, and the embassy's that pale-yellow building along there, giving a good imitation of Buckingham Palace."

I told him I was going for a drink with the cultural attaché and he said the best of British luck, and not to miss seeing the ambassador's loo; it had the best view of the Kremlin in the whole of Moscow.

"I say," he said, as we went on over the bridge. "Do you mind telling me what you're actually here for?"

"Didn't they say?"

"No. Only to interpret, if necessary."

I shook my head in frustration. "Chasing a will-of-the-wisp. Looking for a rumor called Alyosha. Some say he doesn't exist and others that he doesn't want to be found. All I have to do is find him, see who he is and what he is, and decide whether he poses any sort of threat to a chap who wants to ride in the Olympics. And since you asked, I will now bore your ears off by telling you the whole story."

He listened with concentration and his ears remained in place. When I'd finished, he was walking with a springier step.

"Count me in, then," he said. "And hang the lectures. I'll borrow someone's notes." He turned at the end of the bridge to go back, and between the snowflakes I saw his dark-brown eyes shining with humorous life. "I thought you were here just fact-finding for the Games. In a general way, and semiofficial. This is more fun."

"I haven't thought so," I said.

He laughed. "Ve have vays of making you sit up and enjoy yourself."

"Ve had better have vays of keeping it all very discreet."

"Oh sure. Do you want the benefit of the immense experience of a lifetime of living in Moscow?"

"Whose?" I said.

"Mine, of course. I've been here eleven weeks. Lifetimes are comparative."

"Fire away," I said.

"Never do anything unusual. Never turn up when you're not expected, and always turn up if you are."

I said, "That doesn't sound very extraordinary."

I received a bright amused shot from the brown eyes. "Some English people touring here by car decided to go to a different town for a night from the one they had originally booked. Just an impulse. They were fined for it."

"Fined?" I was amazed.

"Yes. Can you imagine a foreign tourist being fined in England because he went to Manchester instead of Birmingham? Can you imagine an English hotel doing anything but shrug if he didn't turn up? But everything here is regulated. There are masses of people just standing around watching other people, and they all report what they see, because that's their job. They are employed to watch. There's no unemployment here. Instead of handing a bloke dole money and letting him spend it in civilized ways like soccer and gambling and pubs, they give him a job watching. Two birds with one stone, and all that."

"Standing in groups at airports and in bus shelters, and dotted around outside hotels?"

He grinned. "So right. Those guys at bus stops are there to stop all foreign-registered cars going out of Moscow, to check their destinations and visas, because all foreigners need a visa to go more than thirty kilometers from the center. Sometimes they stop Russian cars, but not often. Anyway, there's a joke here that you always see at least three Russians together when they've any regular contact with foreigners. One alone might be tempted, two might conspire, but if there are three, one will always inform."

"Cynical."

"And practical. What did you say you'd do today? I take it you have Intourist girls looking after you?"

"Natasha and Anna," I said. "I said I'd be in the hotel to lunch and go on a bus tour of the city afterward."

"Then you'd better do it," he said judiciously. "I'm not sure they don't get into trouble if they lose their charge, so to speak."

I paused at the center of the bridge to look over the parapet at the iron-gray water. Snow speckled everything and filled the air like torn tissue paper. To the right along the riverbank stretched the long red beautiful walls of the Kremlin, with golden towers at intervals and vistas of golden onion domes inside. A walled city, a fortress, and defunct churches and active government offices and the daily tread of millions of tourists. To the left, on the opposite bank, the British Embassy.

"Better move on," Stephen said. "Two men standing still on a bridge in the snow—that's suspicious."

"I don't believe it."

"You'd be surprised."

We walked on, however, and went back up the incline to Red Square.

"Job number one," I said. "Will you make a call for me?"

I showed him the Olympic team trainer's name and number, and we stopped at a glass-walled telephone box. Telephone calls, it appeared, were cheap. Stephen brushed away my offered ruble and produced a two-kopeck coin.

"What shall I say?" he asked.

"Say I'd like to see him tomorrow morning. Say I was very impressed with the Russian team at the International Horse Trials and would like to congratulate him and ask his advice. Say I'm frightfully important in the horse world. Lay it on a bit. He doesn't know me." I gave him some well-known eventing names. "Say I'm a colleague of theirs."

"Are you?" he said, dialing the number.

"I know them," I said. "That's why I was sent. Because I know the horse people."

Someone answered at the other end, and Stephen launched into what was to me a vague jumble of noises. A softer-sounding language than I had for some reason expected. Pleasing.

He talked for quite some time, and listened, and talked, and listened, and talked, and finally rang off.

"Success," he said. "Eleven o'clock. Outside the stables, round the far side of the racecourse."

"The Hippodrome," I said.

"That's right." His eyes gleamed. "The Olympic horses exercise there on the track."

"Fantastic," I said, astounded. "Bloody incredible."

"And you were wrong about one thing," Stephen said. "He did know who you are. He said you went to ride in a race called the Pardubice in Czechoslovakia, and he saw you finish third. He seemed, in point of fact, to be quite pleased to be going to meet you."

"Nice of him," I said modestly.

Stephen spoiled it. "Russians love a chance of talking to people from the outside. They see so few that they love it."

We agreed that he should meet me outside the hotel the following morning, and his cheerfulness was catching.

"When you go on that bus tour," he said as we parted, "you'll stop in Derzhinsky Square. With a statute of Derzhinsky on a tall column. There's a big store for children there. What the guide won't tell you, though, is that the building next to it, across the street, is the Lubyanka Prison."

There were taxies waiting outside the hotel but none of the drivers spoke English, and either they didn't understand the words "British Embassy" or the address written in English script, or they understood but refused to take me there. In any case, I got a chorus of shaken heads, so in the end I walked. It was still snowing, but wetly, and what lay on the ground was slush. After a mile and a half of it, my feet were soaking and icy and my mood deepening from cross to vile. Following Stephen's instructions, I found the steps at the far side of the bridge and descended to the lower level, walking along there with dark, heavy buildings on my left and the chest-high river wall on the right. When I at length reached the gateway of the embassy, a Russian soldier stepped out of a sentry box and barred my way.

An odd argument then took place, in which neither antagonist could understand a word the other said. I pointed vigorously at my watch, and to the embassy door, and said, "I am English," several times very loudly, and got even crosser. The Russian finally, dubiously, stood back and let me through into the short driveway. The huge front door of the embassy itself was opened, with a lot less fuss, by a dark-blue uniform with gilt buttons and braid.

Inside, the hall and stairs and visible doorways were rich with the glossy wood and glass and plaster moldings of more elegant ages. There was also a large leather-topped desk behind which sat a one-man reception committee, and standing near him, a tall, languid man with noble bones and graying hair combed carefully backward.

The dark-blue uniform offered to relieve me of my coat and hat, and the man at the desk asked if he could help me.

"The cultural attaché?" I said. "I've an appointment."

The gray-haired man moved gently like a lily in the wind and said that the cultural attaché happened to be himself. He extended a limp hand and a medium smile, and I responded with the merest shade more warmth to both. He murmured platitudes about the weather and air travel while he made some internal judgments about me, but it appeared that I had passed his private tests, because he suddenly changed mental gears and asked with some charm whether I would care to look over the embassy itself before we went to his office for a drink. His office, he explained, was in a separate building.

We climbed the stairs and made a tour of the reception rooms, and duly inspected the loo with the best view of the Kremlin. The cultural attaché, who had identified himself as Oliver Waterman, kept up a genial informed chatter as if he showed visitors round this route every day of the week—which, on reflection, perhaps he did. We ended up, after a short, windy outside walk, in a more mdern-looking first-floor suite of carpeted book-lined offices, where he wasted no time in pouring hefty drinks.

"Don't know what we can do for you," he said, settling deep into a leather armchair and waving me to one similar. "This Farringford business seems to be a fuss over nothing."

"You hope," I said.

He smiled thinly. "True. But there's no fire without smoke, and we haven't had even a whiff."

"Did you yourself interview the three Russian observers?" I asked.

"Er . . ." he said, clearing his throat and looking concerned. "Which observers would those be?"

Resignedly I explained. His expression cleared gradually, as if a responsibility had been taken from him.

"But you see," he said pleasantly, "we in the embassy would not speak to them ourselves. We approached our opposite numbers for relevant information, and were informed that no one knew anything of any significance."

"You couldn't have spoken to those men face to face in their own homes?"

He shook his head. "It is actively discouraged, if

not positively forbidden, for private contacts to take place.''

''Forbidden by them, or by us?''

''Bit of both. But by us, definitely.''

''So you never really get to know the Russian people, even though you live here?''

He shook his head without any visible regret. ''There is always a risk, in unofficial contacts.''

''So xenophobia works both ways?'' I said.

He uncrossed his legs and recrossed them left over right. ''Fear of foreigners is older than the conscious mind,'' he said, smiling as if he had said it often before. ''But, now, about you inquiries—''

The telephone at his elbow interrupted him. He picked up the receiver in a leisurely fashion after the third ring, and said merely, ''Yes?''

A slight frown creased his high, smooth forehead. ''Very well; bring him round.'' He replaced the receiver and continued with his former sentence. ''About your inquiries, we can offer you telex facilities, if you need them, and if you'll give me your room's telephone number, I can ring you if any messages arrive for you.''

''I gave you the number,'' I said.

''Oh, did you?'' He looked vague. ''I'd better take it again, my dear chap.''

I repeated the number from memory, and he wrote it on a notepad.

''Let me see to your glass,'' he said, splashing away with a lavish hand. ''And then perhaps you might meet one or two of my collegaues.''

There were the noises of people arriving downstairs. Oliver Waterman stood up and brushed his smooth hair back with the insides of both wrists—a gesture of preparing himself, I reckoned, more than any need for grooming.

There was one loud intrusive voice rising above a chorus of two others, one male, one female, and as they came up the stairs I found myself putting a name to it. With no sense of surprise I watched Malcolm Herrick advance through the doorway.

"Evening, Oliver," he said confidently, and then, seeing me, "Well, sport, if it isn't our sleuth. Made any progress?"

From a fleeting glance at Oliver Waterman's face I gathered that his reaction to Malcolm Herrick was much like mine. It was impossible not to attend to what Herrick said because of the physical force of his speech, the result, no doubt, of years of journalistic necessity; but there was no visible warmth behind the sociable words, and possibly even a little malice.

"Drink, Malcolm?" Oliver suggested, with true diplomatic civility.

"Couldn't be better."

Oliver Waterman, bottle and glass in hand, made introducing motions between me and the other two newcomers. "Randall Drew . . . Polly Paget, Ian Young. They work here with me in this department."

Polly Paget was a sensible-looking lady in flat shoes, past girlhood but not quite middle-aged, wearing her hair short and her cardigan long. She gave Oliver Waterman a small straightforward smile and accepted her drink before Herrick, as of right. He himself looked as if he thought attachés' assistants should be served after him.

If I hadn't been told Ian Young's name or heard him speak, I would have taken him for a Russian. I looked at him curiously, realizing how familiar I had already become with the skin texture and stillness of expression of the Moscow population. Ian Young had the same white heavyish face in which nothing discernible was going on. His voice, when he spoke, which at that time was very little, was unremarkably English.

Malcolm Herrick effortlessly dominated what conversation there was, telling Oliver Waterman, it seemed to me, just what he should do about a particularly boring row which had just broken out over a forthcoming visit of a prestigious orchestra.

When Polly Paget offered a suggestion, Herrick interrupted without listening and squashed her. Oliver Waterman said, "Well, perhaps, yes, you might be right," at intervals, while not looking Herrick in the eye except in the briefest of flashes, a sure sign of boredom or dislike. Ian Young sat looking at Herrick with an unnerving lack of response, by which Herrick was not in the least unnerved; and I drank my drink and thought of the wet walk back.

All possible juice extracted from the music scandal, Herrick switched his attention back to me.

"Well, then; sport, how's it going?"

"Slow to stop," I said.

He nodded. "Told you so. Too bad. That whole ground's been raked fine and there's not a pebble to be found. Wish there was. I need a decent story."

"Or indecent, for preference," Polly Paget said. Herrick ignored her.

"Did you talk to the *chef d'équipe?*" I said.

"Who?" said Oliver Waterman. I saw from Herrick's face that he hadn't, but also that he wasn't going to admit it unless forced to; and even then, I guessed, he would pooh-pooh the necessity.

I said to Oliver Waterman, "Mr. Kropotkin. The man who oversees the training of the horses and riders for the horse trials. The nonplaying captain, so to speak. I was given his name by Rudolph Hughes-Beckett."

"So you'll be seeing him?" Waterman said.

"Yes; tomorrow morning. He seems to be all that's left."

Ian Young stirred. "I talked with him," he said.

Every head turned his way. Thirty-five or so, I thought. Thick-set, brown-haired, wearing a crumpled gray suit and a blue-and-white-striped shirt with the points of the collar curling up like a dried sandwich. He raised his eyebrows and pursed his mouth, which for him was an excessive change of expression.

"In the course of the discreet preliminary inquiries required by the Foreign Office, I, too, was given his name. I talked with him pretty exhaustively. He knows nothing about any scandal to do with Farringford. A complete dead end."

"There you are, then," Waterman said, shrugging. "As I said before, there's no fire. Not a spark."

"Mm," I said. "It would be best that way. But there is a spark. Or there was, in England." And I told them about Johnny Farringford's being beaten up by two men who warned him to stay away from Alyosha.

Their faces showed differing levels of dismay and disbelief.

"But, my dear chap," said Oliver Waterman, recovering his former certainty. "Surely that means that this Alyosha, whoever he is, is absolutely determined not to be dropped into any sort of mess. So surely that makes it all the safer for Farringford to come to the Olympics."

"Except," I said apologetically, "that of course Farringford was also told in the summer that if he came to Moscow, Alyosha would be waiting to extract revenge for the stress which gave Hans Kramer a heart attack."

There was a short, thoughtful silence.

"People change their minds," said Polly Paget at length, judiciously. "Maybe in the summer, when Kramer died, this Alyosha sounded off a bit hysterically, and now on reflection the last thing he wants is to be involved."

Herrick shook his head impatiently, but it seemed to me the most sensible solution yet advanced.

"I really hope you're right," I said. "The only trouble will be proving it. And the only way to prove it, as it always had been, is for me to find Alyosha and talk to him and get from him his own positive assurance that he means Farringford no harm.''

Polly Paget nodded, Oliver Waterman looked mildly despairing, and Malcolm Herrick unmirthfully laughed.

''Good luck to you, then, sport,'' Herrick said. You'll be here till doomsday. I'll tell you, I've looked for this bloody Alyosha, and he doesn't exist.''

I sighed a little and looked at Ian Young. ''And you?'' I said.

''I've looked, too,'' he said. ''There isn't a trace.''

There seemed little else to say. The party broke up, and I asked Waterman if he could telephone for a taxi.

''My dear chap,'' he said regretfully, ''they won't come here. They don't like to be contaminated by stopping outside the British Embassy. You can probably catch an empty one on the main road, if you walk along to the bridge.''

We shook hands at his outer door, and again swathed in overcoat and fur hat, I set off toward the guarded gate. It had stopped snowing at last, which improved the prospects slightly. Ian Young, however, called out after me and offered me a lift in his car, which I gratefully agreed to. He sat stolidly behind his steering wheel, dealing with darkness, fallen snow, and road-obscuring slush as if emotion had never been invented.

''Malcolm Herrick,'' he said, still deadpan, ''is a pain in the arse.''

He turned left out of the gate, and drove along beside the river.

''And you're stuck with him,'' I said.

His silence was assent. ''He's a persistent burrower,'' he said. ''Gets a story if it's there.''

''You're telling me to go home and forget it?''

''No,'' he said, turning more corners. ''But don't stir up the Russians. They take fright very easily. When they're frightened, they attack. People of great endurance, full of courage. But easily alarmed. Don't forget.''

"Very well," I said.

"You have a man called Frank Jones sitting at your table at the hotel," he said.

I glanced at him. His face was dead calm.

"Yes," I said.

"Did you know he was in the KGB?"

I copied his impassiveness. I said, "Did you know that you are going a very long way round to my hotel?"

He actually reacted; even went so far as to smile. "How did you know?"

"Went on a bus tour. Studied the maps."

"And does Frank Jones sit with you always?"

"So far," I said, nodding. "And a middle-aged couple named Wilkinson from Lancashire. We sat together by chance at dinner yesterday, our first night here, and you know how it is, people tend to return to the same table. So yes, the same four of us have sat together today at breakfast and lunch. What makes you think he is in the KGB? He's as English as they come, and he was thoroughly searched at the airport on the way in."

"Searched so that you could see, I suppose?"

"Yes," I said, thinking. "Everyone on the plane could see."

"Cover," he said. "There's no mistake. He's not sitting at your table by accident. He came with you from England and he'll no doubt go back with you. Has he searched your room yet?"

I said nothing. Ian Young very faintly smiled again.

"I see he has," he said. "What did he find?"

"Clothes and cough mixture."

"No Russian addresses or phone numbers?"

"I had them in my pocket," I said. "Such as they are."

"Frank Jones," he said, driving round back streets, "has a Russian grandmother, who has spoken the language to him all his life. She married a British sailor, but her sympathies were all with the October Revolution. She recruited Frank in the cradle."

"But if he is KGB," I said, "why do you let him . . . operate?"

"Better the devil you know . . ." We swung into yet another deserted street. "Every time he comes back, we are alerted by our passport control people back home. They send a complete passenger list of the flight he comes on, because he always travels with his business. So we scan it. We get someone out pronto to the airport to see where he goes. We follow. Tut tut. We see him book into the Intourist. We drift into the dining room. If it's safe, he also *sits* with his business. We see he's with you. We know all about you. We relax. We wish Frank well. We certainly don't want to disturb him. If his masters discovered we knew all about him, next time they'd send someone else. And then where would we be? When Frank comes, we know to pay attention. Worth his weight in rubles, Frank is, to us."

We went slowly and quietly down a dark road. Snow fell and melted wetly as it touched the ground.

"What is he likely to do?" I said.

"About you? Report where you go, who you see, what you eat, and how many times you crap before breakfast."

"Sod," I said.

"And don't ditch him unless you have to, and if you have to, for God's sake make it look accidental."

I said doubtfully, "I've had no practice at this sort of thing."

"Obvious. You didn't notice him follow you from your hotel."

"Did he?" I said, alarmed.

"He was walking up and down the Naberezhnaya waiting for you to come out. He saw you drive out with me. He'll go back to the Intourist and wait for you there."

The lights from the dashboard shone dimly on his big, impassive face. The economy of muscle movement extended, I had noticed, throughout his body. His head turned little upon his neck; his hands remained in one position on the steering wheel. He didn't shift in his seat, or drum with his fingers. In his heavy raincoat, thick leather gloves, and fur hat with the ear flaps up, he looked every inch a Russian.

"What is your job here?" I said.

"Cultural assistant." His voice gave away as little as his face. Ask silly questions, I thought.

He slowed the car still further and switched off the headlights, and with the engine barely audible, swung into a cobbled courtyard and stopped. Put on the hand brake. Half turned in his seat to face me.

"You'll be a few minutes late for dinner," he said.

5

He seemed to be in no hurry to explain. We sat in complete darkness, listening to the irregular ticking of metal as the engine cooled to zero in the Moscow night. In time, as my eyes adjusted, I could see dark high buildings on each side, and some iron railings ahead, with bushes behind them.

"Where are we?" I said.

He didn't answer.

"Look—" I said.

He interrupted. "When we get out of the car, do not talk. Follow me, but say nothing. There are always people standing in the shadows. If they hear you speak English, they will be suspicious. They'll report our visit."

He opened the car door and stood up outside. He seemed to take it for granted that I should trust him, and I saw no particular reason not to. I stood up after him, closed the door quietly, as he had done, and followed where he led.

We walked toward the railings, which proved to

contain a gate. Ian Young opened it with a click of iron, and it swung on unoiled hinges with desolate little squeaks, falling shut behind us with a positive click. Beyond it, a curving path led away between straggly bare-branched bushes, the dim light showing that in this forlorn public garden the snow lay grayly unmelted, covering everything thinly, like years of undisturbed dust.

There were a few seats beside the path, and glimpses of flat areas which might in summer be grass; but in late November the melancholy of such places could seep into the soul like fungus.

Ian Young walked purposefully onward, neither hurrying nor moving with caution—a man on a normal errand, not arousing suspicion.

At the far side of the garden we reached more railings and another gate. Again the opening click, the squeaks, the closing clink. Ian Young turned without pause to the right and set off along the slushy pavement.

In silence, I followed.

Light from windows overhead revealed us to be in a residential road of large old buildings with alleys and small courtyards in between. Into one of these yards, cobbled and dark, Ian Young abruptly turned.

Again I went with him, unspeaking.

Scaffolding climbed the sides of the buildings there, and heaps of rubble cluttered the ground. We picked our way over broken bricks and metal tubing and scattered planks, going, as far as I could see, nowhere.

There was, however, a destination. To reach it, we had to step through the scaffolding and over an open ditch which looked like the preliminary earthworks of new drains; and on the far side of the mud and slush there was a heavy wooden door in a dark archway. Ian Young pushed the door, which seemed to have no fastening, and it opened with the easy grind of constant use.

Inside, out of the wind, there was a dimmish light

in a bare gray entrance. Gritty concrete underfoot, no paint, no decoration of any kind on the grayish concrete walls. There was a flight of concrete steps leading upward, and, beside them, a small lift in an ancient-looking cage.

Ian Young pulled open the outer and inner folding metal gates of the lift, and we stepped inside. He closed the gates, pushed the fourth-floor button, and forbade me, with his eye, to utter a word.

We emerged from the lift onto a bare landing, wooden-floored, not concrete. There were two closed doors, wooden, long ago varnished, one at each end of the rectangular space. Ian Young stepped to the left and pressed the button of a bell.

The hallway was very quiet. One could not hear the sound of ringing when he pushed the button, as he did again, in a short-short-long rhythm. There were no voices murmuring behind the doors. No feet on the stairs. No feeling of nearby warmth and life. The lobby to limbo, I thought fancifully; and the door quietly opened.

A tall woman stood there, looking out with the lack of expression which I by now regarded as normal. She peered at Ian Young, and then, more lingeringly, at me. Her eyes traveled back again, inquiringly.

Ian Young nodded.

The woman stepped to one side, tacitly inviting us in. Ian Young went steadfastly over the threshold, and it was far too late for me to decide that on the other side of the door was where I had no wish to be. It swung shut behind me, and the woman slid a bolt.

Still no one spoke. Ian Young took off his coat and hat, and gestured for me to do the same. The woman hung them carefully on pegs in a row that already accommodated a good many similar garments.

She put a hand on Ian Young's arm and led the way along the passage of what seemed to be a private flat. Another closed wooden door was opened, and we went into a moderate-sized living room.

There were five men there, standing up. Five pairs of eyes focused steadily on my face, five blank expressions covering who knew what thoughts.

They were all dressed tidily and much alike, in shirts, jackets, trousers, and indoor shoes, but they varied greatly in age and build. One of them, the slimmest, of about my own age, held himself rigid, as if facing an ordeal. The others were simply wary, standing like wild deer scenting the wind.

A man of about fifty, gray-haired and wearing glasses, stepped forward to greet Ian Young and give him a token hug.

He talked to him in Russian, and introduced him to the other four men in a jumble of long names I couldn't begin to catch. They nodded to him, each in turn. A little of the tension went out of the proceedings and small movements occurred in the herd.

"Evgeny Sergeevich," Ian Young said, "this is Randall Drew."

The fiftyish man slowly extended his hand, which I shook. He was neither welcoming nor hostile, and in no hurry to commit himself either way. More dignity than power, I thought; and he was inspecting me with intensity, as if wishing to peer into my soul. He saw instead, I supposed, merely a thinnish, gray-eyed, dark-haired man in glasses, giving his own impression of a stone wall.

To me Ian Young at last spoke. "This is our host, Evgeny Sergeevich Titov. And our hostess, his wife, Olga Ivanovna." He made a small semiformal bow to the woman who had let us in. She gave him a steady look, and it seemed to me that the firmness of her features came from iron reserves within.

"Good evening," I said, and she replied seriously in English, "Good evening."

The rigid young man, still tautly strung, said something urgently in Russian.

Ian Young turned to me. "He is asking if we were followed. You can answer. Were we followed?"

"No," I said.

"Why don't you think so?"

"No one followed us through the garden. The gates made an unmistakable noise. No one came through them after us."

Ian Young turned away from me and spoke to the group in Russian. They listened to him with their eyes on me, and when he had finished they stirred, and began to move apart from each other, and to sit down. Only the rigid one remained standing, ready for flight.

"I have told them they can trust you." Ian Young said. "If I am wrong, I will kill you."

His eyes were cool and steady, looking unwaveringly into mine. I listened to his words, which in other contexts would have been unbelievable and embarrassing, and I saw that he quite simply meant what he said.

"Very well," I said.

A flicker of something I couldn't read moved in his mind.

"Please sit down," Olga Ivanovna said, indicating a deep chair with arms on the far side of the room. "Please sit down there." She spoke the English words with a strong Russian accent, but that she knew any English at all put me to shame.

I walked across and sat where she pointed, knowing that they had discussed and planned that I should be placed there, from where I couldn't escape unless they chose to let me go. The deep chair embraced me softly like a bolstered prison. I looked up and found Ian Young near me, looking down. I half closed my eyes, and faintly smiled.

"What do you expect?" he said.

"To learn why we are here."

"You are not afraid." Half a statement, half a question.

"No," I said. "They are."

He glanced swiftly at the six Russians and then looked back, with concentration at me.

"You are not the usual run of bloody fool," he said.

The rigid young man, still also on his feet, said something impatiently to Ian Young. He nodded, looked from me to the rigid man and back again, took a visible breath, and entrusted me with a lot of dangerous knowledge.

"This is Boris Dmitrevich Telyatnikov," he said.

The rigid young man raised his chin as if the name itself were an honor.

Ian Young said, "Boris Dmitrevich rode in the Russian team at the International Horse Trials in England in September."

It was a piece of information which had me starting automatically to my feet, but even the beginnings of the springing motion reawoke the alarm in all the watchers. Boris Dmitrevich took an actual step backward.

I relaxed into the chair and looked as mild as possible, and the atmosphere of precarious trust crept gingerly back.

"Please tell him," I said, "that I am absolutely delighted to meet him."

The same could obviously not be said for Boris Dmitrevich Telyatnikov, but I was there from their choice, not my own. I reckoned if they hadn't wanted to see me pretty badly, they wouldn't have put themselves at what they clearly felt was considerable risk.

Olga Ivanovna brought a hard wooden chair and placed it facing me, about four feet away. She then fetched another and placed it near me, at right angles. Ian Young took this seat next to me, and Boris Dmitrevich the one opposite.

While this was going on, I took a look round the room, which had bookshelves over much of the wall space, and cupboards over the rest. The single large window was obscured by solid wooden cream-painted shutters, fastened by a flat metal bar through slots. The floor was of bare wooden boards, dark-stained, unpolished and clean. Furniture consisted of a table, an old sofa covered with a rug, several hard chairs, and the ōne deep uncomfortable one in which I sat. All the furniture, except for the two chairs repositioned for Boris Dmitrevich and Ian Young, was ranged round the walls against the bookshelves and cupboards, leaving the center free. There were no softeners: no curtains, cushions, or indoor plants. Nothing extravagant, frivolous, or wasteful. Everything of ancient and sensible worth, giving an overall impression of shabbiness stemming from long use but not from underlying poverty. A room belonging to people who chose to have it that way, not who could not afford anything different.

Ian Young carried on a short conversation with Boris Dmitrevich in impenetrable Russian, and then did a spot of translation, looking more worried than I liked.

"Boris wants to warn us," he said, "that what you are dealing with is not some tomfool scandal but something to do with killing people."

"With *what?*"

He nodded. "That's what he said." He turned his head back to Boris, and then talked some more. It appeared, from the expressions all around me, that what Boris was saying was no news to anyone except Ian Young and myself.

Boris was built like a true horseman, of middle height, with strong shoulders and well-coordinated movements. He was good-looking, with straight black hair and ears very flat to his head. He spoke earnestly to Ian Young, his dark eyes flicking my way every few seconds as if to check that he could still risk my hearing what he had to tell.

"Boris says," Ian Young said, the shock showing, "that the German Hans Kramer, was murdered."

"No," I said confidently. "There was an autopsy. Natural causes."

Ian shook his head. "Boris says that someone has found a way of causing people to drop dead from heart

attacks. He says that the death of Hans Kramer
was"—he turned back briefly to Boris to consult, and
then back to me—"the death of Hans Kramer was a
sort of demonstration."

It seemed ridiculous. "A demonstration of what?"

A longer chat ensued. Ian Young shook his head
and argued. Boris began to make fierce chopping motions with his hands, and spots of color appeared on
his cheeks. I gathered that his information had at this
point entered the realms of guess-work, and that Ian
Young didn't believe what was being said. Time to
take a pull back to the facts.

"Look," I said, interrupting the agitated flow.
"Let's start at the beginning. I'll ask some questions,
and you get me the answers. O.K.?"

"Yes," Ian Young said, subsiding. "Carry on."

"Ask him how he traveled to England, and where
he went, and where he stayed, and how his team fared
in the finals."

"But," he said, puzzled, "what has that to do with
Hans Kramer?"

"Not much," I said. "But I know how the Russians
traveled and where they stayed and how they fared,
and I just want to do my own private bit of checking
that Boris is who he says he is; and also, if he talks
about unloaded things like that he will calm down
again and we can then get the beliefs without the passion."

He blinked. "My God," he said.

"Ask him."

"Yes." He turned to Boris and delivered the question.

Boris answered impatiently that they traveled by
motorized horsecar across Europe to The Hague, and
from there by sea to England, still with the horsecars,
and drove on to Burghley, where they stayed in quarters especially reserved for them.

"How many horses, and how many men?" I said.

Boris said six horses, and stumbled over the number of people. I suggested that this was because the Russians had paid for only seven "human" tickets but had actually taken ten or more men. . . . . Make it a joke, I said to Ian Young, not an insult.

He made it enough of a joke for Boris and everyone else almost to laugh, which handily released much tension all round and steadied the temperature.

"They want to know how you know," Ian said.

"The shipping agent told me. Tickets were bought for six riders and a *chef d'équipe,* but three or four grooms traveled among the legs of the horses. The shipping agents were amused, not angry."

Ian relayed the answer and got another round of appreciative noise in the throat. Boris gave a more detailed account of the Russian team's performance in the trials than I had memorized, and by the end I had no doubt that he was genuine. He had also recovered his temper and lost his rigidity, and I reckoned we might go carefully back to the minefield.

"Right," I said. "Now ask him if he knew Hans Kramer personally. If he ever spoke to him face to face, and if so in what language."

The question at once stiffened up the sinews, but the reply looked only moderately nervous.

Ian Young translated. "Yes, he did talk to Hans Kramer. They spoke German, though Boris says he knows only a little German. He had met Hans Kramer before, when they both rode in the same trials, and they were friendly together."

"Ask him what they talked about," I said.

The answer came easily, predictably, with shrugs. "Horses. The trials. The Olympics. The weather."

"Anything else?"

"No."

"Anything to do with backgammon, gambling clubs, homosexuals, or transvestites?"

I saw by the collective indrawn breaths of disap-

proval that if Boris had been discussing such things,
he had better not say so. His own positive negative,
however, looked real enough.

"Does he know Johnny Farringford?" I said.

It appeared that Boris knew who Johnny was, and
had seen him ride, but had not spoken to him.

"Did he see Hans Kramer and Johnny Farringford
together?"

Boris had not noticed one way or the other.

"Was he there on the spot when Hans Kramer
died?"

Boris's unemotional response told me the answer
before Ian translated.

"No, he wasn't. He had finished his cross-country
section before Hans Kramer set out. He saw Hans
Kramer being *weighed.* . . . Is that right?" Ian Young
looked doubtful.

"Yes," I said. "The horses have to carry minimum
weights, to make it a fairer test. There is a weighing
machine on the course, to weigh the riders with their
saddles, just before they set off, and also as soon as
they come back. The same as in racing."

Boris, it appeared, had had to wait while Hans Kramer was weighed out, before himself weighing in. He
had wished Hans Kramer good luck. *"Alles besten."*
The irony of it lugubriously pleased the listening
friends.

"Please ask Boris why he thinks Hans Kramer was
murdered." I said the words deliberately flatly, and
Ian Young relayed them the same way, but they reproduced in Boris the old high alarm.

"Did he hear anyone say so?" I asked decisively,
to cut off the emotion.

"Yes."

"Who said so?"

Boris did not know the man who said so.

"Did he say it to Boris face to face?"

No. Boris had overheard it.

I could see why Ian Young had doubted the whole story.

"Ask in what language this man spoke."

In Russian, Boris said, but he was not a Russian.

"Does he mean that the man spoke Russian with a foreign accent?"

That was right.

"What accent?" I said patiently. "From what country?"

Boris didn't know.

"Where was Boris when he overheard this man?"

It seemed a pretty harmless question to me, but it brought an abrupt intense stillness into the room.

Evgeny Sergeevich Titov finally stirred and said something lengthily to Ian.

"They want you to understand that Boris should not have been where he was. That if he tells you, you will hold his future in your power."

"I see," I said.

There was a pause.

Ian said, "I think they're waiting for you to swear you will never reveal where he was."

"Perhaps he had better just tell me what he heard," I said.

There was a brief consultation among all of them, but they must have decided before I came that I would have to know.

Evgeny Sergeevich did the talking. Boris, he said, had been on a train, going to London. It was absolutely against orders. If he had been discovered, he would have been sent home immediately in disgrace. He would never be considered for the Olympic team, and he might even have faced imprisonment, as he was carrying letters and other papers to Russians who had defected to the West. The papers were not political, Evgeny said earnestly, but just personal messages and photographs from the defectors' families still in Russia, and a few small writings for publication in

literary magazines. Not state secrets, but highly illegal. There would have been much trouble for many
people, not just for Boris, if he had been stopped and
searched. So that when he heard someone speaking
Russian on the train he had been very frightened, and
his first urgent priority had been to keep out of sight
himself, not to see who had been speaking. He had
crept out of the carriage he was in, and walked forward
as far as he could through the train. When it reached
London, he left it fast, and was met by friends at the
barrier.

"I understand all that," I said, when Ian Young
finished translating. "Tell them I won't tell."

Encouraged, Boris came to the nub.

"There were two men," Ian Young relayed.
"Because of the noise of the train, Boris could only
hear one of them."

"Right. Go on."

Boris spoke into a breath-held attentive silence. Ian
Young listened with his former skepticism showing
once again.

"He says," he said, "that he overheard a man say,
'It was a perfect demonstration. You could kill half
the Olympic riders the same way, if that's what you
want. But it will cost you.' Then the other man said
something inaudible, and the voice Boris could hear
said, 'I have another client.' The other man spoke,
and then the man Boris could hear said, 'Kramer took
ninety seconds.' "

Bloody hell, I thought. Shimmering scarlet *hell*.

Boris crept away at that point, Ian said. Boris was
too worried about being discovered himself for the
meaning of what he had heard to sink in. And in any
case, it was not until the next day that he learned of
Kramer's death. When he did hear, he was shattered.
Before that, he had thought the ninety seconds was
something to do with timing on the event course."

"Ask him to repeat what he heard the man say,"
I said.

The exchanges took place.

"Did Boris use exactly the same words as the first time?" I said.

"Yes, exactly."

"But you don't believe him?"

"He half heard something perfectly innocent and the rest's imagination."

"But he believes it," I said. "He got angry when you argued. He certainly believes that's what he heard."

I thought it over, all too aware of seven pairs of eyes directed unwaveringly at my face.

"Please ask Mr. Titov," I said, "why he has persuaded Boris to tell us all this. I might guess, but I would like him to confirm it."

Evgeny Sergeevich, sitting on a wooden chair in front of a bookcase, answered with responsibility visibly bowing his shoulders. Lines ridged his forehead. His eyes were somber.

Ian said, "He has been very worried since Boris came home from England and told him what he had heard. There was the possibility that Boris was mistaken, and also the possibility that he was not. If he did really hear what he thought he heard, there might be another murder at the Olympics. Or more than one. As a good Russian, Evgeny was anxious that nothing should harm his country in the eyes of the world. It wouldn't do for competitors to be murdered on Russian soil. A way had to be found of warning someone who could get an investigation made, but Evgeny knew no one in England or Germany to write to, even if you could entrust such a letter to the mail. He couldn't explain how he had come by such knowledge, because Boris's whole life would be spoiled, and yet he couldn't see anyone believing the story without Boris's own testimony, so he was up a creek without a paddle."

"Or words to that effect?"

"You got it."

"Ask if they know anyone called Alyosha who is even remotely concerned with the Russian team, or the trials, or the Olympics, or Hans Kramer, or anything."

There was a general unhurried discussion, and the answer was no.

"Is Boris related to Evgeny?" I said.

The question was asked and answered.

"No. Boris just values Evgeny's advice. Evgeny consulted the others."

I looked thoughtfully at Ian. His face, as always, gave away as much as a slab of granite, and I found it disconcerting to have no clue at all to what he was thinking.

"You yourself knew Mr. Titov before this evening, didn't you?" I said. "And you'd been here before?"

"Yes, two or three times. Olga Ivanovna works in Cultural Relations, and she's a good friend. But I have to be careful. I'm not allowed to be here."

"Complicated," I agreed.

"Evgeny rang me this afternoon and said you were in Moscow, and would I bring you here this evening. I said I would if I could, after you'd been to the embassy."

The speed of communications had me gasping. "Just how did Evgeny know I was in Moscow?"

"Nikolai Alexandrovich happened to tell Boris—"

"*Who?*"

"Nikolai Alexandrovich Kropotkin. The *chef d'équipe*. You have an appointment with him tomorrow morning."

"For Christ's sake."

"Kropotkin told Boris, Boris told Evgeny, Evgeny rang me, and I had heard from Oliver Waterman that you would be round for a drink."

"So simple," I said, shaking my head. "And if Evgeny knew you, why didn't he tell you all this weeks ago?"

Ian Young gave me a cool stare and relayed the question.

"Evgeny says it was because Boris wouldn't talk to me."

"Well, go on," I said, as he stopped. "Why did Boris decide he *would* talk to *me?*"

Ian shrugged, and asked, and translated Boris's reply.

"Because you are a rider. A man who knows horses. Boris trusts you because you are a comrade."

6

The lifts at the Intourist Hotel did not stop at the lower of the two restaurant floors, which was where the English tourists ate. One could either walk up one story from the lobby, or stop the lift at the floor above and walk down. I did that, after parking my coat in my room, and walked down the shallow treads of the broad circular staircase, where through the handrail I could see the faces in the dining room before they looked up and saw me.

Natasha was on her feet, consulting her watch and looking worried. The Lancashire Wilkinsons were drinking coffee, unaffected; and if I read anxiety and anger into the fidgets of Frank Jones, it was probably only because I guessed they were there.

"Evening," I said, reaching the bottom. "Am I too late? Is there anything left?"

Natasha sped across with visible relief. "We thought you were lost."

I gave her a full and ingenuous story about a friend driving me up to the university to look down on the lights of the city by night. The Wilkinsons listened with interest, and Frank with slowly evaporating tenseness, as they all, like me, had been up at the semiofficial lookout spot in the afternoon on the bus tour. Indeed, I almost convinced myself. "Afraid we were a bit longer than I expected," I said apologetically.

The Wilkinsons and Frank stayed for company while I ate, and kept up a thoroughly touristy flow of chat. I looked at Frank with a great deal more interest than before, trying to see behind the mask, and failing to do so. Outwardly he was still a raw-boned twenty-eight or so with an undercombed generosity of reddish-brown curls and the pits and scars of long-term acne. His views were still diluted Marx and his manner still based on a belief in his own superiority to the bulk of mankind.

There were four courses to the evening meal, and the only choice was eat it or don't. The meat looked identical to the tasteless rubber of the evening before, and when it arrived I stared at it gloomily.

"Aren't you going to eat that?" Frank demanded, pointing fiercely at my plate.

"Are you still hungry? Would you care for it?" I said.

"Do you mean it?" He took me at my word, slid the plate in front of him, and set to, proving that both his appetite and his molars were a lot stronger than mine.

"Did you know," he said with his mouth full, giving us a by now accustomed lecture, "that in this country rents are very low, and electricity and transport and telephone calls are cheap. And when I say cheap, I mean cheap."

Mrs. Wilkinson sighed with envy over so perfect a world.

"But then," I said, "if you're a retired welder from Novosibirsk, you can't go on a package tour of London, just for a bit of interest."

"There, Dad," Mrs. Wilkinson said. "That's true."

Frank chewed on the meat and made no comment.

"Isn't it term time?" I asked him innocently.

He ruminated over his answer, then asserted he was between jobs. Left one school back in July, starting at another in January.

"What do you teach?" I said.

He was vague. "You know. This and that. A bit of everything. Junior school, of course."

Mrs. Wilkinson told him that her nephew, who had ingrowing toenails, had always wanted to be a teacher. Frank opened his mouth and then decided not to ask what ingrowing toenails had to do with it, and I smothered my laughter in ice cream and black-currant jam.

I needed something to laugh about, however inwardly. The intensity and fear that had vibrated among the Russians in Evgeny Titov's flat remained with me as a sort of hovering claustrophobic depression. Even leaving the place had had to be carefully managed. It would never have done, I gathered, for so many people to have left at once. Evgeny and Olga had pressed Ian Young and me to stay for a further ten minutes after Boris had gone, so that if anyone was watching, we should not be connected.

"Is it always like this?" I had asked Ian Young, and he had said prosaically, "Pretty much."

Evgeny, having shifted the burden of his knowledge squarely onto me, had shaken hands gravely in farewell, clasping my hands in both of his. He had done his best, I supposed. He had passed on the flaming torch, and if now the Olympics were scorched by it, it would be my fault, not his.

Olga had seen us out with the same prudence with which she had let us in. We picked our way through the scaffolding—"Old apartment building being renovated," Ian explained in the car later—and walked back through the garden. There were still only two sets of black footprints in the snow on the path, our own from the outward journey; and no one came after us through the gates. Two dark, silent figures, we eased our way into the car, and the noise of the engine's starting seemed suddenly too loud for safety. To have to live like that, constantly wary, seemed to me dreadful. Yet the Russians and even Ian Young considered it normal; and perhaps that was most dreadful of all.

"What are you going to do?" Ian asked, driving back toward the city center. "About this story of Boris's?"

"Ask around," I said vaguely. "What are you?"

"Nothing. It's just his overheated imagination."

I didn't altogether agree with him, but I didn't argue.

"And I'd be glad if you'd do me a favor, my old son."

"What's that?" I said, internally amused.

"Don't mention Evgeny or his apartment to anyone from the embassy. Don't mention our visit. I like our good Oliver to be able to put his hand on his heart among the natives and swear he has no knowledge of any of his staff making private visits to Russian homes."

"All right."

He turned into a wide, well-lit divided highway which at eight-thirty held as much traffic as one would at four in the morning back home.

"And don't get them into trouble," he said. "Evgeny and Boris."

"Or you'll kill me."

"Yeah." He laughed awkwardly. "Well ... it sounds stupid, out here."

I didn't ask if he really meant it. It was a question to which there was no answer, and I hadn't any intention of putting him to the test.

With the image of Ian Young in my mind, I glanced across the table at Frank Jones. One looked Russian and walked carefully on the wrong side of the regulations; the other looked English and harmless and could throw you to the spikes.

Natasha brought her marvelous eyebrows to the table and drew up a chair. She wore a neat pink wool dress, which went with the lipstick and displayed curves where they looked best. Her voice had a small disarming lisp, and she was achieving a slightly anxious smile.

"Tomorrow," she said, "the Exhibition of Economic Achievements . . ."

"Tomorrow," I said, providing my best giving-no-offense expression, "I'm going to see some horses. I'm sure the exhibition is great, but I'm much better at horses, and I have this absolutely wonderful chance to see some of your very best, your really top horses, the ones that are being trained for the Olympics, and that will be such a treat for me that I simply can't miss it."

The floweriness more or less did the trick, and it was Frank who asked, with natural-looking interest, where the horses were that I was going to see.

"At the racecourse," I said. "They are stabled near there, I believe."

I saw no point in not telling him. It would have looked odd if I hadn't, and in any case he could have found out by following.

Stephen Luce appeared promptly at ten the following morning outside the hotel, his round, cheerful face the brightest thing under the gray Moscow sky. I made the passage from hot air to cold through the double entrance to join him, passing at least six men standing around doing nothing.

"Metro and bus to the Hippodrome," Stephen said. "I've looked up the stops."

"Taxi," I said firmly.

"But taxis are expensive, and the metro's cheap."

"And the far side of the Hippodrome could be two miles' walk from the front entrance."

We took a taxi. Pale greenish-gray sedan, with a meter. Stephen carefully explained where we wanted to go, but the driver had to stop and ask twice when we reached the area. Passengers, it appeared, very seldom asked to be driven to the back of the race-course. I resisted two attempts to decant us with vague assurances that the place we wanted was "just down there," and finally, with a scowl or two and some muttering under the breath, we were driven right into the stable area, with the track itself lying a hundred yards ahead.

"You're very persistent," Stephen said, as I counted out the fare.

"I don't like wet feet."

The air temperature must have been about one degree centigrade and the humidity 95 percent: a damp, icy near-drizzle. The slushy snow lay around sullenly melting, lying in puddles on the packed clay surface in the centers of the stable roadways, banked up in ruts along the edges.

To left and right a double row of lengthy stable blocks stretched away, built of concrete on the barn principle, with the horses totally enclosed, and not sticking their heads out into the open air. Ahead, the stable area led directly out through a wide gap onto the railed racing circuit, which was of the sticky consistency of dirt tracks the world over.

In the distance, over on the far side, one could see the line of stands, gray and lifeless at that time of day. All around us, where the morning action lay, horses and men trudged about their business and paid no attention to us at all.

"It's staggering," Stephen said, looking around. "You practically can't get into anywhere in the Soviet Union without talking your way past some sort of guard, and we just drove straight in here."

"People who work with horses are antibureaucratic."

"Are you?" he said.

"Every inch. Stick to essentials, and make your own decisions."

"And to hell with committees?"

"The question nowadays is whether it's possible." I watched some horses without saddles being led by on their way from a stable block out toward the track, their feet plopping splashily in the wet. "You know something? These are not race horses."

"It's a racecourse," he said, as if I were crazy.

"They're trotters."

"What do you mean?"

"Trotting races. The driver sits on a little chariot thing called a sulky, and the horse pulls it along at a fast trot. Like that," I added, pointing, as a horse and sulky came into view on the track.

It wheeled up speedily to the entrance to the stables, and there the handlers unfastened the harness which held the shafts of the sulky, and led the horse away. The sulky was harnessed to the next horse to be exercised, and the driver took up the reins and got on with his job.

"Don't you think we ought to look for Mr. Kropotkin?" Stephen suggested.

"Not really. We're a few minutes early. If we just stand here, maybe he will come and find us."

Stephen looked as if life were full of surprises but not altogether bad ones, and several more horses slopped past. The stablehands leading them all seemed to be small weather-beaten men with unshaven chins and layers of uncoordinated clothes. None of them wore gloves. None of them even looked our way, but they shambled on with stolid, unsmiling faces.

A new and larger string of horses appeared, coming not from one of the stable blocks, but across the road we had arrived by, and in through the unguarded, ungated entrance. Instead of being led, these were ridden; and the riders were neatly dressed in jodhpurs and quilted jackets. On their heads they wore not leather caps but crash helmets, with the chin straps meticulously fastened.

"What are those?" Stephen said, as they approached.

"They're not thoroughbreds—not race horses. I should think those might be the eventers."

"How can you tell they're not race horses?"

"Thicker bones," I said. "The more solid shape of the head. And more hair around the fetlocks."

Stephen said, "Oh," as if he wasn't much wiser. I noticed that behind the horses walked a purposeful man in a dark overcoat and a fur hat. His gaze had fallen upon us, and he changed course ten degrees to starboard and came our way.

Stephen went a step to meet him.

"Mr. Nikolai Alexandrovich Kropotkin?" he said.

"*Da*," said the newcomer. "That is so."

His voice was as deep as chocolate and the Russian intonation very pronounced. He looked at me closely. "And you are Randall Drew," he said, carefully stressing each word separately.

"Mr. Kropotkin, I am very pleased to meet you," I said.

He clasped my outstretched hand and gave it a good pump with both of his own.

"Randall Drew. Pardubice. You are three."

"Third," I said, nodding.

Words failed him in English and he rumbled away in his own language.

"He is saying," Stephen said, his eyes grinning, "that you are a great horseman with a bold heart and hands of silk, and he is honored to see you here."

Mr. Kropotkin broke off the exaggerations to shake hands in a perfunctory way with Stephen, giving him the fast head-to-toe inspection of a horseman for a horse. He said something to him abruptly, which Stephen said afterward was "Do you ride?" and on receiving a negative, treated him henceforth merely as a translating machine, not as a valued friend.

"Please tell Mr. Kropotkin that the Russian team rode with great courage and skill at the International Trials, and the fitness of his horses here today does his management great credit."

Mr. Kropotkin's appreciation of the compliments showed in a general aura of pleased complacency. He was a big man of about sixty, carrying a good deal of excess weight but still light on his feet. A heavy graying mustache overhung his upper lip, and he had a habit of smoothing the outer edges downward with his forefinger and thumb.

"You watch horses," he said, his way with English putting the words halfway between a command and an invitation. I would be pleased to, I said, and we walked forward onto the track.

His five charges were circling there, waiting for the instructions which he gave decisively but briefly in his rolling bass. The riders stopped circling and divided into two groups.

"Horses canter," Kropotkin said, sweeping out an arm. "Round."

"Yes," I said.

He and I stood side by side in the manner of horse watchers the world over, and eyed the training exercises. There was a lot of muscle, I thought, and all five had good free-flowing actions; but it was impossible to tell how good each was at eventing, because speed alone had little to do with it.

Kropotkin launched into several sentences and waited impatiently for Stephen to translate.

"These are a few of the Olympic possibles. It is too soon to decide yet. There are other horses in the south, where it is warmer. All the flat race horses from the track have gone south to the Caucasus for the winter. Some horses are training there for the Olympics also, but he will have them back in Moscow next summer."

''Tell him I am very interested.''

Kropotkin received the news with what I took to be satisfaction. He, too, had the inexpressive face and unsmiling eyes which were the Moscow norm. Mobility of features, I supposed, was something one did or didn't learn in childhood from the faces all around; and the fact that they didn't show didn't conclusively prove that admiration and contempt and hate and glee weren't going on inside. It had become, I dared say, imprudent to show them. The unmoving countenance was the first law of survival.

The horses came back from circling the mile-long track without a flutter of the nostril. The riders dismounted and spoke to Kropotkin with respect. They didn't look to me like Olympic material either on horseback or on their feet—nothing of the self-confident presence of Boris—but I asked all the same.

''*Niet,*'' Kropotkin said. ''Misha is young. Is good.''

He pointed at a boy of about nineteen who was, like the others, leading his horse round in a circle under Kropotkin's stony gaze. Kropotkin added more in Russian, and Stephen translated.

''He says they are all grooms, but he is teaching Misha, because he is brave and has good hands and can get horses to jump.''

A dark-green horsecar was driven in through the stable area behind us, its engine making an untuned clatter which stirred up the horses. Kropotkin stolidly watched while it made a bad job of reversing down between the two rows of stable blocks, its old-fashioned wooden sides rattling from the vibration of the engine. The noise abated slightly once it was out of sight on the other side of the concrete barn, and when Kropotkin could once again make himself heard, he said a good deal to Stephen.

''Mr. Kropotkin says,'' Stephen said, ''that Misha went to the International Trials in September as a groom, and perhaps you would like to talk to him also. Mr. Kropotkin said that when a man from the British

Embassy came to ask him some questions about Lord Farringford and Hans Kramer, he said he knew nothing, and that was true. But he has remembered since then that Misha does know something about Hans Kramer, but not Lord Farringford, and he arranged for Misha to be riding this morning in case you should wish to see him.''

"Yes," I said. "Thank you very much indeed."

Kropotkin made a small inclination of the head, and addressed himself to the riders.

"He's telling them to lead the horses back to the stable, and to be careful crossing the road outside. He's telling Misha to stay behind."

Kropotkin turned back to me and stroked his mustache. "Horse of Misha is good. Go to Olympics," he said.

I looked at Misha's charge with interest, though there was no way in which it stood out from the others. A hardy chestnut with a white blaze down its nose, and two white socks; a rough coat, which would be normal at that time of year, and a kind eye.

"Good," Kropotkin said, slapping its rump.

"He looks bold and tough," I said. Stephen translated and Kropotkin did not demur.

The four other horses were led away, and Kropotkin introduced Misha formally but without flourish.

"Mikhail Alexeevich Tarevsky," he said, and to the boy added what was clearly an instruction to answer whatever I asked.

"*Da*, Nikolai Alexandrovich," he said.

I thought there were better places for conducting interviews than in near-freezing semidrizzle on an open dirt track, but neither Kropotkin nor Misha seemed aware of the weather, and the fact that Stephen and I were shifting from one cold foot to the other evoked no offers of adjourning to a warm office.

"In England," said the boy, "I learn little English."

His voice and manner were serious, and his accent a great deal lighter than Kropotkin's. His eyes, unexpectedly blue in his weather-tanned face, looked full of unguarded intelligence. I smiled at him involuntarily, but he only stared gravely back.

"Please tell me what you know of Hans Kramer," I said.

Kropotkin instantly rumbled something positive, and Stephen said, "He wishes Misha to speak in Russian, so that he may hear. He wishes me to translate what you ask."

"O.K.," I said. "Ask Misha what he knows of Kramer. And for God's sake let's get on. I'm congealing."

Misha stood beside his horse, pulling the reins over the chestnut's head to hold them more easily below the mouth for leading, and stroking his neck from time to time to soothe him. I couldn't see that it was doing any good for an Olympic-type horse to stand around getting chilled so soon after exercise, but it wasn't my problem. The chestnut certainly didn't seem to mind.

Stephen said, "Mikhail Alexeevich—that is, Misha—says that he was near Hans Kramer when he died."

It was amazing how suddenly I no longer felt the cold.

"How near?"

The answer was lengthy. Stephen listened and translated.

"Misha says he was holding the horse of one of the Russian team who was being weighed—is that right?—and Hans Kramer was there. He had just finished his cross-country, and had done well, and people were there round him, congratulating him. Misha was half watching, and half watching for the rider of the horse."

"I understand," I said. "Go on."

Misha talked. Stephen said, "Hans Kramer staggered and fell to the ground. He fell not far from Misha; about three meters. An English girl went to help him and someone else ran to fetch the doctor.

Hans Kramer looked very ill. He could not breathe properly. But he was trying to say something. Trying to tell the English girl something. He was lying flat on the ground. He could hardly breathe. He was saying words as loudly as he could. Like trying to shout.''

Misha waited until Stephen had finished, clearly understanding what Stephen was saying and punctuating the translation with nods.

"Hans Kramer was saying these words in German?'' I said.

"Da," said Misha, but Kropotkin interrupted, wanting to be told the question. He made an assenting gesture with his hand to allow Misha to proceed.

"And does Misha speak German?"

Misha, it appeared, had learned German in school, and had been with the teams' horses to East Germany, and knew enough to make himself understood.

"All right," I said. "What did Hans Kramer say?"

Misha said the words in German, and then in Russian, and one word flared out of both like a beacon.

Alyosha.

Stephen lit up strongly with excitement, and I thought there was probably a good deal to be said for a face that gave nothing away. His enthusiasm seemed to bother Kropotkin, who made uneasy movements as if on the point of retreat.

"Cool it," I said to Stephen flatly. "You're frightening the birds."

He gave me a quick surprised look, but dampened his manner immediately.

"Hans Kramer said," he reported in a quiet voice, " 'I am dying. It is Alyosha. Moscow.' And then he said, 'God help me.' And then he died."

"How did he die?" I said.

Misha, via Stephen, said that he turned blue, and seemed to stop breathing, and then there was a sort of small jolt right through his body, and someone said it was his heart stopping; it was a heart attack. The doctor came, and agreed it was a heart attack. He tried to bring Hans Kramer back to life, but it was useless."

The four of us stood in the Russian drizzle thinking about the death of a German in England on a sunny September day.

"Ask him what else he remembers," I said.

Misha shrugged.

"The English girl and some of the people near had understood what Hans Kramer had said. The English girl was saying to other people that he had said he was dying because of Alyosha, who came from Moscow, and other people were agreeing. It was very sad. Then the Russian rider came back from being weighed, and Misha had to attend to him and the horse, and he saw from a little way off that the ambulance people came with a stretcher. They put Hans Kramer on the stretcher and put a rug right over him and over his face, and carried him off."

"Um . . ." I said, thinking. "Ask him again what Hans Kramer said."

Hans Kramer had said, "I am dying. It is Alyosha. Moscow. God help me." He had not had time to say any more, although Misha thought he had been trying to.

"Is Misha sure that Hans Kramer did not say, 'I am dying because of Alyosha from Moscow'?"

Misha, it seemed, was positive. There had deen no "because" and no "from." Only "I am dying. It is Alyosha. Moscow. God help me." Misha remembered very clearly, he said, because Alyosha was his own father's name.

"Is it really?" I said, interested.

Misha said that he himself was Mikhail Alexeevich Tarevsky. Mikhail, son of Alexei. And Alyosha was the affectionate form of Alexei. Misha was certain Hans Kramer had said. "It is Alyosha." *"Es ist Alyosha."*

I looked unseeingly over the sodden racecourse.

"Ask Misha," I said slowly, "if he can describe

any of the people who were with Kramer before he staggered and fell down. Ask if he remembers if any of them was carrying anything, or doing anything, which did not fit into the normal scene. Ask if anyone gave Kramer anything to eat or drink.''

Stephen stared. ''But it was a heart attack.''

''There might have been,'' I said mildly, ''contributive factors. A shock. An argument. An accidental blow. An allergy. A sting from a wasp.''

''Oh, I see.'' He asked the alarming questions as if they were indeed harmless. Misha answered straightforwardly, taking them the same way.

''Misha says,'' Stephen reported, ''that he did not know any of the people round Hans Kramer, except that he had seen them at the trials that day and the day before. The Russians are not allowed to mix with the other grooms and competitors, so he had not spoken to them. He himself had seen nothing which could have given anybody a heart attack, but of course, he had not been watching closely. But he couldn't remember any argument, or blow, or wasp. He couldn't remember for certain whether Hans Kramer had eaten or drunk anything, but he didn't think so.

''Well,'' I said, pondering, ''was there anyone there who Misha considers could have been Alyosha?''

The answer to that was that he didn't really think so, because when Hans Kramer was saying that name he was not saying it *to* anyone, except perhaps to the English girl, but *she* couldn't have been Alyosha, because it was a man's name.

The cold was creeping back. If Misha knew any more, I didn't know how to unlock it.

I said, ''Please thank Misha for his very intelligent help, and tell Mr. Kropotkin how much I value his assistance in letting me speak to Misha in this way.''

The compliments were received as due, and Kropotkin, Stephen, and I began to walk off the track, back toward the main stable area and the road beyond.

Misha, leading the horse, followed a few paces behind us.

As we passed the opening between the two rows of stable blocks, the green wooden horsecar, whose engine had been grumbling away in the background all the while we had been talking, suddenly revved up into a shattering roar.

Misha's horse reared with fright, and Misha cried out. Automatically I turned back to help him. Misha, facing me, was tugging downward on the reins, with the chestnut rearing yet again above him, and the horse's bunched quarters were, so to speak, staring me in the face.

As I came toward him, Misha's gaze slid over me and fastened on something behind my back. His eyes opened wide in fear. He yelled something to me in Russian, and then he simply dropped the reins and ran.

7

From a purely reflex action I grabbed the reins which he had left dangling to the ground and at the same time glanced back over my shoulder.

The time to death looked like three seconds.

The towering top of the green horsecar blotted out the sky. The engine accelerated to a scream. I shall remember the pattern of the radiator grille forever after. Six tons unladen weight, I thought. One had time, I found, for the most useless thoughts. Thoughts could be measured in fizzing ten-thousandths of a second. Action took a little longer.

I grabbed the horse's mane with my left hand and the front of the saddle with my right, and half jumped, half hauled myself onto his back.

The horse was terrified already by the noise and the proximity of the horsecar, but horses don't altogether understand about the necessity of removing themselves pronto from under the wheels of thundering juggernauts. Frightened horses, on the whole, are more apt to run *into* the paths of vehicles than away.

Horses, on the other hand, are immensely receptive to human emotions, especially when the human is on their back, and scared out of his wits. The chestnut unerringly got the unadulterated message of fear, and bolted.

From a standing start a fit horse can beat most cars over a hundred yards, but the horsecar was a long way from standing. The chestnut's blast-off kept him merely a few yards ahead of the crushing green killer roaring on our heels.

If the horse had had the right sort of sense, he would have darted away to the left or right down some narrow cranny where the horsecar couldn't follow. Instead he galloped ahead in a straight true line, making disaster easy.

It was of only moderate help that I was still grasping a section of rein. Owing to the fact that Misha had taken the reins over the horse's head to lead him, they were not now neatly to hand, with each rein leading tidily to its own side of the bit; they were both on the left side and came from below the horse's mouth. Since horses are normally steered by pulling the bit upward against the mouth's sensitive corners, any urgent instructions from me had little chance of getting through. There were also the difficulties that my feet were not in the stirrups, I was wearing a heavy overcoat, and my fur hat was tipping forward over my spectacles. The chestnut took his own line and burst out onto the open spaces of the track.

He swerved instinctively to the right, which was the way he always trained, and his quarters thrust him onward with the vigor of a full-blown stampede. His hurtling feet sent up clouds of spray behind us, and it was while I was wondering how long he could keep up the pace, and hoping it was forever, that I first thought that perhaps the sound of the motor had diminished.

Too good to be true, I thought. On the straight and level, a horsecar could go faster than a horse; perhaps it was in overdrive and simply made less noise that way.

I risked a look over my shoulder, and my spirits went up as swiftly as a helium balloon. The horsecar had given up the chase. It was turning on the track, and going back the way it had come.

"Glory be," I thought, and "Hallelujah," and "O noble beast"—jumbled thanks to the horse and his putative maker.

There was still the problem of getting the noble beast to stop. Panic had infected him easily. Nonpanic was not getting through.

My hat fell completely off. Speed drove cold air through my hair, and stung my ears. The drizzle misted my glasses. Heavy double-breasted close-but-toned·overcoats were definitely bad news on bolters. Flapping trousers never reassured any horse. I thought that if I didn't do something about the pedals and steering, I could very well ignominiously fall off—and what would Mr. Kropotkin have to say if I let his Olympic horse go loose?

Little by little, a vestige of control returned to the proceedings. It was after all a mile-long, left-hand cir-cuit, and the one way I had a chance of influencing our direction was to the left. Constant pressure on the reins pulled the chestnut's head all the time toward the inner rails, and once I'd managed to put my feet in the stirrups, pressure from my right knee did the same. Some soothing exhortations, like "Whoa there, boy—whoa there, you old beauty," also seemed to help; even if the words were English, the tone and intention were universal.

Somewhere on the home stretch, in front of the stands, the steam went out of the flight, and in a few strides after that he was walking. I patted his neck and made further conversation, and after a bit he stood still.

This time, unlike after his training canter, he showed great signs of exertion, taking breaths in gusts through his nostrils and heaving out his ribs to inflate his lungs. I brushed the wet off my glasses, and undid a couple of buttons on my coat.

"There you are, then, chum," I said. "You're a good old boy, my old fellow," and I patted his neck some more.

He shifted only a little while I cautiously leaned far forward to his ears, and put my arms under his chin, and brought the reins back over his head. It seemed to me that he was almost relieved to have his headgear returned to its normal riding configuration, because he trotted off along the track again at my signal with all the sweetness of a horse well schooled in dressage.

Kropotkin had come a little way out to meet us, but no man walked far on that sticky dirt from choice, and he was back by the stable entrance when the chestnut and I completed the circuit.

Kropotkin showed considerable emotion, which was not surprisingly all for his horse. After I had dismounted and handed the reins to a stunned-looking Misha, he rumbled away in basso profundo, anxiously feeling each leg and standing back to assess the overall damage. Finally he spoke at some length to Stephen, and waved an arm in a gesture which was neither anger nor apology, but perhaps somewhere between the two.

"Mr. Kropotkin says," Stephen relayed, "that he doesn't know what the horsecar was doing here today. It is one of the horsecars which take the Olympic horses, when they travel. Mr. Kropotkin had not ordered one to come to the track. They are always parked beside the stables he is in charge of, across the road. He is sure that none of the drivers would drive so badly in a stable area. He cannot understand how you and the horse came to be in the way when the horsecar prepared to leave the stables." Stephen's eyebrows were rising. "I say," he said dubiously. "You weren't in its way. The bloody thing drove straight at you."

"Never mind," I said. "Tell Mr. Kropotkin that I

quite understand what he is saying. Tell him I regret having stood in the way of the horsecar. Tell him that I am glad the horse is unharmed, and that I see no reason why I should need to mention this morning's happenings to any other person."

Stephen stared. "You learn fast."

"Tell him what I said."

Stephen obliged, Kropotkin's manner lost so much tension that I only then realized the extent of his anxiety. He even went so far as to produce a definite lightening of the features, almost a smile. He also said something about which Stephen seemed less doubtful.

"He says you ride like a Cossack. Is that a compliment?"

"Near enough."

Kropotkin spoke again, and Stephen translated.

"Mr. Kropotkin says he will give you any further help he can, if you ask."

"Thank you very much," I said.

"Friend," the deep voice said in its slow, heavy English, "you ride good."

I pushed my glasses hard against the bridge of my nose and thought murderous thoughts about the people who had stopped me from racing.

Stephen and I trudged about half a mile to where Kropotkin had said there was a taxi rank.

"I thought you'd be one for rushing off to the police," Stephen said.

"No." I picked some of the dirt off my fur hat, which someone had retrieved. "Not this trip."

"Not this country," he said. "If you complain to the fuzz here, you as likely as not surface in the clink."

I gave up cleanliness in favor of a warm head. "Hughes-Beckett would have a fit."

"All the same," Stephen said, "whatever Kropotkin may say, that horsecar was trying to kill you."

"Or Misha. Or the horse," I said, untying the ear flaps.

"Do you really believe that?"

"Did you see the driver?" I asked.

"Yes and no. He had one of those balaclava things on under a fur hat with the ear flaps down. Everything covered except his eyes."

"He took a hell of a risk," I said thoughtfully. "But then he darn near succeeded."

"You take it incredibly calmly," Stephen said.

"Would you prefer screaming hysterics?"

"I guess not."

"There's a taxi." I waved, and the green-gray sedan swerved our way and slowed. We piled aboard.

"I've never seen anyone jump on a horse like you did," Stephen said, as we set off to the Intourist. "One second on the ground; the next galloping."

"You never know what you can do until Nemesis breathes down your neck."

"You look," Stephen said, "like one of those useless la-di-das in the telly ads, and you perform . . ." Words failed him.

"Yeah," I said. "Depressing, isn't it?"

He laughed. "And by the way . . . Misha gave me a telephone number." He put a hand in a pocket and brought out a crumpled scrap of paper. "He gave it to me while Kropotkin was chasing after you on the track. He says he wants to tell you something without Kropotkin knowing."

"Does the taxi driver speak English?" I asked.

Stephen looked only faintly and transiently alarmed. "They never do," he said. "You could tell them they stink like untreated sewage and they wouldn't turn a hair. Just try it."

I tried it.

The taxi driver didn't turn a hair.

On the principle of turning up where and when expected, I arrived on time for lunch in the Intourist dining room. The soup and the blinis were all right, and the ice cream with black-currant jam was fine, but the meat with its attendant teaspoonfuls of chopped carrot, chopped lettuce, and inch-long chips went across the table to Frank.

"You'll fade away," said Mrs. Wilkinson, without too much concern. "Don't you like meat?"

"I grow it," I said. "Beef, that is. On a farm. So I suppose I get too fussy over stuff like this."

Mrs. Wilkinson looked at me doubtfully. "I would never have guessed you worked on a farm."

"Er . . . well, I do. But it's my own, passed down from my father."

"Can you milk a cow?" Frank said, with a hint of challenge.

"Yes," I said mildly. "Milk. Plow. The lot."

He gave me a sharp look from over my chips, but in fact I spoke the truth. I had started learning the practical side of farming from about the age of two, and had emerged from agricultural college twenty years later with the technology. Since then, under government sponsorship, I'd done some work on the interacting chemistry of land and food, and had set aside some experimental acres for research. After racing, this work had been my chief interest—and from now on, I suppose, my only one.

Mrs. Wilkinson said disapprovingly, "You don't keep calves in those nasty crate things, do you?"

"No, I don't."

"I never do like to think of all the poor animals being killed, when I buy the weekend chops."

"How were the economic achievements?"

"We saw a space capsule." She launched into a grudgingly admiring outline of the exhibition. "Pity we don't have one in England," she said. "Exhibition like that, I mean. Permanent. Blowing our own trumpet for a change, like."

"Did you go?" I asked Frank.

"No." He shook his head, munching. "Been before, of course."

He didn't say where he had been instead. I hadn't noticed him following Stephen and me, but he might have done so. If he had, what had he seen?

"Tomorrow we're going to Zagorsk," Mrs. Wilkinson said.

"Where's that?" I asked, watching Frank chew and learning nothing from his face.

"A lot of churches, I think," she said vaguely. "We're going in a bus, with visas, because it's out of Moscow."

I glanced at her as she sat beside me, divining a note of disappointment in her voice. She was a short woman, solid, late fifties, with the well-intentioned face of the bulk of the English population. An equally typical shrewdness lived inside and poked its nose out occasionally in tellingly direct remarks. The more I saw of Mrs. Wilkinson, the more I saw to respect.

Opposite her, next to Frank, Mr. Wilkinson ate his lunch and as usual said nothing. I had gathered he had come on the trip to please his wife, and would as soon be at home with a pint and watching a Manchester United soccer game on the telly.

"Quite a few people are going to the Bolshoi this evening, to the ballet," said Mrs. Wilkinson a little wistfully. "But Dad doesn't like that sort of thing, do you, Dad?"

Dad shook his head.

Mrs. Wilkinson said in a lower voice to me, confidingly, "He doesn't like those things the men wear. Those tights. You know, showing all the muscles of their behinds . . . and those things in front."

"Codpieces," I said, straight-faced.

"What?" She looked embarrassed, as if I'd used too strong a swear word for her shock threshold.

"That's what they're called. Those things which disguise the outlines of nature."

"Oh." She was relieved. "It would be much nicer if they wore *tunics*, that's what I think. Then they wouldn't be so *obvious*. And you could concentrate on the dancing."

Mr. Wilkinson muttered something which might or might not have been "Poncing about," and filled his mouth with ice cream.

Mrs. Wilkinson looked as if she'd heard that before, and instead said to me, "Did you see your horses?"

Frank's concentration on food skipped a beat.

"They were great," I said, and enlarged for two minutes on the turnout and the training exercise. There was nothing else in Frank's reactions to say he knew I was giving an incomplete account, but then I supposed if there had been, he would have been bad at his job.

Natasha drifted up purposefully to complicate my life.

"We have been lucky," she said earnestly. "We have a ticket for you in a box at the Bolshoi tomorrow evening, for the opera."

I caught Mr. Wilkinson's eye, with its message of sardonic sympathy, as I started feebly to thank her.

"It is *The Queen of Spades*," Natasha said firmly.

"Er . . . " I said.

"Everyone enjoys the opera at the Bolshoi," she said. "There is no better opera in the world."

"How splendid," I said. "I will look forward to it."

She began to look approving and I seized the moment to say I would be going out with friends for the evening, and not to expect me in for dinner. She tried very delicately to lead me into saying exactly where I was going, but as at that moment I didn't actually know, except that it was anywhere for some decent grub, she was out of luck.

"And this afternoon," I said, forestalling her, "the Lenin Museum."

She brightened a good deal. At last, she was no doubt thinking, I was behaving as a good tourist should.

"Mind if I tag along?" Frank said, shoveling in the last of my lunch. His face looked utterly guileless, and I understood the full beauty of his method of working. If following a person might raise their suspicions, tag along in full sight.

"Pleasure," I said. "Meet you in the lobby, in half an hour"; and I vanished as soon as he'd started his specially ordered double portion of ice cream. It would take a good deal to shift him before he had finished it.

I made fast tracks out of the hotel and along to the main post office, which was conveniently nearby.

Telephoned to the embassy. Reached Oliver Waterman.

"This is Randall Drew," I said.

"Where are you calling from?" he said, interrupting.

"The post office."

"Ah. Right. Carry on, then."

"Have there been any telex messages for me, from Hughes-Beckett, or anyone in London?"

"Ah, yes," he said vaguely. "There was something, I think, my dear chap. Hang on. . . ." He put the receiver down and I could hear searching sounds and consulting voices. "Here we are," he said, coming back. "Got a pencil?"

"Yes," I said patiently.

"Yuri Ivanovich Chulitsky."

"Please spell it," I said.

He did so.

"Got it," I said, "Go on."

"There isn't any more."

"Is that the whole of the message?" I asked incredulously.

His voice sounded dubious. "The whole message,

as received by us from the telex people, is 'Inform
Randall Drew Yuri Ivanovich Chulitsky,' and there
are a few numbers, and that's all.''

''Numbers?''

''Could be a telephone number, perhaps. Anyway,
here they are: 180-19-16. Got that?''

I read them back, to check.

''That's right, my dear chap. How's it going?''

''Fair,'' I said. ''Can you send a telex for me, if I
give you the message?''

''Ah,'' he said. ''I think I should warn you that
there's a spot of trouble brewing on the international
scene, and the telex is pretty busy. They told us pretty
shirtily just now not to bother them with unessentials,
like music. Unessentials, I ask you. Anyway, my dear
chap, if you want to be sure your message gets off, I
should take it along there yourself.''

''Take it where?'' I said.

''Oh, yes, I was forgetting you wouldn't know. The
telex machine is not here in the embassy, but along
with the commercial section in Kutuzovsky Prospect.
That's the continuation of Kalinin Prospect. Do you
have a map?''

''I'll find it,'' I said.

''Tell them I sent you. They can check with me, if
they want. And I should stand over them, my dear
chap. Make yourself a bit of a nuisance, so they send
it to get rid of you.''

''I'll take your advice,'' I said, smiling to myself.

''The British Club is along there in Kutuzovsky
Prospect,'' he said languidly. ''Full of temporary ex-
iles, wallowing in nostalgia. Sad little place. I don't go
there much.''

''If any more messages come for me,'' I said,
''please would you ring me at the Intourist Hotel?''

''Certainly,'' he said civilly. ''Do give me your
number.''

I stifled the urge to tell him I'd given it to him twice

already. I repeated it again, and wondered whether, by the time I left, he would find his office scattered with small pieces of paper all bearing the same number, which he would peer at with willowy bewilderment while smoothing back his gray-winged hair.

I rang off and debated whether or not to lose Frank there and then, and make tracks for the telex; but the message would keep for an hour or two and wasn't worth the stirring up of trouble. I hurried back to the Intourist, went upstairs, came downstairs, and strolled out of the lift to find Frank waiting.

"Oh, there you are," he said. "Thought I'd missed you."

"Off we go, then," I said fatuously, and we walked out of the hotel, down into the long pedestrian tunnel which led under Fiftieth Anniversary of the October Revolution Square, and up into a cobbled street with the red walls of the Kremlin away to the right.

On the underground walk he gave me his thoughts on Comrade Lenin, who was, according to Frank, the only genius of the twentieth century.

"Born, of course, in the nineteenth," I said.

"He brought freedom to the masses," Frank declared reverently.

"Freedom to do what?" I said.

Frank ignored me. Somewhere under the wet and woolly sociological guff which he ladled so unstintingly over the Wilkinsons and me, there had to be a hard-core card-carrying fully indoctrinated Communist. I looked at Frank's angular pitted face framed in a long striped college scarf, and thought he was marvelous: he was giving a faultless performance as a poorly educated left-wing encumbrance of the National Union of Teachers, so convincing that it was hard to believe he was acting.

It flickered across my mind that perhaps Ian Young was wrong, and Frank was not KGB after all; but then if Ian was what I thought, he would be right. If Frank were not KGB, why should Ian say he was?

I wondered how many lies I had been told since I had arrived in Moscow, and how many more I had yet to hear.

Frank more or less genuflected on the threshold of the Lenin Museum, and we went inside to have our ears bent about the clothes, desk, car, and so on that the liberator of the masses had personally used. And this was the face, I thought, looking at the prim little bearded visage reproduced without stint on paintings and posters and booklets and cards, who had launched a million murders and left his disciples bloodily empire-building round the world. This was the visionary who had unleashed the holocausts: the man who had meant to do good.

I looked at my watch and told Frank I'd had enough of the place; I needed some fresh air. He ignored the implied insult and followed me out, simply saying that he had visited the museum every time he'd been to Moscow and never tired of it. Easy enough to believe that that, at least, was true.

Stephen, back from lunch and an unmissable tutorial, was waiting, as arranged, outside. He had arranged, that is, to meet only me. Frank was surplus to requirements.

I introduced them without explanations: "Frank Jones . . . Stephen Luce," and they disliked each other at once.

Had they been dogs, there would have been some unfriendly sniffing and menacing show of teeth; as it was, their noses actually wrinkled. I wondered whether Stephen's instinctive response was to the real Frank or to the cover Frank—to an individual or to a type.

Frank, I supposed, merely guessed that any friend of mine was no friend of his; and if Ian was right about him following me, he had certainly seen Stephen before.

Neither of them wanted to say anything to the other.

"Well, Frank," I said cheerfully, hiding my amusement, "thank you for your company. I'm off now with

Stephen for the rest of the day. See you at breakfast, I guess.''

''You bet.''

We turned away, but after a step or two Stephen glanced back, frowning. I looked where he did: Frank's back view, walking off.

''Haven't I seen him before?'' Stephen said.

''Where?''

''Couldn't say. Yesterday morning, up here in the Square, maybe.''

We were walking along the side of Red Square, toward the GUM department store.

''He's staying at the Intourist,'' I said.

Stephen nodded, dismissing it. ''Where to?'' he said.

''Phone box.''

We found one and inserted the two kopecks, but there was no answer from the number Misha had given us. Tried again, this time for Yuri Ivanovich Chulitsky. Same result.

''Telex in Kutuzovsky Prospect,'' I said. ''Where do we get a taxi?''

''The metro is cheap. Only five kopecks, however far you go.''

He couldn't understand why I should want to spend money when I didn't have to; incredulity halfway to exasperation filled his eyes and voice. I gave in with a shrug and we went by metro, with me battling as usual against the claustrophobic feeling I always got from hurtling through mole runs far underground. The cathedrallike stations of the Moscow metro seemed to have been built in the greater glory of technology (Down with churches!), but on the achingly long and boring escalators I found myself quite missing London's vulgar advertisements for bras. Ritzy, jazzy, noisy, dirty, uninhibited old London, greedy and gutsy and grabbing at life. Gold coaches and white horses along the Mall instead of tanks, and garbage collectors on strike.

"Do the dustbin men ever strike here?" I said to Stephen.

"Strikes? Don't be silly. Strikes are not allowed in Russia."

We finally resurfaced, and after a good deal of asking and walking, arrived at the commercial section, which was guarded, as was the embassy, by a soldier. We talked our way in, and by following Oliver Waterman's advice and making a nuisance of myself, I persuaded the inmates to telex my message, which was: *Request details of life and background of Hans Kramer. Also whereabouts of his body. Also name and telephone number of the pathologist who did the autopsy.*

"Don't expect an answer," I was told brusquely. "There's all hell breaking loose in some place in Africa which is chock-a-block with Soviet guns and so-called advisers. The telex is steaming. The diplomats have priority. You'll be way, way down the list."

Thanks very much, I said, and we trudged our way back to the pavement outside.

"Now what?" Stephen said.

"Try those numbers again."

We found a glass-walled box nearby and put the kopecks in the slot. No answers, as before.

"Probably not home from work yet," Stephen said.

I nodded. At four in the afternoon, the daylight was fading fast to dusk, the lit windows shining brighter with every minute.

"What do you want to do now?" Stephen said.

"I don't know."

"Like to come up to the university, then? We're not all that far away, actually. Nearer than to your hotel."

"No hope of anything to eat there, I suppose?" I said.

He looked surprised. "Yes, if you like. There's a sort of supermarket for students in the basement, and kitchens upstairs. We can buy something and eat in my room, if you like." He seemed doubtful. "It won't be as good as the Intourist Hotel, though."

"I'll risk it."

"I'll ring up and say you're coming," he said, turning back to the telephone box.

"Can't we just go?"

He shook his head. "In Russia, everything has to be arranged first. If it is arranged, it is O.K. If it's not arranged, it's irregular, suspicious, or subversive, and what's more, you won't get in."

Coming out of the telephone box and saying my visit was fixed, he began planning a route via the metro, but I was no longer listening. Two men were walking toward us, talking intently. From thinking there was something familiar about one of them, I progressed by a series of mental jumps to realizing that I knew them both.

They were Ian Young and Malcolm Herrick.

8

They were, if anything, more surprised to see me.

"Randall!" Ian said. "What are you doing here?"

"If it isn't the sleuth!" Malcolm Herrick's English voice boomed confidently into Kutuzovsky Prospect, scorning discretion. "Found Alyosha yet, sport?"

"Afraid not," I said. "This is Stephen Luce. A friend. English."

"Malcolm Herrick," said the Moscow correspondent of *The Watch*, introducing himself, shaking hands, and waiting for a reaction. None came. He must have been used to it. "Moscow correspondent of *The Watch*," he said.

"Great stuff," said Stephen vaguely, obviously not having read a word from the Herrick pen.

"Are you going to the British Club?" Ian asked. "We're just on our way there."

His watchful eyes waited for a reply.

There were some replies I saw no harm in giving. "I came to send a telex," I said. "Oliver's suggestion."

"The snake," Herrick said unexpectedly, narrowing his eyes. "He usual y gives messages for the telex to the guy in the hall."

"And the guy in the hall relays them to you?" I said.

"Sources, sources, sport." He tapped the side of his nose.

Ian was unmoved. "If an answer comes," he said to me, "I'll see that you get it."

"I'd be grateful."

"Where are you going now, sport?" Malcolm said, loud and direct as always.

"To the university, with Stephen, for tea."

"Tea!" He made a face. "Look, why don't we meet later for a decent meal? All of us," he added expansively, including Ian and Stephen. "The Aragvi do you, Ian?"

Ian, who had not reacted visibly to the original suggestion, seemed to find favor with the choice of place, and nodded silently. Malcolm started giving me directions, but Stephen said he knew the way.

"Great, then," Malcolm said. "Eight-thirty. Don't be late."

The faint drizzle which had persisted all day seemed to be intensifying into sleet. It put, anyway, an effective damper on further conversation in the street, and by common consent we split up and went our own ways.

"Who is the man who looks Russian?" Stephen asked, ducking his head down and sideways to avoid the stinging drops. "The one emulating the Sphinx."

"Let's get that taxi," I said, waving to an approaching gray-green car with the green light indicating availability shining in its windshield.

"Expensive," he protested automatically, slithering into the back seat beside me. "Ve vill have to cure this disgusting bourgeois habit." He had a rich way of imitating a Russian accent while sardonically putting forward the Russian point of view. "Vorkers of the vorld, unite—and go on the metro."

"Caviar is immoral," I said dryly.

"Caviar is not bourgeois. Caviar is for everyone who can scrape up a fortune in rubles." He considered me, relapsing into ordinary English. "Why did you say caviar is immoral? It's not like you."

"Not my idea. A friend's."

"Girl?"

I nodded.

"Aha," he said. "I diagnose a rich middle-class socialist rebelling against mummy."

"Not far off," I said, a touch sadly.

He peered anxiously at my face. "I haven't offended you?"

"No."

I got him to ask the taxi driver to stop by a telephone kiosk, and to wait while we tried our numbers again. There was still no answer from Misha, but the second number was answered at the first ring. Stephen, holding the receiver, made a brief thumbs-up sign to me, and spoke. Listened, spoke again, and handed the receiver to me. "It is Yuri Ivanovich Chulitsky himself. He says he speaks English."

I took the instrument. "Mr. Chulitsky?" I said.

"Yes."

"I am an Englishman visiting Moscow," I said. "My name is Randall Drew. I have been given your name and telephone number by the British Embassy. I wonder if I could talk with you."

There was a longish pause. Then the voice at the other end, calm and with an accent that was a carbon copy of Stephen's imitation, said, "Upon what subject?"

Owing to the meagerness of the telex bearing his name, I couldn't entirely answer. I said hopefully, "Horses?"

"Horses." He sounded unenthusiastic. "Always horses. I do not know horses. I am architect."

"Er . . ." I said, "have you already talked about horses to another Englishman?"

A pause. Then the voice, measured and still calm. "That is so. In Moscow, yes. And in England, yes. Many times." Bits of light began to dawn.

"You were at the International Horse Trials? At Burghley, in September?"

The pause. Then, "At many horse trials. September . . . and August."

Bingo, I thought. One of the observers.

"Mr. Chulitsky," I said persuasively, "please may I meet you? I've been talking to Mr. Nikolai Alexandrovich Kropotkin, and if you want to check up on me, I think he will tell you it would be all right for you to talk to me."

A very long pause. Then he said, "Are you writing for newspaper?"

"No," I said.

"I telephone Nikolai Alexandrovich," he said. "I find his number."

"I have it here," I said, and read it out slowly.

"You telephone again. One hour."

The receiver came down at his end with a decisive crash, and Stephen and I went back to the taxi.

Stephen said, "When we get up to my room, don't say anything you don't want overheard. Or not until I tell you it's O.K."

"Are you serious?"

"I'm a foreigner. I live in the section of the university reserved for foreign students. Every room in Moscow which is used by foreigners should be considered bugged until proved different."

The university building, of vast blocks of narrow windows punctuated by soaring fluted towers, like an immense gray stone blancmange, looked from its hill to the river and the city center beyond; and on the far bank lay, spread out, the Lenin Stadium, where the Olympic athletes were scheduled to run and jump and throw things.

"How will they manage with the whole city full of foreigners?" I said.

"Apartheid will prevail." The Russian accent made it a wicked joke. "Segregation will be ruthlessly maintained."

"Why did you come to Russia," I said, "feeling as you do?"

He gave me a quick bright glance. "I love the place and hate the regime, the same as everyone else. And nowhere's a prison when you can get out."

The taxi shed us at the gate, and we walked to the foreign students' entrance, a door dwarfed by the sheer height of the adjoining walls. Inside, coming down to human scale, there was a dumpy middle-aged woman behind a desk. She looked at Stephen with a lack of reaction which meant she knew him, and then at me; and she was out of her seat and barring my way with the speed of a rattlesnake.

Stephen spoke to her in Russian. She dourly shook her head. Together they consulted a list on her desk; and with severe looks she let me through.

"Dragons like that guard doorways all over Russia," Stephen said. "The only way past is to be expected. Short of slaying them, of course."

We went for a long walk which ended one floor down in a help-yourself food shop. All the packages were unfamiliar, and owing to the Cyrillic alphabet, which made restaurants look like РЕСТОРАН to Western eyes, I couldn't even guess at the contents. Stephen went round unerringly, choosing what later turned out to be crisp-sided cream cakes, and ending with a bottle of milk.

A girl stood at the cash desk before us, paying for her groceries. A pretty girl, with light-brown hair curling onto her shoulders, and the sort of waist Victorian young ladies swooned over. When Stephen greeted her, she turned her head and gave him a flashing smile with a fair view of excellent teeth. The smile, I saw, of at least good friends.

Stephen introduced her as Gudrun, and the unpretty

lady behind the cash register pointed to her packages
and clearly told her to pick them up and go.

The girl picked up her bottle of milk, and the bottom
fell out of it. Milk cascaded onto the floor. Gudrun
stood looking bewildered, with the whole-looking bottle still in her hand and milk stains all over her legs.

I watched the pantomime that follqwed. Stephen
was saying she should have another bottle. The unpretty lady shook her head and pointed to the cash
register. Everyone engaged in battle, and the unpretty
lady won.

"She made her *buy* another bottle," said Stephen,
disgusted, as we set off on further interior tramp.

"So I gathered."

"They make the bottles like tubes here, and just
stick a disk in for the bottoms. Anyway," he finished
cheerfully, "she's coming along to my room for a cup
of tea."

Gudrun was West German, from Bonn. She filled
and illuminated Stephen's tiny cell, which was eight
feet long by six across, and contained a bed, a table
covered with books, a chair, and a glass-fronted bookcase. On the bare wooden floor there was one small
imitation Brussels rug, and at the tall, narrow window,
some skimpy green curtains.

"The Ritz," I said ironically.

"I'm lucky," Stephen said, taking three mugs from
the bookcase and making a space for them on the table. "A lot of the Russian students are two to a room
this size."

"If you had two beds in here you couldn't open the
door," I said.

Gudrun nodded. "They stand the beds up against
the wall in the daytime."

"No protest marches?" I said. "No demos for better conditions?"

"They are not allowed," Gudrun said seriously.
"Anyone who tried would lose his place."

She spoke English perfectly, with hardly a trace of accent. Her Russian, Stephen said, was just as good. His own German was passable, his French excellent. I sighed, internally, for a skill I'd never acquired.

Stephen went off to make the tea.

"Don't come," he said. "The kitchen is filthy. About twenty of us share it, and we're all supposed to clean it, so nobody does."

Gudrun sat on the bed and asked me how I was enjoying Moscow, and I sat on the chair and said fine. I asked her how she was enjoying her course, and she said fine.

"If the Russians are so keen to keep foreigners at arm's length," I said, "why do they allow foreign students in the university?"

She glanced involuntarily round the walls, a revealing glimpse into the way they all lived. The walls had ears; literally.

"We are exchange students," she said. "For Stephen, there is a Russian student in London. For me a Russian student in Bonn. Those students are dedicated Communists."

"Spreading the gospel and recruiting?"

She nodded a shade unhappily, again glancing at the walls and not liking my frankness. I went back to harmless chitchat, and Stephen presently arrived to distribute the goodies, which, for me at least, nicely filled an aching void.

"Show you something," he said, stuffing the last of the cake into his mouth and shifting along to the end of the bed, on which he was sitting. "A little trick."

He picked up what I saw was a tape recorder, and switched it on. Then with a theatrical flourish, he stood up and pressed it against the wall beside my head.

Nothing happened. He removed it and pressed it to another spot. Again nothing. He took it away, and put it delicately against a spot above his bed. From the tape recorder came a high-pitched whine.

"Abracadabra," he said, taking the tape recorder down and switching it off. "From ordinary walls you get nothing. From a live mike inside a wall, you get feedback."

"Do they know?" I said.

"Who can tell? Like to borrow it?" He pointed to the recorder.

"Very much."

"Then I'll dash to get a chit to take it out."

"A chit?"

"Yes. You can't just walk out of here carrying things. They say it's to stop people stealing, but it's just the usual phobia about knowing what goes on."

I glanced at the wall behind his head. Stephen laughed. "If you *don't* complain about the whole bloody repressive Soviet system, they suspect you're putting on an act."

In the corridor, from the telephone installed for the students, I called Yuri Ivanovich Chulitsky. The telephone was safe, Stephen said. The only telephones which were tapped were those in the houses of known dissidents; and Yuri Chulitsky would be anything but a dissident if he had been sent to England as an observer.

He answered at once.

"I talk with Nikolai Alexandrovich," he said. "I meet you tomorrow."

"Thank you very much."

"I drive car. I come outside National Hotel, ten o'clock, tomorrow morning. Is right?"

"Is right," I said.

"Ten o'clock." Down went the receiver with the same crash, before I could ask him how I would know him or his car. I supposed that when I saw him, I would know.

Stephen tried the other number. The bell rang hollowly at the far end, and after ten rings we prepared to give up. Then the ringing stopped and I overheard a sudden breathless voice on the line.

"It's Misha," Stephen said.

"You talk to him. It's easier."

Stephen listened. "He wants to see you again, and it must be tonight. He says he is going to Rostov to-morrow with two horses. The snow is coming, and the horses are going south. Nikolai Alexandrovich—that is, Mr. Kropotkin—is going next week. It was decided today."

"All right," I said. "When and where?"

Stephen asked, and was told. He wrote it down, and the directions took some time.

"Well," he said, slowly replacing the receiver and looking at what he had written. "It is miles out of the center. I think it must be an apartment block. He says he will wait outside, and when you arrive, don't speak English until he says it's O.K."

"Aren't you coming?"

"You don't really need me. Misha does speak some English." He handed me the address, written in Russian script. "Show that to a taxi driver. He'll find it. And I'll meet you later, at the Aragvi."

I looked beyond him to the open door of his room. Gudrun half sat, half lay on the bed, her long legs sprawled in invitation.

I hesitated, but finally I said, "I wish you could come. Someone did try to kill Misha or me this morning. I expect you'll laugh, but if I'm going off into the wilds to meet him, I would feel safer with a backup system."

He didn't laugh. He said goodbye to Gudrun, and came. He also said, "Ve have vays of postponing our pleasures until tomorrow," and made a joke of it; and I thought that for plain good nature he would be hard to beat.

"It's very difficult to think of a good meeting place, if you're an ordinary Russian and you want to talk to a foreigner," Stephen said. "There are no pubs in Russia. No discreet little cafés. And there are always watchers, with tongues. You'd have to be pretty solid with the hierarchy to be seen anywhere public with a foreigner."

We flagged a passing taxi, again without much of a wait.

"No shortage of these," I said, climbing in. Then, as Stephen's mouth opened, I interrupted. "Don't say it. Taxis are dear, the metro's cheap."

"And the taxi charges have practically doubled recently."

"Ask the driver to go via the Intourist Hotel, so that I can drop off the recorder."

"Right."

We sped down the Komosomolsky Prospect and I looked out of the back window two or three times. A medium-sized black car followed us faithfully, but we were on a main road, where that was likely to happen anyway.

"When we get to the Intourist," I said, "I will get out and say good night to you unmistakably. I'll then go into the hotel, and you and the taxi will drive off, and go round the corner, and wait for me outside the National Hotel entrance. I'll dump the tape recorder, and come and meet you there."

Stephen looked out of the rear window. "Seriously," he said, "do you think you're being followed?"

"Seriously," I said, "most of the time."

"But . . . who by?"

"Would you believe, the KGB?"

For all his guided tour to the prying state, he was staggered. "What makes you think so?"

"The Sphinx told me."

It reduced him to silence. Ve have vays of making you stop talking, I thought facetiously. We arrived in due course at the Intourist, and went through the act.

I spent some time on the pavement talking to Stephen through the taxi window, and then bade him good night in ringing tones. I waved a farewell as I went through the double glass entrance; overdoing it, no doubt. I collected my key from the desk, removed hat and coat, and went up in the lift. Then I parked the tape recorder in my room, and without hurrying, so as not to alert the old biddy sitting watchfully at her desk by the lifts, walked back, still carrying outdoor clothes, and descended to the ground floor. There were several routes from the lifts to the front door, as it was a very large hotel. I took the most roundabout, putting on hat and coat on the way, and wafted at an ordinary pace out again onto the pavement. No doubt the watchers there took general note, but no one broke away to bob in my wake.

I stopped at the corner and glanced back. No one seemed to be peeling off to look in nonexistent shop-windows. I walked on, thinking that if the followers were determined as well as professional, my amateur attempts at evasion would have been useless. But they would have had no reason to suppose I knew they were there, or that I would try to duck them, as I had given no signs so far of wanting to; so perhaps they might think I was still somewhere inside the hotel.

The taxi driver was agitated and grumbling at having had to wait a long time where he was not supposed to. Stephen greeted my arrival with sighs of relief, and we set off again with a jerk.

"Your friend Frank went into the hotel just after you," Stephen said. "Did you see him?"

"No," I said tranquilly.

He didn't pursue it. "The driver says the temperature is dropping. It has been warm for November, he says."

"It's December today."

"He says it will snow."

We motored a good way northward, and then north-east, through the wide, well-lit, mostly empty streets.

When the roads became narrower, I said, "Ask the driver to stop for a moment."

"What now?" Stephen said.

"See if we've a tail."

No car stopped behind us, however, and when we went on, we found no stationary car waiting ahead. I asked Stephen to get the driver to circle a fairly large block. The driver, thoroughly disillusioned by these junketings, began muttering under his breath.

"Get him to drop us before we reach the address," I said. "We don't want him undoing the good work by reporting our exact destination."

A large tip on top of the big fare cured most of the driver's grumbles, but wouldn't, I guessed, keep his mouth shut. He sped off back to the brighter lights as if glad to be rid of us. But no black cars, or any others, passed or stopped. As far as we could tell, we were on our own.

We stood in an area which was being developed. On each side, end on to the road, were ranks of newly built apartment blocks, all about forty feet wide and nine stories high, clad in gray-white pebble dash and stretching away into the darkness with ranks of windows front and back.

"Standard-issue housing," Stephen said. "Egg boxes for the masses. Six square meters of floor space per person; the maximum regulation allowance."

We walked along the slushy pavement, the only people in sight. The block we were currently passing was unfinished, with its walls in place but empty holes for windows. The one after that, although still uninhabited, had glass. The one after that looked furnished, and the one after that had residents. It proved also to be where we were going.

A last look at the street showed no one taking the slightest notice of us. We wheeled into the broad space between the two blocks and discovered from the numbers that the entrance we wanted was the second door along. We went toward it without haste, and stopped a few paces short.

We waited. A minute ticked past, and another. No Misha. With every lungful, the wet freezing air chilled from the inside out. If we had traveled all this way for nothing, I thought, I would be less than amused.

A voice spoke softly, from behind us.

"Come."

9

We turned, startled. We hadn't heard him, but there
he stood in his leather coat and his leather cap, young
and neat. He made a small beckoning movement with
his head, and turned on his heel. We followed him out
into the street, along the pavement, and round into the
space between the next two blocks. He made steadily
for one of the entrances, and in silence we traipsed in
his footsteps.

Inside, the brightly lit and warm hall smelled of new
paint. There were two lifts, both not working, and a
flight of stairs. Misha addressed himself to the stairs.
We followed.

On the landing above there were four doors, all
closed. Misha continued up the stairs. On the next
landing, four identical doors, again all closed. Misha
went on climbing. On the fourth floor, we stopped for
breath.

Between the fifth and sixth floors we came across
two young men struggling to carry upward an electric
range. They had ropes and protective wadding around

it, and leather straps with carrying handles to help them, but they were both sweating and panting from exertion. They stopped work, with the range poised precariously half on and half off a step, to let us pass. Misha said something which sounded consoling, and on we went at a slower and slower pace.

It had to be the ninth floor, I thought. Or the roof.

The ninth floor. Misha produced a key, unlocked one of the uninformative doors, and led us in.

The apartment consisted of kitchen, bathroom, and two meager rooms, and was almost unfurnished. There were some rather gloomy green tiles in the kitchen, and nothing much else; certainly no range. The bare necessities in the bathroom. Bare floors, bare windows, and bare walls in the two rooms, with two wooden chairs and a table in one of them, and the frame of a bed in the other. But, like everywhere indoors in Moscow, it was warm.

Misha closed the door behind us, and we took off our hats and coats. Misha swept an arm around, embracing the flat, and Stephen translated what he said.

"It is his sister's flat. When the flats are ready, the people on the list draw lots for them. His sister and her husband drew the ninth floor, and she hates it and is very depressed. They have a baby. Until the lifts are working she will have to carry the baby and her shopping up nine floors all the time. The range for the flat is provided, but it has to be carried up, like we saw the others doing. All the furniture has to be carried up, by friends."

"Why don't the lifts work?" I said.

Misha said (via Stephen) that it was because the caretaker claimed the interiors of the lifts would be damaged if people used them for taking up ranges and furniture, so the lifts would not be switched on until all the flats were furnished and occupied. It seemed monstrous, but it was quite true.

"Why don't they put a temporary lining inside the lifts, and remove it later?" I said.

Misha shrugged. It was impossible to argue, he said. The caretaker would not listen, and he was in control. He gestured to us to sit on the chairs, and he himself perched half on and half off the table. He was thin but strong, fit rather than undernourished. The vivid blue eyes in the tanned face looked at us with more friendliness than in the morning and reinforced my belief in his brains.

"Thank you for coming," he said. "Tomorrow, I go. I speak again."

"Tell Stephen in Russian," I said. "It will be easier for you. And you can say more."

He nodded a shade regretfully, but saw the sense of it. He spoke in bursts, waiting for Stephen to catch up, and again nodding as he heard his intentions put into English.

"Later, after we had gone," Stephen translated, "Nikolai Alexandrovich, Mr. Kropotkin, had more visitors—your friend the English journalist, Malcolm Herrick, and someone who sounds like the Sphinx. They came together. Mr. Kropotkin got Misha to repeat to them what he had just told us. Misha thinks that Mr. Kropotkin knew the Sphinx quite well."

"His name is Ian," I said. "And yes, they had talked together before."

"Mr. Kropotkin thinks you need help," Stephen went on. "He sent Misha to fetch his little book with telephone numbers, and he telephoned to several people to ask if they knew anything about Alyosha, and if they did, to tell him, and he would tell you. Boris Dmitrevich Telyatnikov, who is one of the possible Olympic riders, came in the afternoon to see the horses, and Mr. Kropotkin asked him also. Boris said he didn't know anything about Alyosha, but Misha thinks Boris was worried."

"Yes," I said. "Carry on."

"Practically everyone in Moscow who has anything to do with the Olympic equestrian games now seems to be looking for Alyosha."

"My God," I said.

Misha looked a little anxious. "Nikolai Alexandrovich help," he said. "You save horse. Nikolai Alexandrovich help."

"It is kind of him," I said dazedly.

Stephen listened, and reported. "The Sphinx—Ian—told Mr. Kropotkin that once you had found Alyosha and talked to him, you could go home. Mr. Kropotkin said, 'Then we will find Alyosha for him. He saved our best horse. Nothing is too much.' "

"My God," I said again.

"According to what Mr. Kropotkin told everybody, the horse swung unexpectedly in front of the horsecar as it approached. The driver had no time to swerve, but you rescued the horse."

"Is that what Misha thinks?" I said.

"*Niet.*" Misha understood and was positive. "Driver go . . . boom." He smashed his fist unmistakably into his hand.

"Did you know him?" I asked.

"*Niet.* No see."

It was the horsecar, Misha told Stephen, in which he and the chestnut and another horse were to travel the next day to Rostov. When he had led the chestnut back to its stable, the horsecar had been parked in its usual place. Mr. Kropotkin had felt the engine, to make sure it was the horsecar we had seen, and yes, the engine was warm. No one could be found who had driven it. Mr. K.'s view of things was that the driver was ashamed of his carelessness and afraid of being disciplined.

"Well," Stephen said, standing up and straightening his spine, "thank you for telling us."

Misha hopped off the table and waved him back to his chair, talking earnestly.

"That is not why he asked us to come here," Stephen relayed.

"No," I said. "He gave you his phone number before all this happened."

"Never miss a trick, do you?"

"I don't really know," I said.

"That figures."

"I speak to German," Misha said.

"What?" I looked at him with quickened interest. "Do you mean you spoke to Hans Kramer?"

Misha regretfully did not. Misha told Stephen that he had become friends with the boy who had looked after Hans Kramer's horse. He had been unable to tell us that in the morning, because of course it was forbidden to talk to the foreigners and he had disobeyed orders.

"Yes," I said resignedly. "Go on."

It appeared that the two young men had formed a pleasant habit of retiring to a disused hayloft to talk and smoke cigarettes. Smoking in the stables was forbidden also. Misha had enjoyed both talk and smoke, because they were forbidden.

Misha's blue eyes were brightly alive, full of pleasure at his own daring, and totally unsophisticated.

"What did you talk about? ' I prompted.

Horses, of course. And Hans Kramer. The German boy disliked Kramer, who was, Stephen translated succinctly, a bastard.

"In what way?"

Misha talked. Stephen translated. "Kramer was apparently O.K. with horses, but he liked to play nasty little jokes on people."

"Yes, I was told of one," I said, thinking of Johnny and the pink-boa girl-boy. "Go on."

"He was also a thief."

I showed disbelief. Misha nodded vigorously, not just with his head, but from halfway up his back.

"Misha says," Stephen went on, "that Kramer stole a case from the veterinary surgeon's car when he called to see the horses of the British team, before the trials began."

"A case containing drugs?" I said.

"Da," Misha said. "Drug."

"People are always stealing cases from doctors and vets," I said. "You'd think they would chain them up like bicycles, not leave them around in cars. Well . . . so was Kramer an addict?"

I felt doubtful as I said it, because heavy drug addiction and international-standard riding didn't seem to be happy bedfellows. Misha, however, didn't know. The German boy had told him there was a fuss when the vet discovered his loss, but Kramer had hidden the case.

"How did the German boy know?"

"He found it somewhere in the stable, hidden in Kramer's kit. Four days later, when Kramer died, the German boy took the case to the hayloft, and he and Misha shared out the contents."

"For God's sake," I said.

"It sounds to me," said Stephen, speaking frankly after another long tale from Misha, "that the German boy took the case itself and all the salable items like barbiturates, and gave Misha the rubbish. Not surprising, really. Our Misha is a proper little innocent at large."

"What did he do with his share?"

Stephen consulted. "Brought it back to Moscow with some other stuff—souvenirs of the trip, that's all. To remind him of the happy talks in the hayloft."

I stared vacantly at the double-glazed window, seeing in my mind not an uncurtained black square, but an old-world cottage in England.

Johnny Farringford, I thought, had not wanted to be thought to be connected too much with Kramer. He had not wanted me to seek or find Alyosha; had wanted the rumors forgotten, and had denied there was any scandal to hush up. Suppose, I thought bleakly, that the Alyosha business was after all unimportant, and the thing Johnny desperately did not want uncovered had nothing to do with unorthodox sex but all to do with drugs.

"Has Misha still got the stuff he brought back?" I said.

Misha had.

"Would you let me see it?" I asked him.

Misha was not unwilling, but said he would be going away first thing in the morning.

"Is it important?" Stephen said.

"Only in a negative sort of way." I sighed. "If Kramer had the case for four days before he died, he probably took out of it what he wanted. Then the German boy took his share. . . . Whatever Misha still has, it is not what Kramer wanted—which might tell us something. Besides barbiturates, vets usually carry other things. Pethidine, for example. It's a painkiller, but I believe it is so addictive for humans that you can get hooked by using it only a very few times. And Butazolidin . . . and steroids . . ."

"Got you," Stephen said, and spoke to Misha. Between them they had a long chat, which ended in evident agreement.

"Misha says his souvenirs are at his mother's flat, but he himself has a room with the other grooms, near the stable. He has to be back there soon, and tomorrow morning he goes. He can't get to his mother's. But he will telephone, and ask his sister, who lives at home until she moves into this place, to bring the stuff to you tomorrow morning. But she cannot come to the hotel, as it would not do to be seen talking to foreigners, so she will meet you inside the main entrance of GUM. She will wear a red woolen hat with a white pompon, which Misha gave her last week for her birthday, and a long red scarf. She speaks some English, because she learned it in school."

"Great," I said. "Could she make it fairly early? I have to meet Chulitsky outside the National Hotel at ten."

Misha said he thought she could get there by half-past nine, and on that we agreed.

I thanked Misha for all his trouble and kindness in giving us this information. I enthusiastically shook his hand.

"Is good," he said, looking pleased. "You save horse. Nikolai Alexandrovich say help. I help."

We arrived outside the Aragvi restaurant ten minutes late because of an absence of taxis in the far-flung suburb, and a scarcity of buses. The metro, we had discovered, came to an end three miles short of the flat. Misha traveled toward the city center with us, but apart, not looking at us, not speaking. He left us on the train, when he reached his interchange station, without a flicker of farewell, his face as stolid as the others ranged about.

"Don't tell Malcolm Herrick what Misha has just told us," I said, as we hurried the last hundred yards on foot. "He's a newspaperman. My brief is to hush up what I can, not get it printed in *The Watch*. And we'd get Misha into trouble."

"Silent as the sepulcher," Stephen promised, in a voice which spoke of teaching grandmothers something about eggs.

The Aragvi turned out to be less than half a mile from the Intourist Hotel: up Gorky Street, and turn right at the traffic lights. Malcolm and Ian were waiting just a little short of it and Malcolm grumbled, quietly for him, that we had kept them waiting in the cold.

There was a short queue outside the restaurant, shivering.

"Follow me, and don't talk until we are inside," Malcolm said. He by-passed the queue and opened the firmly shut door. The by now familiar argument took place, and finally, grudgingly, we were let in.

"I booked," Malcolm said as we peeled off our coats. "I come here often. You'd never think it."

The place was full, and somewhere there was some music. We were led to the one vacant table and a bottle of vodka materialized within five seconds.

"Of the two decent restaurants in Moscow," Malcolm said, "I like this the better."

"Two?" I said.

"That's right. What do you want to eat?" He peered into the large menu. "The food is Georgian. It is a Georgian restaurant. Most of the customers are from Georgia."

"For Georgia, U.S.S.R., read Texas, U.S.A.," Ian said.

The menu was written exclusively in Russian, and while the other three chose from it, I used my eyes instead on the customers. There were three men at the next table, and beyond them, sitting with their backs to the wall, two more. Very few women. The faces, I realized, were livelier, and varied. The two men over by the wall, for instance, were not Moscow types; they had sallower skins, fierce dark eyes, black curling hair. They ate with concentration, intent on their food.

The three men at the table next to ours were, on the other hand, intent on their drink. Not much tablecloth showed between full bottles, empty bottles, full and empty glasses. The men, one huge, one medium, one small, were diving into vast tulip-shaped glasses of champagne.

Malcolm looked up from the menu and followed my gaze. "Georgians," he said, "born with hollow legs." I watched with fascination while the gold liquid disappeared like beer. The eyes of the smallest were faintly glazed. The huge one looked as sober as his gray flannel suit; and there were three empty vodka bottles on the table.

Ian, Malcolm, and Stephen all ordered expertly, and I told Stephen just to double his for me. The food when it came was strange and spicy, and light-years away from the gray chunks down the road. The huge man at the next table roared at the waiter, who hurried to bring a second bottle of champagne.

"Well, how's it going, sport?" Malcolm said, forking some chicken in bean sauce into his mouth.

"The smallest one's legs are full," I said.

"What?" He looked round at the three men. "No, I meant the Sherlock Holmes bit. What've you come up with so far?"

"The German who died at Burghley called on Alyosha with his dying breath," I said. "And that's about all."

"And anyway, you knew that," said Stephen.

I kicked him under the table. He gave me a sharp inquiring look and then realized that except for Misha, we wouldn't have been aware that they knew. Neither Malcolm nor Ian commented, however. The four of us ate thoughtfully.

"Not much in that, is there, sport?" Malcolm said.

"Alyosha must exist," I said, "Alyosha. Moscow." I sighed. "I'll have to go on looking."

"What'll you do next?" Ian said.

I took off my glasses, and squinted at them, and polished some nonexistent smears with my handkerchief.

"Er . . ." I said.

"How bad are your eyes, sport?" Malcolm said, interrupting. "Let's look through your windows."

Short of breaking the frames, I couldn't have prevented him. He took the glasses firmly out of my hand and placed them on his own nose.

To me, his face, and all the others in the place, looked a distorted blur. Colors told me roughly where hair, eyes, and clothes were, but outlines had vanished.

"Christ," Malcolm said. "You must have corkscrew vision."

"Astigmatism," I said.

"And some."

They all had a go at looking at the world through my eyes, and then handed them back. Everything became nicely sharp again.

"In both eyes?" Ian said.

I nodded. "And both different. Frightfully handy."

The small man at the next table was propping his head up with his champagne glass and seemed to be going to sleep. The friends kept up a steady intake and ignored him. The huge one roared at the waiter again and held up three fingers, and with my mouth open I watched three more bottles of vodka arrive at the table.

Coffee was brought for us, but I was glued to the scene in front. The small man's head, still balanced on the glass of champagne, sank lower and lower. The glass came to rest on the table, and the hand holding it dropped away, and the little man sat there with his head on the glass fast asleep.

"Georgians," said Malcolm, glancing at them, as if that explained everything.

The huge man paid the bill and stood up, rising to a good seven feet tall. He tucked the three full bottles of vodka under one arm and the sleeping friend under the other, and made the stateliest of exits.

"Bloody marvelous," I said.

The waiter who had served them came and spoke to us, watching the departure with respect.

Malcolm said, "The waiter says they started with a whole bottle of vodka each. Then they had two more bottles of vodka between them. Five in all. Then the two bottles of champagne. No one but Georgians could do that."

I said mildly, "I thought you didn't know Russian."

He gave me a startled glance and a short burst of the flat hard stare of the first evening.

"Yeah, sport, I remember. I told you I don't *speak* Russian. . . . Well, I don't. That doesn't mean I don't know it. It means I don't let the Russkies in general cotton on. Right, sport?"

"Right," I agreed.

"It's not in your file," Ian said conversationally.

"Dead right. The Russkies have my file, too, don't forget. I learned the lingo in private from twelve long-playing records and some textbooks, and you just forget that piece of information pronto."

"Never misses a trick," Stephen said.

"Who doesn't?"

"Our friend Randall."

Ian regarded me with slightly narrowed eyes, and Malcolm called for the bill.

The two sallow men from over by the wall had gone in the wake of the Georgians, and the place was emptying fast. We collected our coats and hats and shuddered out into the saturated air. It seemed colder to me than ever. The other three made off for the metro, and I risked a fine by crossing Gorky Street above ground instead of tunneling under. At after eleven at night there were even fewer cars than usual to mow one down, and not another pedestrian in sight, let alone a policeman.

The Intourist Hotel lay in the distance down the slight hill, with its large canopy stretching out over the pavement. I turned up my coat collar, wondering, for about the tenth time, why most of the center of the canopy was an intentional rectangular hole, like a skylight without glass, open to every drop of rain or snow which cared to fall. As a shelter for people arriving and departing, the canopy was a nonstarter. Of as much practical use as a bath with no plug.

A mind floating along in neutral is in rotten shape for battle. A black car rolled quietly down the road beside me and came to a halt ten paces ahead. The driver got out of the car, and the front passenger door opened. The front passenger stood up onto the pavement, and as I approached, he sprang at me.

The surprise was absolute. His hand snaked out toward my spectacles, and I hit it violently aside as one would a wasp. When it came to saving my sight, my reflexes were always instantaneous; but for the rest, I was unbalanced.

He crowded after me across the pavement to pin me against the unyielding stone of the flanking build-

ing. His friend hustled to help. There was a fierce
brutal strength in their manner, and there was also no
doubt that, whatever they intended next, their first
target was still my eyes.

One wouldn't actually choose to fight while wearing
a thick overcoat and a fur hat, even if the opposition
were similarly handicapped. To fight, however, seemed
imperative.

I kicked the storming passenger very viciously on
the knee, and when his head came forward I grabbed
hold of the wool balaclava he wore under his hat and
swung him round so that his head hit the wall.

The driver arrived like a whirlwind and grabbed my
arm, his other hand aiming at my glasses. I ducked.
His fingers sank only into fur. My hat, dislodged, fell
off. I let go with a kick at him, which connected but
not very effectively, and I also opened my mouth and
started shouting.

I shouted, "Ya-ya-ya-ya-ya!" at the top of my
voice, roaring into the empty street, which had no
traffic noise to drown the decibels.

They hadn't expected such a racket. I felt the im-
petus slacken in them fractionally, and I tore myself
out of their grasp and ran. Ran downhill, toward the
Intourist. Ran with all the power I could bring to every
muscle. Ran like the Olympics.

I heard one of the car doors slam. Heard the car
coming behind me. Went on running.

There was life and waiting taxis and people outside
the Intourist. There were also the watchers, earning
their keep. I wondered fleetingly if watchers ever went
to the help of people running away from other people
in black cars, and supposed not.

Not in Moscow.

I didn't bother to yell for their help. I simply ran.
And I made it. Just.

The men in the car must have decided it was too
near the Intourist for them to make another attack,
especially as I was now running flat out and not walk-

ing along with woolly thoughts. In any case, after it had passed me, the car didn't stop, but accelerated away past the hotel, and turned right at the end of the street, and went out of sight.

I slowed to a fast walk for the last hundred yards, heart thumping madly and chest heaving to take in vast lungfuls of cold wet air. I was not as fit, I thought grimly, as I would have been in any other autumn, when I'd been racing.

I covered the last few yards at ordinary walking pace, and attracted no more eyes than usual when I went in through the big double airlock-type glass entrance. The warmth inside seemed suddenly cloying, stoking up the sweat of exertion. I peeled off my coat and collected my room key, and thought that nothing on earth would persuade me to go back up Gorky Street to retrieve my hat.

My room looked calm and sane, as if to reassure me that hotel guests could not be frighteningly attacked in one of the main streets of the city.

It could happen in Piccadilly, I thought. It could happen on Park Avenue and the Champs Élysées and the Via Veneto. What was so different about Gorky Street?

I threw my coat and room key on the bed, poured a large reviver from the duty-free Scotch, and sank onto the sofa to drink it.

Two attacks in one day. Too bloody much.

The first had been a definite attempt to cripple or kill. The second had been—perhaps—an attempt at abduction. Without glasses, I would have been a push-over. They could have got me into the car. And after the drive . . . what destination?

Did the Prince expect me to stick to the task until I was dead? Probably not, I thought; but then the Prince hadn't known what he was sending me into.

More than anything, I'd been lucky. I could be lucky again. Failing that, I had better be careful. My heart gradually steadied. My breath quietened to normal. I drank the Scotch, and felt better.

After a while I put down my glass and picked up the tape recorder. Switched it on. Started methodically beside the window, and made slow comprehensive sweeps of the walls. Top to bottom. Every inch.

There was no whine.

I switched the recorder off and put it down. No whine was inconclusive. It didn't mean no listening probe embedded in the plaster; it meant no listening probe switched on.

I went slowly to bed and lay awake in the dark, thinking about the driver and the passenger in the black car. Apart from general awareness of their age, twenty to thirty, and height, five nine, they had left me with three clear impressions. The first was that they knew about my eyesight. The second, that the savage quality I had sensed in their attack was a measure of the ferocity in their minds. And third, that they were not Russian.

They had not spoken, so their voices had given me no clue. They had worn only the sober garb of the Russian man in the street. Their faces had been three-quarters covered, with the result that I had seen only their eyes, and even those very briefly.

So why did I think . . . ? I pulled the duvet over my shoulders and turned comfortably onto one side. The Russians, I thought drowsily, didn't behave like that unless they were KGB, and if the KGB had wanted to arrest me they would not have done it in that way, and they would not have failed. Other Russians were tamed by deterrents like labor camps, psychiatric hospitals, and the death sentence. Frank's voice drifted back to me from breakfast. "There are no muggings in Russia. The crime rate is very low indeed. There are practically no murders."

"Repression is always the outcome of revolution," I said.

"Are you sure you've got it the right way round?" Mrs. Wilkinson asked me, looking puzzled.

"People don't actually like being purged of their lazy and libertine old ways," I said. "So you have to force their mouths open, to give them the medicine. Revolutionaries everywhere are by nature aggressive, oppressive, and repressive. All for your own good, of course."

I got no rise out of Frank. He merely repeated that in a perfect socialist state like Russia, there was no need for crime. The state supplied all needs, and gave to the people whatever it was good for them to have.

Sixty years or so after the October Revolution (now confusingly celebrated in November owing to the updating of the calendar), its wind-sown seeds were germinating their bloody crops around the world, but way back where it all started, the second and third generation were not given to acts of private violence.

The eyes looking out of the balaclavas had burned with a hunger for a harvest yet to come: sixty years younger than the blank, dull look of a people for whom everything was provided.

10

Frank followed me to GUM the following morning.

When I had gone in through the main door without once looking back, I stood still in the shadows, and watched, and presently he appeared, hurrying a little.

At breakfast, upon Natasha's insistent inquiry, I had said I was going to see some more horse people, but before that I was going to GUM to buy a new hat, as I had lost my last one.

The tiniest frown crossed Frank's face, and he looked at me with a shade of speculation. I remembered that when he had followed me into the hotel the evening before, after I had ostensibly said good night to Stephen, I had been wearing the hat. How careful one had to be, I thought, over the most innocent remarks.

"Where did you loss your hat?" he said, showing only friendly interest.

"Must have dropped it in the foyer or the lift," I said easily. "I don't know."

Natasha suggested I ask at the desk. I would, I said; and did. One learned. If not fast enough, one learned in the end.

I turned away from GUM's main door while Frank was still a little way off, and saw the red woolen hat with a white pompon immediately. Below the hat there were two blue-gray eyes in an elfin face, and straight hair in escaping wisps. She looked too young and slight to be married and a mother, and I could see why nine stories up with no lifts was a crying disaster.

"Elena?" I said, tentatively.

She nodded a fraction, and turned to walk purposefully away. I followed a few paces behind. For talking to a foreigner she would have to pick her own moment, and it suited me well for it to be out of Frank's sight.

She wore a gray coat with a red scarf falling jauntily over her shoulder, and carried a string bag with a paper-wrapped parcel inside it. I shortened the distance between us and said, so that she could hear, "I want to buy a hat." She gave no sign of understanding, but when she stopped it was, in fact, outside a shop selling hats.

The inside of GUM was not a department store along Western lines but like those in the Far East, a huge collection of small shops all under one roof. A covered market, two stories high, with intersecting alleys and a glassed roof far above. Drips of melted snow fell through the cracks in the heavens and made small puddles underfoot.

I bought the hat. Elena waited outside in the alley displaying no interest in me, and set off again when I came out. I looked carefully around for Frank, but couldn't see him. Shoppers blocked every long perspective; and it worked both ways. If I couldn't see him, very likely he couldn't see me.

Elena squeezed through a long queue of stolid people and stopped outside a shop selling folk arts and crafts. She transferred the plastic carrier to my hand with the smallest of movements and no ceremony whatsoever. Her gaze was directed toward the goods in the window, not at me.

"Misha say give you this." Her accent was light and pretty, but I gathered from the disapproval in her tone that she was on this errand strictly for her brother's sake, and not for mine.

I thanked her for coming.

"Please not bring trouble for him."

"I promise I won't," I said.

She nodded briefly, glancing quickly at my face, and away.

"You go now, please," she said. "I queue."

"What is the queue for?"

"Boots. Warm boots, for winter."

I looked at the queue, which stretched a good way along one of the ground-floor alleys, and up a staircase, and along the gallery above, and away out of sight. It hadn't moved a step forward in five minutes.

"But it will take you all day," I said.

"Yes. I need boots. When boots come in shop, everyone come to buy. It is normal. In England, the peasants have no boots. In Soviet Union, we are fortunate."

She walked away without any more farewell than her brother had given on the metro, and attached herself to the end of the patient line. The only thing that I could think of that England's bootless peasantry would so willingly queue all day for would be Cup Final tickets.

A glance into the tissue-wrapped parcel revealed that what Misha had sent, or what Elena had brought, was a painted wooden doll.

Frank picked me up somewhere between GUM and the pedestrian tunnel under Fiftieth Anniversary et cetera Square. I caught a glimpse of him behind me underground—a split second of unruly curls and college scarf bobbing along in the crowd. If I hadn't been looking, I would never have noticed.

It was already after ten. I lengthened my stride and finished the journey fairly fast, surfacing on the north side of the square and veering left toward the National Hotel.

Parked just beyond the entrance was a small bright-yellow car, with, inside it, a large Russian in a high state of fuss.

"Seven minutes late," he said. "For seven minutes I sit here illegally. Get in, get in, do not apologize."

I eased in beside him and he shot off with a crash of gears and a fine disregard for other traffic.

"You have been to GUM," he said accusingly, "and therefore you are late."

I followed the direction of his gaze and began to feel less bewildered by his clairvoyance: he was looking at the printed tissue paper inside the string bag which Elena had given me. How cautious of her, I thought, to have brought Misha's souvenirs in a wrapping to suit the rendezvous, in a bag any foreign tourist could acquire. A bag, too, I thought contentedly, that friend Frank would not query. The secret of survival in Russia was to be unremarkable.

Yuri Ivanovich Chulitsky revealed himself, during the time I spent with him, as a highly intelligent man with a guilt-ridden love of luxury and a repressed sense of humor. The wrong man for the regime, I thought, but striving to live honorably within its framework. In a country where an out-of-line opinion was a treachery, even if unspoken, he was an unwilling mental traitor. Not to believe what one believes one should believe is a spiritual torment as old as doctrine, and Yuri Chulitsky, I grew to understand, suffered from it dismally.

He was about forty, plumply unfit, with pouches already under his eyes, and a habit of raising the center of his upper lip to reveal the incisors beneath. He spoke with deliberation, forming the words carefully and precisely, but that might have been only the effect of using English, and as on the telephone, he gave the impression that every utterance was double checked internally before being allowed to escape.

"Cigarette?" he said, offering a packet.

"No. Thank you."

"I smoke," he said, flicking a lighter one-handed with the dexterity of long practice. "You smoke?"

"Cigars, sometimes."

He grunted. The fingers of his left hand with the cigarette stuck between them, resting on the steering wheel, were stained yellowish brown, but otherwise his fingers were white and flexible, with spatulate tips and short, well-tended nails.

"I go see Olympic building," he said. "You come?"

"Sure," I said.

"At Chertanovo."

"Where?"

"Place for equestrian games. I am architect. I design buildings at Chertanovo." He pronounced design like *dess-in,* but his meaning was clear. "I go today see progress. You understand?"

"Every word," I said.

"Good. I see in England how equestrian games go. I see need for sort buildings . . ." He stopped and shook his head in frustration.

"You went to see what sort of things happened during international equestrian games, so that you would know what buildings would be needed, and how they should best be designed for dealing with the needs and numbers of the Olympics."

He smiled lopsidedly. "Is right. I go also Montreal. Is not good. Moscow games, we build good."

The leisurely one-way system in central Moscow meant, it seemed to me, mile-long detours to return to where one started, but facing the other way. Yuri Chulitsky swung his bright little conveyance round the corners without taking his foot noticeably off the accelerator, the bulk of his body making the car's skin seem not much more than a metal overcoat.

At one point, arriving at a junction with a main road,

we were stopped dead by a policeman. Yuri Chulitsky shrugged a trifle and switched off the engine.

"What's the matter?" I said.

The main road had, I saw, been totally cleared of traffic. Nothing moved on it. Chulitsky said something under his breath, so I asked again, "What's the matter? Has there been an accident?"

"No," he said. "See lines in road?"

"Do you mean those white ones?"

There were two parallel white lines painted down the center of the main road, with a space of about six feet between them. I had noticed them on many of the widest streets, but thought of them vaguely as some sort of no man's land between the two-way lines of traffic.

"White lines go to Kremlin," Chulitsky said. "Politburo people drive to Kremlin in white lines. Every peoples car stop."

I sat and watched. After three or four minutes a long black car appeared, driving fairly fast in lonely state up the center of the road, between the white lines.

"Chaika," Chulitsky said, as the limousine slid lengthily past, showing curtains drawn across the rear windows. "Is official car. *Chaika*, in English, is 'seagull.'"

He started his engine, and presently the policeman stepped out of the middle of the side road and waved us on our way.

"Was that the Chairman?" I asked.

"No. Many Politburo peoples go in Chaika on white lines. All peoples cars always stop."

Democratic, I thought.

The small yellow car sped south of the city, along what he told me was the road to Warsaw.

He said, "Nikolai Alexandrovich Kropotkin say tell you when you ask. You ask. I tell."

"I'm looking for someone called Alyosha."

"Alyosha? Many people called Alyosha. Nikolai Alexandrovich say find Alyosha for Randall Drew. Who is this Alyosha?"

"That's the problem," I said. "I don't know, and I haven't been able to find out. No one seems to know who he is." I paused. "Did you meet Hans Kramer, in England?"

"*Da*. German. He die."

"That's right. Well . . . he knew Alyosha. The autopsy said Kramer died of a heart attack, but people near him when he died thought he was saying that Alyosha had caused him to have a heart attack. Er . . . have I said that clearly enough?"

"Yes. Is clear. About Alyosha, I cannot help."

I supposed I would have been surprised if he had said anything different.

"You have been asked before, about Alyosha?" I said.

"Please?"

"An Englishman came to see you at the Olympic Committee building. He saw you and the two colleagues who went with you to England."

"Is right," he agreed gruffly. "Is writing for newspaper."

"Malcolm Herrick."

"*Da*."

"You all said you knew nothing at all about anything."

A long pause; then he said, "Herrick is foreigner. Comrades not say things to Herrick."

He relapsed into silence, and we drove steadily along the Warsaw highway, leaving the city center behind and making for another lot of egg box suburbs. Some light powdery snow began to fall, and Yuri switched on the windshield wipers.

"Today, tomorrow, it snow. This snow not melt. Stay all winter."

"Do you like the winter?" I said.

"No. Winter is bad for building. Today is last day is possible see progress of buildings at Chertanovo. So I go now."

I said I would be most interested in the buildings, if he felt like showing me round. He laughed in a small, deep, throaty rumble, but offered no explanation.

I asked him if he had personally known Hans Kramer, but he had spoken to him only about buildings. "Well . . . Johnny Farringford?" I asked.

"Johnny . . . Farringford. Are you saying *Lord* Farringford? Is a man with red hairs? Ride in British team?"

"That's the one," I said.

"I see him many times. Many places. I talk with him. I ask him about buildings. He is no good about buildings. I ask other peoples. Other peoples is more good." He stopped, obviously unimpressed by the planning ability of earls, and we drove four or five miles while he seemed to be thinking deeply about anything except my mission; but finally, as if coming to a difficult decision, he said, "Is not good Lord Farringford come to Olympics."

I held my breath. Damped down every quick and excited question. Managed in the end to say without even a quaver, "Why?"

He had relapsed, however, into further deep thought.

"Tell me," I said, without pressure.

"It is for my country good if he come. It is for your country not good. If I tell you, I speak against the good for my country. It is difficult for me."

"Yes," I said.

After a long way he turned abruptly off the highway to the right, along a somewhat lesser dual roadway. There was, as usual, very little traffic, and without much ado he swung round in a U-turn across the center strip, to face the way we had come. He pulled in by the roadside and stopped with a jerk.

On our left the road was lined as far as the eye could see with rows of apartment buildings, grayish white.

On our right there was a large, flat, snow-sprinkled space bordered on the far side by a stretch of black-looking forest consisting of spindly young trees packed tightly together. On the side near the road there was a wire fence, and between the fence and the road itself, a wide ditch full of white half-melted slush.

"Is there," Yuri said, pointing into this far from promising landscape with a gleam of relaxed humor. "Equestrian games."

"Ye gods," I said.

We got out of the car into the bitter air. I looked away down the road in the direction we had originally been traveling. There were tall concrete lamp standards, electricity pylons, dense black forest on the left, white unending impersonal apartment blocks on the right, a gray double road with no traffic, and at the side, wet white snow. Over it all softly fell the powdery forerunners of the winter freeze. It was silent and ugly and as desolate as a desert.

"In summer," Yuri said, "forest is green. Is beautiful place for equestrian games. Is grass. Everything beautiful."

"I'll take your word for it," I said.

Farther along, on the side of the road where we had stopped, there were two large billboards, one bearing a long announcement about the Olympics, and the other sporting a big picture of the stadium as it was one day going to be. The stands looked most ingenious, shaped like a Z, with the top and bottom ranks of the seats facing one way, and the center rank facing the other. Events, it appeared, would take place on both sides of the stands.

Yuri gestured to me to return to the car, and he drove us through a gate in the wire, onto the site itself. There were a few men there driving mechanical earth-movers, though how they knew what they were moving was a mystery to me, as the whole place looked a sea of jumbled mud with pools of icy slush amid the usual broken white blanket of half-melted snow.

Yuri reached into the space behind my seat and brought forth a huge pair of thigh-high rubber boots. These he put on by planting them firmly outside the opened car door, removing his walking shoes, wrapping his trousers round his legs, and sinking his feet into the depths as he stood up.

"I talk to men," he said. "You wait."

Superfluous advice, I thought. Yuri unfastened his ear flaps against the chill wind and talked to his men, trudging about and making sweeping gestures with his arms. After a fair while he returned and reversed the boot process, tucking the now wet and muddy objects in behind his own seat.

"Is good," he said, lifting the center of his lip and giving me a gleam of teeth. "We finish foundations. In spring, when snow melt, we build quickly. Stadium." He pointed. "Stables." He pointed again. "Restaurants, buildings for riders, buildings for officials, buildings for television. There"—he waved an arm at a huge, slightly undulating area bordered by forest—"is cross-country for trials, like Badminton and Burghley. In summer, is beautiful."

"Will everyone who wants to come to Games get visas?" I said.

"*Da*. All peoples have visas."

"It isn't always like that," I said neutrally, and he replied in the same level tone. "For Olympics, all peoples have visas. Stay in hotels. Is good."

"What about the press?" I said. "And the television people?"

"We build press building for foreign press. Also television building for foreign television peoples, near Moscow television building. Use same . . ." He described a transmitting mast with his hands. "Foreign peoples go only in these buildings. In England, we ask press peoples about press buildings. We see what press peoples need. We ask many press peoples. We ask Herrick."

"Herrick?" I said. "Did you ask him in England, or in Moscow?"

"In England. He help us. He come to Burghley. We see him with Lord Farringford. So we ask him. We ask many peoples about buildings. We ask Hans Kramer about buildings. He was . . ." Words failed him but gestures did not. Hans Kramer, I gathered, had given the Russian observers a decisively rude brush-off.

He tied up the ear flaps of his hat without taking it off. I spent the time scanning the road for anything that looked like a following car, but saw nothing of note. A bus passed, its tires making a swishing noise on the slushy tarmac. I thought that the low level of traffic on most roads would make a following car conspicuous; but on the other hand, there seemed to be very little variety in make, so that one car tended to look exactly like the next. Difficult to spot a tail. Easy, however, to follow a bright yellow box on wheels.

"What sort of car is this?" I said.

"Zhiguli," he said. "Is my car." He seemed proud of it. "Not many peoples have car. I am architect, have car."

"Is it expensive?" I asked.

"Car expensive. Petrol cheap. Driving examination, very difficult."

He finished the bow on his hat, checked that his boots were inside, slammed the door, and backed briskly out onto the road.

"How is everyone going to get there?" I said. "Competitors and spectators."

"We build metro. New station." He thought. "Metro on top of ground, not deep. New metro for Chertanovo peoples. Many new buildings here. Chertanovo is new place. I show you."

We set off back toward the Warsaw highway, but before we reached it he turned off to the right, and drove up another wide road, where apartment blocks were springing up like mushrooms. All whitish gray; all nine stories high, marching away into the distance.

"In Soviet all peoples have house," Yuri said. "Rent is cheap. In England, expensive." He shot me an amused look as if challenging me to argue with his simplistic statement. In a country where everything was owned by the state, there was no point in charging high rents. To enable people to pay high rents, or high prices for electricity, transport, and telephones, for that matter, it would be necessary to pay higher wages. Yuri Chulitsky knew it as well as I did. I would have to be careful, I told myself, not to underestimate the subtlety of his thoughts because of the limitations of the English they were expressed in.

"Can I make a trade with you?" I said. "A bargain? One piece of information in exchange for another?"

For that I got a quick, sharp, piercing glance, but all he said was, "Car need petrol." He pulled off the road into a station with pumps, and removed himself from the car to talk to the attendant.

I found myself taking off my glasses and polishing the already clean lenses. The playing-for-time gesture, which was not at that moment needed. I wondered if it had been intuitively sparked off by Yuri's purchase of petrol, which seemed hardly urgent, as the tank was well over half full, according to the gauge.

While I watched, the needle crept round to full. Yuri paid and returned to the car, and we set off back toward the city center.

"What information you exchange?" he said.

"I don't have it all yet."

A muscle twitched beside his mouth. "You diplomat?" he said.

"A patriot. Like you."

"You tell me information."

I told him a great deal. I told him what had really happened at the Hippodrome, not Kropotkin's watered-down version, and I told him of the attack in

Gorky Street. I also told him, though without names
or places or details, the gist of what Boris Telyatnikov
had overheard, and the inferences one could draw
from it. He listened, as any faithful Russian would,
with a growing sense of dismay. When I stopped, he
drove a good way without speaking, and in the end his
comment was oblique.

"You want lunch?" he said.

11

He took me to what he called the Architects' Circle
and in the big basement restaurant there gave me food
I hadn't believed existed in Moscow. Prime smoked
salmon, delicious ham off the bone, tender red beef.
An apple and some grapes. Vodka to toss off for starters, followed by excellent red wine. Good strong coffee at the end. He himself ate and drank with as much
enjoyment as I did.

"Marvelous," I said appreciatively. "Superb."

Yuri leaned back at last and lit a cigarette, and told
me that every profession had its circle. There was a
Writers' Circle, for instance, to which all Soviet writers belonged. If they did not belong to the circle, they
did not get published. They could of course be ex-
pelled from the circle, if it was considered that what
they wrote was not suitable. Yuri's manner dared me
to suggest that he didn't entirely agree with this system.

"What about architects?" I asked mildly.

Architects, I gathered, had to be politically sound

if they wished to be members of the Architects' Circle. Naturally, if one did not belong to the circle, one was not allotted anything to design.

Naturally.

I drank my coffee and made no remark. Yuri watched me, and smiled with a touch of melancholy.

"I give information," he said. "About Lord Farringford."

"Thank you."

"You are clever man." He sighed and shrugged resignedly, and kept his side of the bargain. "Lord Farringford is foolish man. With Hans Kramer, he go bad places. Sex places." Distaste showed in his face, and the top lip lifted even further off the incisors. "In London, is disgusting pictures. In the street. All people can see. Disgusting." He searched for a word. "Dirty."

"Yes," I said.

"Lord Farringford and Hans Kramer go into these places. Three, four times."

"Are you sure it was more than once?" I said attentively.

"Sure. We see. We . . . follow." The confession came out on a downward inflection, drifting off into silence, as if he hadn't quite said what he had.

Wow, I thought; and what I said, without emphasis of any sort, was "Why did you follow?"

He struggled a great deal with his conscience, but he told me what I was sure was the truth.

"Comrade with me, he look in England and in many country for foolish peoples. When foolish peoples come to Soviet Union, comrade use . . . make . . ."

"Your comrade makes use of them through their liking for pornography?"

He blew out a sharp breath.

"And if Farringford comes to the Olympics, your comrade will make use of him?"

Silence.

"What use could Farringford be? He isn't a diplomat. . . ." I stopped, thought, and went on more slowly. "Do you mean," I said, "that in return for not . . . embarrassing the British people, for not exposing a scandalous misdemeanor into which your comrade has lured him, your comrade will demand some concession from the British government?"

"Say again," he said.

I said it again, more forthrightly. "Your comrade traps Farringford into a dirty mess. Your comrade says to the British government, give me what I want, or I publish the mess."

He didn't directly admit it. "The comrades of my comrade," he said.

"Yes," I agreed. "Those comrades."

"Farringford is rich man," Yuri said. "For rich man, comrade feel . . ." He didn't know the word, but his meaning was unmistakable, and it was contempt.

"For all rich men?" I said.

"Of course. Rich man bad. Poor man good." He spoke with utter conviction and no suggestion of cynicism, stating, I supposed, one of humanity's most fundamental beliefs. Camels through eyes of needles, and all that. Rich men never got to heaven, and serve them right. Which left absolutely no hope of eternal bliss for Randall Drew, who had an unequal share of this world's goods. . . . If I warned Johnny Farringford, I wondered, putting a stop to my dribbling thoughts, would it be enough? Or would it really be wiser for him to stay at home?

"Yuri," I said, "how about another bargain?"

"Explain."

"If I learn more here, I will exchange it for a promise that your comrade will not try to trap Farringford, if he comes to the Olympics."

He stared. "You ask things impossible."

"A promise in writing," I said.

"Is impossible. Comrade with me . . . impossible."

"Yeah . . . well, it was just a thought." I reflected.

"Then if I learn more, I would exchange it for information about Alyosha."

Yuri studied the tablecloth and I studied Yuri.

"I cannot help," he said.

He stubbed out his cigarette and raised his eyes to meet mine. I was aware of a fierce intensity of thought going on behind the steady gaze, but upon what subject I couldn't guess.

"I take you," he said finally, "to Intourist Hotel."

He dropped me, in fact, around the corner, outside the National, where he had picked me up, implying, though not saying, that there was no sense in engaging the attention of the watchers unnecessarily.

It was by that time growing dark, as for various reasons our lunch had been delayed in arrival and leisurely in the eating, not least because of a wedding party going on in the next room. The bride had worn a long white dress and a minuscule veil. Did they get married in church? I asked. Of course not, Yuri said; it was not allowed. Pagan rituals, it seemed, had survived the rise and fall of Christianity.

The powdery snowfall of the morning had thickened into a determined regularity, but by no means into a raging blizzard. The wind had actually dropped, but so had the temperature, and there was a threatening bite to the cold. I walked the short distance from one hotel to the other among a crowd of hurrying pedestrians, and no men in black cars attempted to pick me off.

I arrived at the Intourist entrance at the same time as the Wilkinsons and their package tour, fresh back from the coach trip to Zagorsk.

"It was quite interesting," said Mrs. Wilkinson gamely, pushing through into the suddenly crowded foyer. "I couldn't hear the guide very well, and it seemed wrong somehow, guided tours going in through churches, when there were people in there praying. Did you know that they don't have any chairs in Rus-

sian churches? No pews. Everyone has to stand all
the time. My feet are fair killing me. There's a lot of
snow out in the country. Dad slept most of the way,
didn't you, Dad?"

Dad morosely nodded.

Mrs. Wilkinson, along with nearly everyone else on
the bus tour, carried a white plastic bag with a green
and orange swirly pattern on it.

"There was a tourist shop there. You know, foreign
currency shop. I bought ever such a pretty matroshka."

"What's a matroshka?" I said, waiting beside her
at the desk to collect our room keys.

"One of these," she said, fishing into the white plastic depths and tearing off some tissue paper. "These
dolls."

She produced with a small flourish an almost identical double of the fat, brightly colored wooden doll I,
too, carried in the string bag dangling from my left
hand.

"I think *matroshka* means 'little mother,' " she
said. "Anyway, you know, they pull apart and there's
another, smaller one inside, and you go right down to
a tiny one in the middle. There are nine inside here.
I'm going to give it to my grandchildren." She beamed
with simple pleasure, and I beamed right back. If only
all the world, I thought regretfully, were as wholesome
and as harmless as the Wilkinsons.

Wholesome and harmless did, I supposed, describe
the outward appearance of my tidy room upstairs, but
this time, when I swept the walls with the tape recorder, I heard the whine. High-pitched, assaulting
the ear, and originating from a spot about five feet up
from the floor, and about midway along the bed. I
switched off the recorder and wondered who, if anyone, was listening.

The matroshka doll which Elena had handed me
proved, on a closer look, to be a well-worn specimen
with paint scratched off all over her pink-cheeked face

and bright-blue dress and yellow apron. In shape she
was a very large elongated egg, slightly smaller round
the head than lower down, and flat at the bottom, in
order to stand. In all, about ten inches high and rotund
in circumference.

Pull apart she should, Mrs. Wilkinson had said, and
pull apart she did, across the middle, though either the
two halves were a naturally tight fit, or else Misha or
Elena had used some sort of glue. I tugged and
wrenched, and the little mother finally gave birth with
a reluctant jerk and scattered her closepacked secrets
all over the sofa.

I collected Misha's souvenirs of England and laid
them out on the dressing-table shelf, a row of valueless
bits and pieces brought home by an unsophisticated
young rider.

Easily the largest in size was the official program of
the international event, printed in English but with the
results and winners written in, in several places, in
Russian script. The program had been rolled to fit into
the matroshka doll, and lay in an opening tube with
the pages curling.

There were two picture postcards, unused, with
views of London. A brown envelope containing a
small bunch of wilted grass. An empty packet of Players cigarettes. A small metal ashtray with a horse's
head painted on the front, and "Made in England"
stamped into the back. A flat tin of mentholated cough
pastilles. Several pieces of paper and small cards with
writing on them, and finally, the things that had come
from the vet's stolen case.

Stephen had been right in thinking that Misha's
share had not been very much, and I wondered what
he had made of it, all the wording on the labels being
in English.

There were four flat two-by-two-inch sachets of a
powder called Equipalazone, each sachet containing
one gram of phenylbutazone B Vet C, known succinctly in the horse world as "bute."

I had used the drug countless times myself, in ten years of training my own horses, as it was tops at reducing inflammation and pain in strained and injured legs. In eventing and show jumping, one could give it to the horses up to the minute they performed, but in British racing, though not in some other countries, it had to be out of the system before the "off." Bute might be the subject of controversy and dope tests, but it was also about as easy to get hold of as aspirins, and one did not have to get it through a vet. The amount that Misha had brought home was roughly a single day's dose.

There was next a small plastic tub of sulfanilamide powder, which was useful for putting on wounds, to dry and heal them; and a sample-sized round tin of gamma benzine hexachloride, which, as far as I could remember, was anti-louse powder. There was a small, much folded advertisement leaflet extolling a cure for ringworm; and that was all.

No barbiturates. No Pethidine. No steroids. Either Kramer, or the German lad, had cleaned out the lot.

Well, I thought, as I began to pack everything back into the doll; so much for that. I went through everything again, more thoroughly, just to make sure. Opened up the sample-sized tin of louse powder, which contained louse powder, and the small plastic tub of sulfanilamide power, which contained sulfanilamide power. Or at least I supposed they did. If the two white powders were actually LSD or heroin, I wasn't sure that I would know.

The Equipalazone sachets were foil-packed, straight from the manufacturers, and hadn't been tampered with. I stuffed them back into the doll.

There was nothing lodged between the leaves of the program. I shook it; nothing fell out. The writings on the pieces of card and paper were some in Russian and some in German, and I laid these aside for a translation from Stephen. The empty cigarette packet contained no cigarettes, or anything else, and the small tin of cough lozenges contained—er—no cough lozenges. The tin of cough lozenges contained another piece of paper, much handled and wrinkled, and three very small glass vials in a bed of cotton wool.

The vials were of the same size and shape as those I had for Adrenalin: tiny glass capsules less than two inches in length, with a much-narrowed neck a third of the way along, which snapped off so that one could put a hypodermic needle through the resulting opening and down into the liquid, to draw it up. Each vial in the tin contained one milliliter of colorless liquid, enough for one human-sized injection. Half a teaspoonful. Not enough, to my mind, for a horse.

I held one of the vials up to the light, to see the printing on it, but as usual with such baby ampules, it was difficult to see the lettering. Not Adrenalin. As far as I could make out, it said 0.4 mg naloxone, which was spectacularly unhelpful, as I'd never heard of the stuff. I unfolded the piece of paper, and that was no better, as whatever was written there was written in Russian script. I put the paper back in the tin and closed it, and set it aside with the other mysteries for Stephen to look at.

Stephen himself had planned to spend the day between lectures and Gudrun, but had said he would be near the telephone from four o'clock onward, if I should want him. It frankly didn't seem worthwhile for me to traipse up to the university, or for him to come down, to decipher Misha's bits of paper, without first seeing if it could be done by wires; so I rang him.

"How's it going?" he said.

"The walls are whining."

"Oh, cripes."

"Anyway," I said, "if I spell some German words out to you, can you tell me what they mean?"

"If you think it's wise."

"Stop me if you don't think so," I said.

"O.K."

"Right. Here goes with the first." I read out, letter

by letter, as far as I could judge, the three lines of German handwriting on one of the cards.

Stephen was laughing by the end. "It says: 'With all good wishes for today and the future, Volker Springer.' That's a man's name."

"Good God."

I looked at the other cards more attentively, and saw something I had entirely missed. At the bottom of one of them, signed with a flourish, was a name I knew.

I read out that card, too, letter by letter.

"It says," Stephen said, " 'Best memories of a very good time in England. Your friend . . .' Your friend who?"

"Hans Kramer," I said.

"Bull's-eye." Stephen's voice crackled in my ear. "Are those by any chance Misha's souvenirs?"

"Yes."

"Autographs, no less. Anything else?"

"One or two things in Russian. They'll have to wait until tomorrow morning."

"I'll be with you at ten, then. Gudrun sends her love."

I put the receiver down, and almost immediately the bell rang again. A female English voice, calm, cultured, and on the verge of boredom.

"Is that Randall Drew?"

"Yes," I said.

"Polly Paget here," she said. "Cultural attaché's office, at the embassy."

"How nice to speak to you."

I had a vivid picture of her; short hair, long cardigan, flat shoes, and common sense.

"A telex has just come for you. Ian Young asked me to phone and tell you, in case you were waiting for it."

"Yes, please," I said. "Could you read it to me?"

"Actually, it is complicated, and very long. It really

would be better, I think, if you came to collect it. It would take a good half hour for me to dictate it while you write it down, and to be honest, I don't want to waste the time. I've a lot still to do, and it's Friday evening, and we're shutting down soon for the week-end."

"Is Ian there?" I asked.

"No, he left a few minutes ago. And Oliver is out on official business. There's just me holding the fort. If you want your message before Monday, I'm afraid it means coming to get it."

"How does it start?"

With an audible sigh and a rustle of paper, she began: " 'Hans Wilhelm Kramer, born July 3, 1941, in Düsseldorf, Germany, only child of Heinrich Johannes Kramer, industrialist—' "

"Yes, all right," I said, interrupting. "I'll come. How long will you be there?" I had visions of un-cooperative taxis, of having to walk.

"An hour or so. If you're definitely coming, I'll wait for you."

"You're on," I said. "Warm the Scotch."

Having grown a little wilier, I engaged a taxi to drive me to the far side of the bridge, pointing to a street map to show where I meant. The road over the bridge, I had found, extended into the Warsaw highway and was the road we had taken to Chertanovo. In another couple of days I would have Moscow's geography in my head forever.

I paid off the driver and stepped out into the falling snow, which had increased to the point of flakes as big as rose petals and as clinging as love. They settled on my sleeve as I shut the taxi's door, and on my shoulders, and on every flat surface within sight. I found I had stupidly forgotten my gloves. I thrust my hands in my pockets and turned down the steps to the lower road, to turn there along to the embassy.

It had seemed to me that I was unfollowed and safe;
but I was wrong. The tigers were waiting under the
bridge.

They had learned a few lessons from the abortive
mission in Gorky Street.

For a start, they had chosen a less public place. The
only sanctuary within running distance was now not
the big bustling well-lit mouth of the Intourist Hotel,
but the heavily closed front door of the embassy, with
an obstructive guard outside at the gate.

They had learned that my reflexes weren't the slow-
est on record, and also that I had no inhibitions about
kicking them back.

There were still only two of them, but this time they
were armed. Not with guns, but with riot sticks. Nasty
hard things like baseball bats, swinging from a loop of
leather round the wrist.

The first I knew of it was when one chunk of timber
connected shatteringly with the side of my head. The
fur ear flaps perhaps saved my skull from being
cracked right open, but I reeled dizzily, bewildered,
not realizing what had happened, spinning under the
weight of the blow.

I had a second's clear view of them, like a snapshot.
Two figures in the streetlights against the dark shadows under the bridge. The snow falling more sparsely
in the bridge's shelter. The arms raised, with the
heavy truncheons swinging.

They were the same men; no doubt of it. The same
brutal quality, the same quick ferocity, the same un-
merciful eyes looking out of the same balaclavas. The
same message that human rights were a laugh.

I stumbled, and my hat fell off, and I tried to protect
myself with my arms, but it wasn't much good.
There's a limit to the damage even a riot stick can do
through thick layers of jacket and overcoat, so that to
an extent the onslaught was disorientating more than
lethal, but bash number three or four by-passed my

feeble barriers and knocked off my glasses. I stretched for them, tried to catch them, got hit on the hand, and lost them entirely in the falling snow.

It seemed to be all they were waiting for. The battering stopped, and they grabbed me instead. I kicked and punched at targets I could no longer properly see, and did too little damage to stop the rot.

It felt as though they were trying to lift me up, and for a fraction of time I couldn't think why. Then I remembered where we were: on the road beside the river, which flowed along uncaringly on the other side of the breast-high wall.

Desperation kept me struggling when there was absolutely no reasonable hope.

I had seen the Moscow River from several bridges, and everywhere its banks were the same. Not sloping grassy affairs shading gently into the water, but gray perpendicular walls rising straight from the riverbed to about eight feet above the surface of the water. They looked like defenses against flooding, more than tourist attractions, designed to keep everything between them from getting out.

I clung grimly to whatever I could reach. I tore at their faces. At their hands. I raised from one of them a grunt and from the other a muttered word in a language I didn't recognize.

I didn't rationally think that anyone would come along the road and beat them off. I fought only because while I was still on the road I was alive, but if I hit the water I would be as good as dead. Instinct and anger, and nothing else.

It was hopeless, really. They had me off my feet, and I was being bundled over. I carried on with the limpet act. I pulled the knitted balaclava clean off one of them, but whatever he might have feared, I still couldn't have sworn to a positive identification. One of the streetlights was shining full on his face and I saw him as if he'd been drawn by Picasso during his cubist period.

In my racing days I had kept my glasses anchored by a double head strap of elastic, a handy gadget now gathering dust with my five-pound saddle. It had never crossed my mind that it might mean the difference between life or death in Moscow.

They pushed and shoved, and more and more of my weight was transferred over the wall. It all seemed both agonizingly fast and painfully endless: a few seconds of physical flurry that stretched in my mind like eternity.

I was hanging onto the parapet and life with one hand, the rest of me dangling over the water.

They swung, as I had time to realize, one of the riot sticks. There was an excruciating slam on my fingers. I stopped being able to use them, and dropped off the wall like a leech detached.

12

Winter had already penetrated the Moscow River. I went down under the surface, and the sudden incredible cold was the sort of numbing, punching shock which Arctic Ocean bathers don't survive.

I kicked my way up into the air, but I knew in my heart that the battle was lost. I felt weak and half blind, and it was dark, and thickly snowing. The temperature made me breathless, and my right hand had no feeling. My clothes got heavier as they became saturated. Soon they would drag me under. The current carried me downriver, under the bridge and out the other side, away from the embassy; and even while I tried to shout for help, I thought that the only people who would hear me would be the two who wouldn't give it.

The yell, in any case, turned into a mouthful of icy water; and that seemed the final reality.

Lethargy began slowing my attempts to swim and dulling my brain. Resolution ebbed away. Coherent thought was ending. I was anesthetized by cold, a lump of already mindless matter with all other bodily systems freezing fast to a halt, sinking without will or means to struggle.

I began, in fact, to die.

I dimly heard a voice calling.

"Randall . . . Randall . . ."

A bright light shone on my face.

"Randall, this way. Hold on. . . ."

I couldn't hold on. My legs had given their last feeble kick. The only direction left was downward, into a deep, numbing death.

Something fluffy fell on my face. Fluffier and of more substance than snow. I was past using a hand to grab it, past even thinking that I should. But somewhere in the last vestiges of consciousness an instinct must still have been working, because I opened my mouth to whatever had fallen across it, and bit it.

I held a lot of soft stuff between my teeth. There was a tug on it, as if something was pulling. I gripped it tighter.

Another tug. My head, which had been almost under water, came up again a few inches.

A sluggish thought crept back along the old mental pathways. If I held on to the line, I might be pulled out onto the bank, like a fish.

I should hold on, I vaguely thought, with more than my teeth.

Hands.

There was a problem about hands.

Couldn't feel them.

"Randall, hold on. There's a ladder along here."

I heard the words, and they sounded silly. How could I climb a ladder when I couldn't feel my hands?

All the same, I was awake enough to know that I had been given one last tiny chance, and I clenched my jaws over the soft lifeline with a grip that only total blackout might loosen.

The line pulled me against the wall.

"Hold on," yelled the voice. "It's along here. Not far. Just hold on."

I was bumping along the wall. Not far might be too far. Not far was as far as the sun.

"Here it is," shouted the voice. "Can you see it? Just beside you. I'll shine the torch on it. There. Grab hold, can't you?"

Grab hold. Of what?

I lay there like a log.

"Jesus Christ," said the voice. The light came on my face again, and then went off. I heard sounds coming nearer, coming down the river side of the wall.

"Give me your hands."

I couldn't.

I felt someone lift up my right arm, pulling it by the sleeve out of the water.

"Jesus Christ," he said again; and dropped it back.

He pulled my left arm out.

"Hold on with that," he commanded, and I felt him trying to curl my fingers round some sort of horizontal bar.

"Look," he said. "You've got to climb out of the bloody river. You're bloody nearly dead, do you know that? You've been in there too bloody long. And if you don't get out within a minute, bloody nothing will save you. Do you hear that? For Christ's sake . . . *climb*."

I couldn't see what I was supposed to climb, even if I had the strength. I felt him put my right arm up again out of the water, and I thought he was trying to thread my right hand behind the horizontal bar until I had the bar against my wrist.

"Put your feet on one of the steps under the water," he said. "Feel for them. The ladder goes down a long way."

I began vaguely—to understand. Tried to lodge a foot on an underwater horizontal bar, and by some miracle found one. He felt the faint support to my weight.

"Right. The bars are only a foot apart. I'll pull your left hand up to the next one. And whatever you do, don't let your right hand slip out."

I dredged up the last remnants of refrigerated strength and pushed, and rose twelve inches up the wall.

"That's right," said the voice above me, sounding heartily relieved. "Now keep bloody going, and don't fall off."

I kept bloody going and I didn't fall off, though it seemed like Mount Everest and the Matterhorn rolled into one. At some point when half of me was out of the water, I opened my mouth and let the fluffy but now sodden thing fall out; and there was an exclamation from above and presently the line was tied round my left wrist instead.

He went up the ladder above me, still cursing, still instructing, still yelling at me to hurry up.

Step by slow step, we ascended. When I reached the top he was standing on the far side, grabbing hold of me to roll me over onto the flat solid land. My legs buckled helplessly as they touched down, and I ended in a dripping heap on the snow-covered ground.

"Take your coats off," he commanded. "Don't you realize cold kills as fast as bloody bullets?"

I could crookedly see him in the streetlights, but it was his voice I at last conclusively recognized, though I supposed that at some point up the wall I had subconsciously known.

"Frank," I said.

"Yes? Get on with it. Look, let my unbutton this." His fingers were strong and quick. "Take them off." He tugged fiercely and stripped off the clinging wet sleeves. "Shirt, too." He ripped it off, so that the snow fell onto my bare skin. "Now put this on." He guided my arms into something dry and warm, and he buttoned up the front.

"Right," he said. "Now you'll bloody well have to

walk back to the bridge. It's only about a hundred yards. Get up, Randall, and *come on*."

There was a sharp edge to his voice, and it struck me that it was because he, too, was feeling cold, because whatever it was that was sheltering me had come off him. I stumbled along with him on rubbery knees and kept wanting to laugh weakly at the irony of things in general. Didn't have enough breath, however, for such frivolities.

When I nearly walked into a lamppost, he said irritably, "Can't you see?"

"Lost my g-glasses," I said.

"Do you mean," he said incredulously, "that you can't even see a bloody big lamp standard without them?"

"Not . . . reliably."

"Jesus Christ."

Inside his coat, my whole body was shuddering, chilled deep into the realms of hypothermia. Although they were apparently functioning, my legs didn't feel as if they belonged to me, and there was still a pervading wuzziness in the thinking department.

We arrived at a flight of steps and toiled upward to the main road. A black car rolled up and stopped beside us with amazing promptness. Frank threw my wet coats into the back of the car and shoveled me in after them. He himself sat in the front, instructing the driver briefly in Russian, with the result that we went round the by now familiar and lengthy one-way system and arrived in due course outside the Intourist Hotel.

Frank took my coats and escorted me through the front doors into the embrace of the central heating. He collected my room key without asking me the number. Shoveled me into the lift, pressed the button for the eighth floor, and saw me to my door. He fitted the key, and turned it, and steered me inside.

"What are you going to do, if you can't see?" he said.

"G-got a s-spare pair."

"Where?"

"T-top drawer."

"Sit down," he said, practically pushing me onto the sofa; and only the tiniest push was necessary. I heard him opening the drawer, and presently he put the reserves into my hands. I fumbled them onto my nose and again the world took on its proper shape.

He was looking at me with unexpected concern, his face firm and intelligent; but even while I watched, the hawklike quality dissolved, and the features slackened into the mediocrity we saw at meals.

He was wearing, I saw, only a sweater over his shirt, and, wound round his neck, his long striped college scarf. My lifeline.

I said, "I'd b-better give you your coat," and tried to undo the buttons. The fingers of my right hand seemed both feeble and painful, so I did them with the left.

"You'd better have a hot bath," he said diffidently. No decision, no swearing, no immense effectiveness in sight.

"Yes," I said. "Thanks."

His eyes flickered. "Lucky I happened along."

"Luckiest thing in my life."

"I was just out for a walk," he said. "I saw you get out of a taxi ahead and go down those steps. Then I heard a shout and a splash, and I thought it couldn't possibly be you, of course, but anyway I thought I'd better see. So I went down after you, and luckily I had my torch with me, and—well—there you are."

He had omitted to ask how I could have fallen accidentally over a breast-high wall.

I said obligingly, "It's all a bit of a blank, actually," and it undoubtedly pleased him.

He helped me out of his coat and into my dressing gown.

"Will you be all right, then?" he said.

"Fine."

He seemed to want to go, and I made no move to stop him. He picked up his flashlight and his hat, from where they were lying on the sofa, and his coat, and murmuring something about me getting the hotel to dry my clothes, he extricated himself from what must have been to him a slightly embarrassing proximity.

I felt very odd indeed. Hot and cold at the same time, and a little light-headed. I took off the rest of my clammy clothes and left them in a damp heap on the bathroom floor.

The fingers on my right hand were in dead trouble. They hadn't bled much because of their immersion in ice water, but there were nasty tears in the skin of three of them from nails to knuckles, and no strength anywhere at all.

I looked at my watch, but it had stopped.

I really had to get a grip on things, I thought. I really had to start functioning. It was imperative.

I went over to the telephone and with my left hand dialed the number of the university, foreign students department. Stephen was fetched, sounding amiable.

"Something else?" he said.

"What time is it? My watch has stopped."

"You didn't ring just to ask me that? It's five past six, actually."

Five past six . . . It seemed incredible. It was only three-quarters of an hour since I had set off to the embassy. Seemed more like three-quarters of a century.

"Look," I said. "Will you do me a great favor? Will you go . . ." I stopped. A wave of malaise traveled dizzily around my outraged nervous system. My breath came out in a weird groaning cough.

Stephen said slowly, "Are you all right?"

"No," I said. "Look . . . will you go to the British Embassy, and pick up a telex which is waiting there for me, and bring it to the Intourist? I wouldn't ask, but . . . if I don't get it tonight I can't have it until Monday . . . and be careful, because we have rough friends. . . . At the embassy, ask for Polly Paget in the cultural attaché's office.''

"Have the rough friends had another go with a horsecar?" he said anxiously. "Is that why you can't go yourself?"

"Sort of."

"All right," he said. "I'm on my way."

I put the receiver back in its cradle and wasted a few minutes feeling sorry for myself. Then I decided to ring Polly Paget, and couldn't remember the number.

The number was on a sheet of paper in my wallet. My wallet was or had been in the inside pocket of my jacket. My jacket was wet, and in the bathroom, where Frank had put it. I screwed up the energy, and went to look.

One wallet, still in the pocket, but, not surprisingly, comprehensively damp. I fished out and unfolded the list of telephone numbers and was relieved to see they could still be read.

Polly Paget sounded annoyed that I had not even started out.

"I've finished my jobs," she said crossly. "I want to leave now."

"A friend is coming instead of me," I said. "Stephen Luce. He'll be there soon. Please do wait."

"Oh, very well."

"And could you give me Ian Young's phone number? Where he lives, I mean."

"Hang on." She went away, and came back, and read out the number. "That's his flat here in the embassy grounds. As far as I know, he'll be home most of the weekend. Like all of us. Nothing much ever happens in Moscow."

Lady, I thought, you're a hundred percent wrong.

Stephen came, and brought Gudrun.

I had spent the interval putting on dry pants, trousers and socks, and lying on the bed. I disregarded

Frank's advice about hot baths, on the Ophelia principle that I'd had too much of water already. It would be just too damned silly to pass out and drown surrounded by white tiles.

Stephen's cheerful grin faded rapidly.

"You look like death. Whatever's happened?"

"Did you bring the telex?"

"Yes, we did. Reams of it. Sit down before you fall down."

Gudrun folded her elegant slimness onto the sofa and Stephen dispensed my Scotch into bathroom tumblers. I went back to sitting on the bed, and pointed to the sensitive spot on the wall. Stephen, nodding, picked up the tape recorder, switched it on, and applied it to the plaster.

No whine.

"Off duty," he said. "So tell us what's happened."

I shook my head slightly. "A dust-up." I didn't particularly want to include Gudrun. "Let's just say . . . I'm still here."

"And ve have vays of not making a fuss?"

I more or less smiled. "Reasons."

"They'd better be good. Anyway, here's your hot news from home." He pulled an envelope out of his pocket and threw it to me. I made the mistake of trying to catch it naturally with my right hand, and dropped it.

"You've hurt your fingers," Gudrun said, showing concern.

"Squashed them a bit." I took the telex message out of the envelope and, as reported, there was reams of it: Hughes-Beckett busy proving, I thought sardonically, that my poor opinion of his staff work was unjustified.

"While I read all this," I said, "would you cast your peepers over that stuff there?" I pointed to the cough lozenge tin and Misha's pieces of paper. "Translate them for me, would you?"

They picked up the little bunch of papers and shuf-

fled through them, murmuring. I read the first section
of the telex, which dealt exhaustively with Hans Kramer's life history, and included far more details than
I'd expected or asked for. He had won prizes on
ponies from the age of three. He had been to eight
different schools. He appeared to have been ill on and
off during his teens and twenties, as there were several
references to doctors and clinics, but he seemed to
have grown out of it at about twenty-eight. His earlier
interest in horses had from that time intensified, and
he had begun to win horse trials at top level. For two
years, until his death, he had traveled extensively
on the international scene, sometimes as an individual and sometimes as part of the West German
team.

Then came a paragraph headed CHARACTER ASSESS-
MENT, which uninhibitedly spoke ill of the dead. TOL-
ERATED BUT NOT MUCH LIKED BY FELLOW MEMBERS OF
EVENT TEAM. UNUSUAL PERSONALITY, COLD, UNABLE
TO MAKE FRIENDS. ATTRACTED BY PORNOGRAPHY, HET-
ERO AND HOMO, BUT HAD NO KNOWN SEXUAL RELA-
TIONSHIP OF ANY LENGTH. LATENT VIOLENCE SUS-
PECTED, BUT BEHAVIOR IN GENERAL SELF-CONTROLLED.

Then a bald, brief statement. BODY RETURNED TO
PARENTS, STILL LIVING IN DÜSSELDORF. BODY CRE-
MATED.

There was a good deal more to read on other sub-
jects, but I looked up from the typed sheets to see
how Stephen and Gudrun were doing.

"What've you got?" I said.

"Four autographs of Germans. A list in Russian of
brushes and things to do with looking after horses.
Another list in Russian of times and places, which I
should think refer to the horse trials, as they say things
like 'cross-country start 2:40 remember weight cloth.'
Both of those must have been written by Misha, because there is also a sort of diary, in which he lists
what he did for his horses, and what feed he gave
them, and so on, and that's all."

"What about the paper in the cough lozenge tin?"
I said.

"Ah. Yes. Well. To be frantically honest, we can't
be much help with that."

"Why not?"

"It doesn't make sense." He raised his eyebrows
at me comically. "Or do ve have vays of sorting out
gibberish?"

"You never know."

"Well, right then. We are of the opinion that the
letters on the paper probably say the same thing twice
over, once in Russian and once in German. But they
aren't ordinary words in either language, and they're
all strung together anyway, without a break."

"Could you write them in English?"

"Anything to oblige."

He picked up the envelope that had contained the
telex and wrote a long series of letters, one by one.

"There are some letters which come near the end,
which do make an actual English word. . . ." He finished writing, and handed me the envelope. "There
you are. Crystal as mud."

I read: Etorphinehydrochloride245mgacepromazi-
nemaleate10mgchlorocresol01dimethylsulphoxide 90ant-
agonistnaloxone.

"Does it mean anything?" Stephen said. "A chemical formula?"

"God knows." My brains felt like scrambled eggs.
"Maybe i's what's in these ampules; they're stamped
with something about naloxone."

Stephen held one of the baby vials up to the light,
to read the lettering. "So they are. Massive chemical
name for a minute little product." He put the vial back
in the tin, and the original paper on top of it. "There
you are, then. That's the lot." He closed the tin and
put it down. "What a dingy-looking matroshka." He
picked up the doll. "Where did you get it?"

"It contains the last of Misha's souvenirs."

"Does it? Can I look?"

He had almost as much difficulty in pulling it apart as I had had the first time, and everything scattered in a shower out of it, as before. Stephen and Gudrun crawled about on the floor, picking up the pieces.

"Hm," he said, reading the veterinary labels. "More of the same gobbledegook. Anything of any use?"

"Not unless you have bedbugs."

He put everything back in the doll, and also the tin and the autographs.

"Do you want me to take this out to Elena's new flat sometime, after she's settled in?" he said.

"That would be great, if you have the time."

"Better to give Misha his bits back again."

"Yes."

Stephen looked at me closely. "Gudrun and I are on our way out to supper with some friends, and I think you'd better come with us." I opened my mouth to say I didn't feel like it and he gave me no chance to get the words out. "Gudrun, be a lamb and go and wait for us in those armchairs by the lifts, while I get our friend here into some clothes and do his buttons up." He waved at my nonfunctioning fingers. "Go on, Gudrun, love. We won't be long."

Good temperedly, she departed, long-legged and liberal.

"Right then," Stephen said, as the door shut behind her. "How bad is your hand? Come on, do come with us. You can't just sit there all evening looking dazed."

I remembered dimly that I was supposed to be going to the opera. Natasha's earnest ticket to fantasy seemed as irrelevant as dust; yet if I stayed alone in my room I should feel worse than I did already, and if I slept, there would be visions of death in balaclavas . . . and hotel bedrooms were not in themselves fortresses.

Frank had not mentioned seeing my attackers, and very likely when he ran to the rescue they had kept out of his sight. But that didn't mean that they hadn't hung around for a bit . . . and they might know that he had fished me out.

"Randall!" Stephen said sharply.

"Sorry." I coughed convulsively, and shivered. "Wouldn't your friends mind, if I came?"

"Of course not." He slid open the wardrobe door and pulled out my spare jacket. "Where's your coat . . . and hat?"

"Shirt first," I said. "That checked one."

I stood up stiffly and took off the dressing gown. There were beginnings of bruise marks on my arms, where the riot sticks had landed, but otherwise, I was glad to see, my skin had returned from an interesting pale turquoise to its more normal faded tan. Stephen helped me speechlessly to the point where he went into the bathroom for something and came out looking incredulous.

"All your clothes are wet!"

"Er . . . yes. I got shoved in the river."

He pointed to my hand. "With that sort of shove?"

"I fear so."

He opened and closed his mouth like a goldfish. "Do you realize that the temperature tonight has dropped way below zero?"

"You don't say."

"And the Moscow River will freeze to solid ice any day now?"

"Too late."

"Are you delirious?"

"Shouldn't be surprised." I struggled into a couple of sweaters, and felt lousy. "Look," I said weakly, "I don't think I can manage the friends . . . but I also don't want to stay in this room. Would there be any chance, do you think, of me booking into a different hotel?"

"Not the faintest. An absolute nonstarter. No other hotel would be allowed to take you without a fortnight's advance booking and a lot of paper work, and probably not even then." He looked around. "What's wrong with this room, though? It looks fine to me."

I rubbed my hand over my forehead, which was sweating. The two sweaters, I thought, were aptly named.

I said, "Three times in two days, someone's tried to kill me. I'm here through luck, but I've a feeling the luck's running out. I just don't want to—to stand up in the butts."

"*Three* times?"

I told him about Gorky Street. "All I want is a safe place to sleep." I pondered. "I think I'll ring Ian Young. He might help."

I dialed the number Polly Paget had given me for Ian's flat in the embassy grounds. The bell rang and rang there, but the Sphinx was apparently out on the town.

"Damn," I said, with feeling, putting down the receiver.

Stephen's brown eyes were full of troubled thought. "We could slip you into the unviersity," he said. "But my bed's so narrow."

"Lend me the floor."

"You're serious?"

"Mm."

"Well . . . all right." He looked at his watch. "It's too late to get you in through the proper channels, so to speak. They'll have knocked off for the day. . . . We'll have to work the three-card trick."

He took his student pass out of his pocket and gave it to me.

"Show it to the dragon when you go in, and keep on going, straight up the stairs. They don't know all the students by sight, and she won't know you aren't me. Just go on up to my room. O.K.?"

I took the pass and stowed it in a pocket in my jacket. "How will you get in, though?" I said.

"I'll ring a friend who has a room in the block," he

said. "He'll collect my pass from you, and bring it out to me, when Gudrun and I get back."

He held my jacket for me to put on, and then picked up the sheets of telex and folded them back into the envelope. I put the envelope in my jacket and thought about black cars.

"I'd awfully like to make sure I'm not followed," I said.

Stephen raised his eyes to heaven. "All in the service," he said. "What do you want me to do?"

What we did was for me to travel in one taxi to University Prospect, the tourist stopping place for the view down over the stadium to the city, and for him and Gudrun to follow in another. We all got out of the cars there in the thickly falling snow and exchanged vehicles.

"I'll swear nothing followed you," Stephen said. "If anyone did, they used about six different cars, in relays."

"Thanks a lot."

"Anytime."

He told the taxi driver where to take me, and disappeared with Gudrun into the night.

13

The dragon on the door was arguing with someone when I went in. I shoved Stephen's pass under her nose closely enough for her to see that it *was* a pass, and kept moving. Her eyes hardly slid my way as her tongue lashed into some unfortunate offender, and I went on up the stairs as if I lived there.

Stephen's cell-like room felt a proper sanctuary. I struggled out of my jacket and one sweater and collapsed gratefully onto his bed.

For quite a long time I simply lay there, waiting for what one might call the life force to flow back. What with illnesses and the inevitable knocks of life on the land, not to mention the crunches involved in jump racing, I was fairly experienced in the way one's body dealt with misfortunes. I was accustomed to the lassitude that damped it down while it put itself to rights, and to the way that this would eventually lift it into a new feeling of vigor. I knew that the fierce soreness of my fingers would get worse for at least another twelve hours, and would then get better. I'd been concussed enough times to know that the sponginess in my mind would go away slowly, like fog clearing, leaving only an externally tender area of bruised scalp.

All that, in fact, would be the way of it if I gave it rest and time; but rest and time were two commodities I was likely to lack. Better to make the most of what I had. Better, I dared say, to sleep; but one factor I was not used to, and had never had to deal with before, was keeping me thoroughly awake. The sharp threat of death.

There wouldn't be any more lucky escapes. The fourth close encounter would be the last. For if my attackers had learned one thing conclusively during the past two days, it must have been that it was necessary to kill at once, and fast. No fooling around with horsecars, kidnappings, or icy rivers. Next time—if there was a next time—I would be dead before I realized what had happened. It was enough, I thought, to send one scurrying to the airport, to leave the battle to be fought by someone else.

After a while I sat up and took the long telex out of my pocket.

Read again the pages about Hans Kramer.

Eight schools. Doctors, hospitals, and clinics. Ill health, like mine. And, like me, success on ponies, and on horses. Like me, a spot of foreign travel to equestrian events: I to the awesome Pardubice in Czechoslovakia and the Maryland Hunt Cup over fixed timber fences in America, and he to top-rank horse trials around Europe: Italy, France, Holland, and England.

Died at Burghley in September of a heart attack, aged thirty-six. Body shipped home, and cremated.

End of story.

I took off my glasses and tiredly rubbed my eyes. If there was anything useful to be gleaned from all the unasked detail, it was totally invisible to my current mental sight.

I tried to clear my mind by shaking it, which was

about as useful as stirring old port with a teaspoon.
Bits of sediment clogged my thoughts and little green
spots slid around behind my eyes.

I read the rest of the telex twice and by the end had
taken in hardly a word.

Start again.

YURI IVANOVICH CHULITSKY, ARCHITECT. PHONE
NUMBER SUPPLIED EARLIER BUT NOW REPEATED. . . .
ONE OF THE RUSSIAN OBSERVERS IN ENGLAND
DURING AUGUST AND SEPTEMBER LAST. FORMERLY
WENT TO OLYMPICS AT MONTREAL, ADVISER ON
BUILDINGS NECESSARY FOR EQUESTRIAN GAMES
AT MOSCOW.

Yes, I knew all that.

IGOR NAUMOVICH VERSHININ, COORDINATOR
OF BROADCASTING. NO TELEPHONE NUMBER
AVAILABLE. RUSSIAN OBSERVER, IN ENGLAND
DURING AUGUST AND SEPTEMBER. HIS BRIEF: TO
LEARN THE BEST GENERAL POSITIONING FOR TV
COVERAGE; TO SEE WHAT OTHER FACILITIES WERE
ESSENTIAL AND WHICH MERELY DESIRABLE; TO SEE
HOW BEST TO GIVE THE WORLD A GOOD VIEW OF
SOVIET SHOWMANSHIP AND EFFICIENCY.

SERGEI ANDREEVICH GORSHKOV. NO TELE-
PHONE NUMBER AVAILABLE. RUSSIAN OBSERVER,
STATED TO BE STUDYING CROWD CONTROL AT BIG
EQUESTRIAN EVENTS, WHERE THE MOBILITY OF
SPECTATORS WAS A PROBLEM, RELIABLY REPORTED
TO BE A FULL COLONEL OF KGB, AN EXTREME
HARD-LINER, WITH A DEEP CONTEMPT FOR WEST-
ERN STANDARDS. SINCE HIS VISIT, INFORMATION
HAS COME TO HAND THAT HE HAS IN THE PAST
ATTEMPTED TO COMPROMISE MEMBERS OF THE EM-
BASSY STAFF, AND THEIR VISITORS, FAMILY, AND
FRIENDS. STRONGLY ADVISE AGAINST CONTACT.

I put the sheets down. Hughes-Beckett, if it was indeed he who had sent the telex, which was unsigned and had no indication of origin, was up to his old tricks of seeming to help while encouraging failure. Flooding me away from the one who really might pose a threat to Johnny Farringford.

Hughes-Beckett, I thought a shade irritably, had not the slightest idea of what was actually going on.

To be fair to him, how could he know if I didn't tell him?

The mechanics of telling him were not that easy. Anything sent from the embassy via the telex ran the gauntlet of Malcolm Herrick's inside informer; and since Malcolm had learned of Oliver's telling me to send a message directly from Kutuzovsky Prospect, he had probably made his arrangements there as well. The one place I did not want my adventures turning up was on the front page of *The Watch.*

There was the telephone, to which someone at either end might listen. There was mail, which was slow, and might be intercepted.

There was Ian, who, if I read it right, probably had his own secure hot line to the ears back home, but might not have the authority to lend it to any odd private citizen who applied.

In the back of my mind, also, there hovered an undefined question mark about the soundness of Ian as an ally.

Stephen's friend duly came to collect Stephen's pass at shortly after eleven, and Stephen and Gudrun returned, full of bonhomie and onions.

"Onions!" Gudrun said. "Back in the shops today after four months without them. No eggs, of course. It's always something."

"Want some tea?" Stephen suggested, and went to make it.

There floated about both of them the glow of an

evening well spent, and perversely their warmth depressed my already low spirits to sinking point, like Scrooge at Christmas.

"What you need," Stephen said, coming back and making an accurate diagnosis with a glance, "is half a pint of vodka and some good news."

"Supply them," I said.

"Have a biscuit."

He unearthed a packet from the recesses of the bookcase and cleared a space on the table for the mugs. Then, seeming to be struck by a thought, he began rigging up a contraption of drawing pins and string, and upon the string he threaded his bedside alarm clock, so that it hung there loudly ticking on the wall. It was only toward the end of this seemingly senseless procedure that I remembered that that exact spot was the lair of the bug.

"Better interference than nothing, if they're listening," he said cheerfully. "And they get a right earful when the alarm goes off."

The tea probably did more good than the unavailable vodka. A certain amount of comfort began to creep along the nerves.

"All visitors have to be gone by ten-thirty," Stephen nonchalantly said.

"Will they check?"

"I've never known it."

Halfway down the mug, a modicum of order returned to my thoughts. Very welcome, like a friend much missed.

"Gudrun," I said lazily, "would you cast your peepers over something for me?"

"Sorry?"

I put down the mug and picked up the telex, and she noticed the up-to-date state of the hand I hadn't used.

"Oh!" she said. "That must really hurt."

Stephen looked from my fingers to my face. "Are they broken?" he said.

"Can't tell."

I could scarcely move them, which proved nothing one way or the other. They had swelled like sausages, and gone dark, and it was a fair certainty the nails would go black, if they didn't actually come off. It was no worse, really, than if one had been galloped on by a horse, and injuries of that order had been all in the day's work. I smiled lopsidedly at their horrified faces and handed Gudrun the telex.

"Would you read all the stuff about Hans Kramer, and see if it means anything to you which it doesn't to me? He was German, and you are a German, and you might see a significance I've missed."

"All right." She looked doubtful, but compliantly read right to the end.

"What strikes you?" I said.

She shook her head. "Nothing very much."

"He went to eight different schools," I said. "Would that be usual?"

"No." She frowned. "Not unless his family moved a lot."

"His father was and is a big industrialist in Düsseldorf."

She read through the schools again, and finally said, "I think one of these places specializes in children who are . . . different. Perhaps they have troubles like epilepsy, or perhaps they are . . ." She made tumbling motions with her hands, at a loss for the word.

"Mixed up?"

"That's right. But they also take people who have a special talent and need special schooling. Like athletes. Perhaps Hans Kramer went there because he was exceptionally good at riding."

"Or because seven other schools slung him out?"

"Perhaps, yes."

"What about the doctors and hospitals?"

She read through the list again with her mouth negatively pursed, and finally shook her head.

"Would they be, for instance," I said, "anything to do with orthopedics?"

"Bones and things?"

"Yes."

Her eyes went back to the list, but the noes had it.

"Anything to do with heart troubles? Are any of those people or places specialists in chest surgery?"

"I honestly don't know."

I thought. "Well," I said, "anything to do with psychiatry?"

"I'm awfully sorry, but I don't know much about—" Her eyes widened suddenly and she looked rather wildly down at the list. "Oh, my goodness . . ."

"What is it?"

"The Heidelberg University clinic."

"What about it?"

"Don't you know?" She saw from my face that I didn't. "Hans Kramer attended it, it says here, for about three months in 1970."

"Yes," I said. "Why is that important?"

"There was a doctor called Wolfgang Huber working there. He was supposed to be great at straightening out . . . mixed-up children from rich families. Not *little* children; teen-agers and young adults, our age. People who were violently rebellious against their parents."

"He seems to have managed it all right with Hans Kramer, then," I said, "because isn't that clinic the last on the list?"

"Yes," Gudrun said. "But you don't understand."

"Tell me."

She could hardly frame the sentences, so intense were her thoughts.

"Dr. Huber taught them that to cure themselves they had to destroy the system which was making them feel the way they did. He told them they would have to destroy the world of their parents. He called it terrorism therapy."

"My God."

"And . . . and . . ." Gudrun practically gasped for

breath. "I don't know what effect it had on Hans Kramer . . . but Dr. Huber was deliberately teaching his
patients . . . to follow in the footsteps of Andreas
Baader and Ulrike Meinhof."

Time, as they say, stood still.
"You've seen a ghost," Stephen said.
"I've seen a pattern . . . and a plan."
The teachings of Dr. Wolfgang Huber, I supposed,
had been a sort of extreme extension of the theories
behind the Communist revolution. Destroy the cor-
rupt capitalist system and you will emerge into a clean,
healthy society run by the workers. A seductive,
idealistic dream which seemed always to appeal most
to intellectuals of the middle class, who had both the
brains and the means to pursue it.

Even in the hands of visionaries the doctrine had
led to widespread killing. People like Dr. Huber, however, had preached their gospel not to reasoning
adults, but to already disturbed youth, and the result
in widening ripples had been the Baader-Meinhof followers, the Palestinian Black September, the Irish
Republican Army, the Argentinian ERP and the Jap-
anese Red Army, with endless virulent offshoots
among small groups like Croatians, South Moluccans,
and Basques.

The place most free from terrorism was the land
which still encouraged and nurtured it, the land where
the seedling had raised its attractive head.

At the Munich Olympics, the world had awakened
in a state of shock to the existence of the growing
crop.

Eight years later, at the Moscow Olympics, someone was planning to carry the fruit home.

14

Stephen lent me his bed and went to share Gudrun's, which seemed to please them both well, and was certainly all right by me. Foreign students were positively encouraged to lie together, he said sardonically, so that they didn't go out and pursue the natives.

I shivered a good deal, and at the same time felt feverish, which boded ill.

I didn't sleep much, though that didn't matter. My hand throbbed like a pile driver but my head was clear, and I much preferred it that way round. I spent most of the time thinking and wondering and guessing, and coming back to the problem of the next day. I had somehow to take some positive steps toward staying permanently alive.

In the morning Stephen fetched some tea, lent me his razor, and bounced cheerfully off to a student breakfast.

He returned with some things like empty hamburger buns from the basement supermarket, and found me studying the long string of letters on the envelope which had held the telex.

"Deciphering the chemical junk?" he said.

"Trying."

"How's it coming?"

"I don't know enough," I said. "Look . . . when all this was written in Russian and German, was it *translated?* I mean . . . are you sure that this is what was meant?"

"It wasn't translated," Stephen said. "It was those letters in that order, but written in formal German script, the sort you see in books. The Russian script version was more or less phonetically the same, but there are more letters in the Russian alphabet, so we adjusted the Russian letters to be the equivalent of the German. Was that all right?"

"Yes," I said. "You see here where it reads 'antagonist'?"

"Uh huh."

"Was that word translated into Russian or German? Or were the letters *a n t a* et cetera written in German script?"

"It wasn't translated, as such, because 'antagonist' is much the same word in all three languages."

"Thanks."

"Is that of any help?"

"Yes, in a way," I said.

"You amaze me."

We buttered and shared the hamburger buns and drank some more tea, and I coughed on and off with an ominous hollowness.

After that I cadged a sheet of paper and wrote the long row of letters into sensible words, adding a few reasonable-looking decimal points. The revised effort read:

> etorphine hydrochloride 2.45 mg
> acepromazine maleate 1.0 mg
> chlorocresol 0.1
> dimethyl sulphoxide 90
> antagonist naloxone

Stephen looked over my shoulder. "That, of course," he said, "makes a world of difference."

"Um . . ." I said thoughtfully. "Would you do me a favor?"

"Fire away."

"Lend me an empty tape for your recorder, and another one with music on it. Or rather, two empty tapes, if you have them."

"Is that all?" He sounded disappointed.

"That's for starters."

He rustled around and produced three tapes in plastic boxes.

"They've all got music on," he said. "But you can record on top, if you like."

"Great." I hesitated, because what I wanted him to do besides sounded melodramatic; but facts had to be faced. I folded the list of chemicals in half and gave it to him. "Would you mind keeping that?" I made my voice as matter-of-fact as possible. "Keep it until after I've got home. I'll send you a postcard to say it's O.K. to tear it up."

He looked puzzled. "I don't see . . ."

"If I don't get home, or you don't get a postcard from me, will you send it to Hughes-Beckett at the Foreign Office. I've put the address on the back. Tell him that Hans Kramer had it, and ask him to show it to a vet."

"A *vet?*"

"That's right."

"Yes, but . . ." He realized exactly what I'd said. "If you don't get home . . ."

"Yeah . . . well, fourth time unlucky and all that."

"For heaven's sake."

"Do you have lectures on Saturdays?" I said.

His eyebrows vanished upward under his hair. "Is that a general invitation to put my head in the trap alongside yours?"

"Probably just to make phone calls and tell taxis where to go."

He gave an exaggerated shrug and a large gesture of surrender, and put on an expression of "Ve have vays of not believing a vord you say." "What first?"

"Ring Mr. Kropotkin," I said. "And if he's in, ask if I can come to see him this morning."

Kropotkin, it seemed, was not only in but anxious. "He says he's been trying to get you at the hotel. He says to arrive at ten o'clock, and we can find him inside the first stable block on the left, on the race-course."

"Fine." I blew a cooling breath onto my hot, swollen fingers. "I think I'll also try Ian Young."

Ian Young was back on British soil and seemed to take a while to realize whom he was talking to. He was feeling fragile, and no one, he said eventually, with a mixture of misery and admiration, could drink like the Russians; and please would I not talk so loudly.

Sorry, I said pianissimo. Could he please tell me how best to make a telephone call to England. Try from the main post office just round the corner from my hotel, he said. Ask for the international operator. He was discouraging, however, about my prospects.

"Sometimes you can get through in ten minutes, but it's usually more like two hours, and with the new flap going on this morning, you'll be lucky if you get through at all."

"Newer than the dust-up in Africa?" I said.

"Oh, sure. Some high-up guy has defected. In Birmingham, of all places. Shock, horror, drama, and all that. Is it important?"

"I want to ring my vet . . . about my horses," I said. "Could I get through from the embassy?"

"I doubt if you'd do any better. There's no one like the Russians for blank obstruction. Brick wall specialists, the Russians." He yawned. "Did you get your telex last night?"

"Yes; thanks."

"Make the most of it; I should." He yawned again.

"Do you feel like swilling the hair of the dog with me? Round about noon?"

"Don't see why not."

"Good. Go past Oliver's office, and past the tennis court, and my flat's in the row at the back of the grounds, second door from the left." He put down the receiver with all the gentleness of the badly hung over.

The snow had temporarily stopped, though the sky was a threatening oily yellow-gray and the air cold enough to freeze the nose's mucus lining in its tracks. I started coughing and gasping for breath before we'd gone a hundred steps, and Stephen thought it extraordinary.

"What's the matter?" he said, his own lungs chugging easily away like an electric bellows.

"Taxi . . ."

We caught one without much difficulty, and immediately, within its comparative warmth and with the help of the pocket bronchodilator inhaler I kept in my pocket like loose change, my chest stopped its infuriating heaving.

"Are you always like this when it's cold?" Stephen said.

"It depends. The river didn't help."

He looked mildly anxious. "You caught a chill? Come to think, it's not surprising."

We stopped twice on the way. The first time, to buy two bottles of vodka; one to give to Kropotkin and one to keep. The second time to buy me yet another hat to top off my assorted clothing, which now consisted, from the skin outward, of an undershirt, a shirt, two sweaters, a jacket, and Stephen's spare coat, which was a size too small and left my forearms sticking out like an orphan's.

The main roads had already been cleared of the overnight snow, but the Hippodrome itself was white. There were horses there all the same, exercising on the track, and even one or two trotters pulling sulkies.

We paid off the taxi practically at the stable door, and went inside to inquire for Kropotkin.

He was waiting for us in a small dark office used by one of the trainers of the trotters. There were heaps of tires everywhere—which seemed stunningly incongruous in a stable until one remembered the sulkies' wheels—and apart from that only a desk with a great deal of scattered paper work, and a chair, and large numbers of photographs pinned to the walls.

Nikolai Alexandrovich cordially grasped my hastily offered left hand and pumped it up and down with both of his own.

"Friend," he said, the heavy bass voice reverberating in the small space. "Good friend."

He accepted the gift of vodka as the courtesy it represented. Then he set the chair ceremoniously for me to sit on, and himself lodged comfortably with his backside half on the desk. Stephen, it seemed, could stand on his own two feet; and, via Stephen, Kropotkin and I exchanged further suitable opening compliments.

We arrived in due course at the meat inside the pastry.

"Mr. Kropotkin says," Stephen said, "that he asked everyone in the world of horses to give any help they could in the matter of Alyosha."

I expressed my warmest appreciations and felt the faintest quickening of the pulse.

"No one, however," Stephen continued, "knows who Alyosha is. No one knows anything about him."

My pulse returned to normal with depressing speed.

"Kind of him to try," I said, sighing slightly.

Kropotkin stroked his mustache downward with his thumb and forefinger and then set off again into a deep rumble.

Stephen did a deadpan translation, although with more interest in his eyes.

"Mr. Kropotkin says that although no one knows who Alyosha is, someone has sent him a piece of pa-

per with the name Alyosha on it, and the piece of
paper originally came from England.''

It hardly sounded the ultimate solution, but definitely better than nothing.

"May I see it?'' I said.

It appeared, though, that Nikolai Alexandrovich
was not to be rushed. Bread and butter first; sweets
after.

"Mr. Kropotkin says,'' Stephen translated, "that
you should understand one or two things about the
Soviet system.'' His eyebrows went upward and his
nostrils twitched with the effort of keeping a straight
face. "He says it is not always possible for Soviet
citizens to speak with total freedom.''

"Tell him I've noticed. Er . . . tell him I understand.''

Kropotkin looked at me broodingly and stroked his
mustache.

"He would like it,'' Stephen said, relaying the next
wedge of rumble, "if you could use everything you
have learned here at the Hippodrome without explain-
ing where you heard it.''

"Give him my most solemn assurance,'' I said sin-
cerely, and I think Kropotkin was probably convinced
more by my tone than the actual words. After a suitable pause, he continued.

"Mr. Kropotkin says,'' Stephen faithfully reported,
"that he doesn't know who sent him the paper. It was
delivered to his flat by hand yesterday evening, with
a brief note of explanation, and a hope that it would
be handed on to you.''

"Does he sound as if he really doesn't know who
sent it, or do you think he's just not telling?''

"Impossible to know,'' Stephen said.

Nikolai Alexandrovich showed signs at last of pro-
ducing the goods. With great deliberation, he drew a
large black wallet from an inside pocket and opened
it wide. His blunt fingers carefully sank into a deep
section at the back, and he slowly drew out a white

envelope. He accompanied the hand-over ceremony with a small speech.

"He says," Stephen said, "that to himself this paper does not seem to be of much significance. He wishes it were. He would like it to be of some use to you, because of his earnest desire to express his thanks for your speed in saving the Olympic horse.'

"Tell him that if it should not turn out to be a significant paper, I will always remember and appreciate the trouble he has taken to help."

Kropotkin received the compliment graciously, and slowly parted with the envelope. I took it from him at the same unhurried pace, and drew out the two smallish sheets of paper which were to be found inside.

They were fastened to each other with a small paper clip. The top one, white and unremarkable, bore a short paragraph written in Russian.

The lower, also white but torn from a notebook and ruled with faint blue lines, was chiefly covered with a variety of geometric doodles, done in pencil. Near the top there were two words: *For Alyosha*, and about an inch lower down, surrounded by doodled stars. *J. Farringford*. Underneath that, one below the other, as in a list, were the words *Americans, Germans, French*, and below that a row of question marks. That seemed to be more or less all, though near the bottom of the page, in their own individual doodled boxes, were four sets of letters and numbers, which were *DEP PET, 1855, K's C*, and *1950*.

On top of all the scribbles, across the whole page from top to bottom, there was the wide, flowing serpentine scrawl of someone crossing out what they had written.

I turned the small page over. The reverse side bore about fifteen lines of what must have been handwriting, written in ballpoint, but this had been meticulously scribbled over, line by line, also in ballpoint but in a slightly different color.

Kropotkin was watching me expectantly. I said, "I

am very pleased. This is most interesting." He understood the words, and looked heavily satisfied.

The business at that point seemed to be over, and
after a few more compliments on both sides we
stepped from the office into the central corridor of the
stable block. Kropotkin invited me to see the horses,
and we walked side by side along to where each side
of the corridor was lined with loose boxes.

Stephen made choking noises behind me as we
reached them, which I guessed was because of the
smell. My own nose twitched a bit over the unusually
piercing stink of ammonia, but the trotters seemed
none the worse for it. They would be racing that evening, Kropotkin said, because the snow was not yet
too deep. Stephen manfully translated to the end, but
gulped at the eventual fresh air as if it were a fountain
in the desert.

There were still several horses exercising on the
track, and to my eyes they came from lower down the
equine class system than race horses or eventers.

"All the riding clubs are here," Kropotkin explained through Stephen. "All stables for horses in
Moscow are in the district, and all exercising is done
at the Hippodrome. All the horses are owned by the
state. The best horses go for racing and breeding, and
the Olympics; then the clubs share what is left. Most
horses stay in Moscow all winter, because they are
very hardy. And I wonder," added Stephen on his
own account, "what it smells like in these barns come
March?"

Kropotkin said a solemn goodbye at the still unat-
tended main entrance. He was a great old guy, I
thought, and through him and Misha I had learned a
good deal.

"Friend," I said, "I wish you well."

He pumped my hand with emotion in both of his,
and then gave me the accolade of a hug.

"My God," said Stephen as we walked away.
"Talk about schmaltzy sob stuff . . ."

"A little sentiment does no harm."

"Ah . . . but did it do any good?"

I handed him the envelope and coughed all the way to the taxi rank.

" 'To Nikolai Alexandrovich, by hand,' " said Stephen, reading the envelope. "So whoever sent it knew Kropotkin fairly well. You'd only use that form of someone's name—the patronymic Alexandrovich without the last name Kropotkin—if you knew him."

"It would be more surprising if they *didn't* know each other."

"I guess so." He picked out the two small clipped-together pages. "This paragraph on the front says, 'Notepaper'—sort of jotting paper, that is 'used at International Horse Trials. Please give it to Randall Drew.' "

"Is that all?"

"That's the lot."

He peered at the second page, and I waved uninhibitedly at a taxi cruising with its windshield light on. Once more on our way, Stephen handed back the treasure trove.

"Not much cop," he said. "A case of the lion straining to produce a gnat."

The taxi driver spoke into my thoughtful silence.

"He wants to know where we're going," Stephen said.

"Back to the hotel."

We stopped, however, on the way at a shop he identified as a chemist. The Russian letters on the shopfront, when approximated into English, read APTEKA. Apothecary. What else? I went inside with him, seeing dampeners for the troubles in fingers and chest, but ended only with the equivalent of aspirins. For his own purchase, he leaned across a counter and spoke low to the ear of a buxom battle-ax.

She replied very loudly, and all the nearby customers turned to stare at him. His face was a scarlet study in embarrassment, but all the same he stood his

ground and brought the transaction to the desired conclusion.

"What did she say?" I asked, as we left.

"She said, 'This foreigner wants *preservativy*.' And
don't bloody laugh."

My chuckle ended in a cough. "*Preservativy* being
contraceptives?"

"Gudrun insists."

"I should darned well think so."

At the hotel we went straight through the foyer to
the lifts, as I had taken my room key with me to the
university so as not to advertise my absence to the
reception desk.

Up to the eighth floor, past the watchful lady at the
desk, and along the corridor . . . and the door of my
room was not locked.

Cleaners?

Not cleaners. The person who was standing inside
was Frank.

He had his back to the door and was over by the
dressing shelf under the window, head bent, looking
down at something in his hands.

"Hello, Frank," I said.

He turned round quickly, looking very startled; and
what he was holding was the matroshka. intact, I saw,
with all her secrets still inside. His fingers were still
tight with the effort of trying to open her.

"Er . . ." he said. "You didn't come to breakfast.
I—er—came to see if you were all right. After last
night. I mean, falling in the river . . ."

Not bad, I thought, as a spot of thinking on the feet.

"I went to the Hippodrome to see the horses
work," I said, playing the game that anyone could
play who had a lying tongue.

Frank relaxed his grip and put the painted doll
slowly down on the shelf, giving his best weak-school-
teacher laugh.

"Right on, then," he said. "Natasha was worried

about you not coming to breakfast. Shall I tell her you'll be in for lunch?"

Lunch. The prosaically normal in the middle of a minefield.

"Why not?" I said. "And I'll have a guest."

Frank looked at Stephen with sustained dislike, and took himself off; and I descended a bit feebly onto the sofa.

"Let's have a drink," I said.

"Scotch or vodka?" He pulled the morning's newly bought bottle out of his overcoat pocket and stood it on the shelf.

"Scotch."

I took two of the *apteka*'s pills with it, without noticeable results.

Looked at my watch, now miraculously ticking again despite immersion. Eleven-thirty. Picked up the telephone.

"Ian?" I said. "How's the hangover?"

From the sound of it, on the mend. The hair of the dog had bitten an hour ago, no doubt. I said I couldn't make it after all before lunch, and how about him tottering along to my room at the hotel at about six?

Totter, he said, might just about describe it, then; but he would come.

Stephen was sweeping the walls with the tape recorder, trying to find the tender spot. I pointed to it, but again there was no whine. And then, just as he was about to give up, the whine suddenly began.

"Switched on, by God," he said under his breath. "Let's have some music."

He pulled the three tapes from the obliging overcoat and slotted in an energetic rendering of *Prince Igor*.

"What next?"

"I bought some paperbacks. Which would you like?"

"And you?" he said, looking at the titles.

"Drink and think."

So the bug listened for an hour to Stephen turning the pages of *The Small Back Room* against the urgencies of Borodin, and I listened inside my head to everything I'd been told, both in England and in Moscow, and tried to see a path through the maze.

Lunch seemed unreal.

The Wilkinsons were there, and Frank was there. Frank hadn't told the Wilkinsons he'd saved my life the evening before, and behaved throughout as if nothing of the sort had ever happened. What he thought of my silence on the subject was a mystery.

Natasha and Anna tried by a mixture of scolding and persuasion to make me promise to stop disappearing without telling them where I was going and I helpfully said I would do my best, without meaning a word of it.

Frank ate my meat.

Mrs. Wilkinson talked. "We've always voted Labour, Dad and me, but isn't it funny—in England it's always the far left people who want more and more immigrants, but here, where it's about as far left as you can get, there aren't any. You don't see black people walking around in Moscow, do you?"

Frank took no notice.

"It just strikes me as funny, that's all," Mrs. Wilkinson said. "Still, I don't suppose there's much of a queue in India for wanting to live in Moscow, come to think."

Mr. Wilkinson muttered to his small-sized chips, "They've got more sense." He doubtless wouldn't say much else for the rest of the day.

Frank came to life with a routine damnation of the anti-black policies of the National Front.

Mrs. Wilkinson gave me a comical look of bewilderment and despair at never being able to get through to Frank.

"Front," I said mildly, "is an overworked word. A cliché. We have Fronts for this and Fronts for that.

One should always ask what—if anything—is *behind* a Front.''

It was again ice cream with black-currant jam. I quite liked it.

Stephen ate like Frank and told me afterward that the Intourist Hotel food was high-class luxury compared with the students' grub.

Apart from all that, which seemed to be going on in a separate life, I was more positively hearing the voices of Boris and Evgeny, and Ian, and Malcolm, and Oliver, and Kropotkin, and Misha and Yuri Chulitsky, and Gudrun and the Prince and Hughes-Beckett and Johnny Farringford . . . and the dead voice of Hans Kramer. I could hear them all clearly.

But where, oh where, was Alyosha?

15

Upstairs in my room, Stephen balanced the chair on my bed, my suitcase on the chair, and the tape recorder on the suitcase, and switched on. The whine came forth, alive and healthy.

He switched off the Record button and pressed the Play, and the listeners got a close earful of a tape of Stravinsky which seemed to be suffering from wow if not flutter.

I spent the time pondering the pieces of paper Kropotkin had given me; the back as much as the front.

"You don't happen to have any blue glass handy, I suppose?" I asked. "Of a certain particular shade?"

"Blue *glass?*"

"Yes . . . a blue filter. You see all this handwriting which has been scribbled out? It was written in a darker color of blue than the scribble; you can see the dark loops underneath."

"Well . . . so what?"

"So if you looked at the page through some blue

glass which was the same color as the lighter scribble, you might be able to see the darker blue writing. The color of the glass, so to speak, would cancel out the color of the scribble, and you could read what was left."

"For crying out loud," he said, "I suppose you could. And where would that get you?"

"I can guess who sent this to Kropotkin, but I'd like to be certain."

"But it could be *anybody*."

I shook my head. "I'll show you something."

I opened the drawer which contained my private pharmacy and brought out the folded piece of paper which lay beneath it. Opening it, and smoothing out the crease, I laid it on the dressing shelf, and put Kropotkin's paper beside it.

"They're the same!" Stephen said.

"That's right. Torn from the same type of notebook: white paper, faint blue lines, spiral binding."

The two notebook pages lay side by side with their ragged torn-off fringes at the top. On one, *For Alyosha, J. Farringford,* and all the rest. And on the other, the name *Malcolm Herrick,* and a telephone number.

"He gave that to me the first night I was in Moscow," I said. "In a bar of the National Hotel."

"Yes, but . . . those notebooks are universal. You can buy them everywhere. Students . . . typists . . . Aren't they especially printed to take shorthand?"

"And constantly used by newspaper reporters," I said, "who have a great habit of crossing out pages when they've finished with them. I've seen them over and over, at the races, talking to me maybe when I've won a race. They flick over the pages to find a fresh one; they go all through the pad one way, and then they turn it over and start on the backs. And to save themselves looking through endless pages afterwards to find just the bits they want, they put a scribble or

a cross over the whole page when they've finished
with it—just like this one, which we got from Kropotkin.''

I turned over the sheet Malcolm had given me with
his telephone number, and there, on the back, were
some notes about a visiting puppet theater, sprawl-
ingly crossed through with a wide flowing *S*.

''*Malcolm*,'' said Stephen, looking bewildered.
''Why should Malcolm send this to Kropotkin?''

''I shouldn't think he did. Maybe he just gave it to
whoever did that writing on the back.''

''But why should he?'' Stephen said frustratedly.
''And what does it matter? It's all *crazy*.''

''It's unlikely that he'll remember who he gave an
odd piece of paper to nearly three months ago,'' I
said, ''But I think . . . we might ask him.''

I dialed the number on the paper, and he was at
home. His big voice positively crackled through the
receiver.

''Where've you been, sport? Been trying to reach
you. Moscow at weekends is like Epsom when they're
racing at Ascot.''

''Out to the Hippodrome,'' I said obligingly.

''Zat so? How's it going? Found Alyosha yet?''

''Not yet.''

''Told you it was a bum steer, sport. I looked. I
told you. If I couldn't find a story, there is no story.
Right?''

''You're an old hand, and I'm not,'' I said. ''But
Kropotkin at the Hippodrome has called on all the
horse people in Moscow to work on it. So we've an
army of allies.''

He grunted, not sounding very pleased. ''Has the
army come up with anything?''

''Only with something pretty small, so far. In fact,''
I said, half making a joke of it, ''a page which looks
as if it came from one of your notebooks.''

''A what?''

"Page, with the name Alyosha on it. And Johnny Farringford's name, ringed with stars. And a lot of doodling. I'm sure you wouldn't remember writing it. But the thing is, do you remember lending or giving a piece of scrap paper to anyone at Burghley who could now be here in Moscow?"

"Christ, sport, you ask damn silly questions."

"Yeah . . ." I said, coughing on a sigh. "Um . . . if you're dead bored, care to come to the Intourist Hotel for a drink in my room, around six? I'm going out for a bit, but I'll be back by then."

"Sure," he said easily. "Bloody good idea. Saturday night's made for drinking. What's the room number?"

I told him and he said fine, and disconnected. I put the receiver down slowly and reflected that I'd done some silly things in my time but that that probably topped the lot.

"I thought you didn't much like him," Stephen said.

I made a face and shrugged. "Maybe I owe him for the dinner in the Aragvi."

I sat on the sofa and gingerly explored my right-hand fingers with those on the left. The worst of the soreness was beginning to wear off, and I could bend and unbend them a bit. It seemed probable that a couple of bones were cracked, though one often couldn't tell for sure without x-rays. I supposed I should count myself lucky they weren't splintered.

"When do you doodle?" I said.

"Doodle?"

"Like that." I nodded toward the page of Malcolm's notebook.

"Oh. During lectures, mostly. I do zigzags, and triangles, not boxes, stars, and question marks. Anytime when I'm listening with a pencil in my hand, I suppose. On the telephone, for instance. Or listening to the radio."

"Mm . . . Well . . ." I stopped unsuccessfully doc-

toring my fingers and got through on the telephone to
the international operator. Calls to England, I was
told, would entail a long delay. How long was a long
delay? Calls to England were not at present being connected. Did that mean hours or days? The international operator couldn't or wouldn't say. Frustrated,
I stood up. "Let's go out."

"Where to?"

"Anywhere. Round and round Moscow in a taxi."

"Out of thugs' reach?"

"Sometimes," I said with mock disparagement,
"you're quite bright."

We took with us the matroshka in its string bag, and
also (in my pocket along with the telex) the two pages
from Malcolm's notebook, on the basis that as these
four treasurers were the only tangible results of my
efforts, they should not be carelessly left around to be
pinched by Frank or anyone else who could open my
bedroom door.

Even though he'd stopped saying it was cheaper on
the metro, Stephen boggled a bit at the expense of that
afternoon. The Prince was paying, I said, dealing out
rubles in hefty installments at half-hour intervals to a
taxi driver who thought I was mad. Stephen had suggested going to the university, for which in the morning he had got me a visitor's pass in order to avoid the
juggling of the day before; but for some reason I always thought best on wheels, and had planned many
a campaign while driving continually up and down on
a tractor. There was something about a moving background that triggered shifts of mind, and let new ideas
standing sharp and clear where they hadn't existed
before. I was an outdoor man, after all.

We saw a lot of Moscow, old parts and new. Old
elegance and new functionalism, historically at odds
but united in the silent white freezing slide into hiber-
nation. Thick white caps on the golden domes. Shops
with more space than goods. Huge advertisements saying GLORY TO THE COMMUNIST PARTY over the roof-

tops. On me the cumulative effect was a powerful pervading melancholy, a sadness for so great a city entangled in such suffocating bureaucracy, such denial of liberty, such a need to look over its shoulder before it spoke.

When darkness closed in we stopped once, to buy a couple of glasses and some reinforcements to the booze line, and a souvenir for me to take home to Emma: and I chose a bright new matroshka with all its little matroshkas nestling inside, because it seemed to me that what I had been doing in Moscow had been in effect like opening that sort of doll. When one pulled off one layer, there was another layer underneath. Remove that, and another layer was revealed. Under that another; and under that, another. And in the center, not a tiny wooden mama with rosy cheeks, but a germinating seed of terror.

When we finally returned to my room it looked uninvaded, undisturbed.

Perhaps we could have stayed there safely; but wasted precautions were never to be regretted. "If only" are the saddest words in the language.

The tape recorder still stood silently on its precarious tower, and when Stephen pressed the Record button, it told us mutely that the listeners slept.

It was five to six. We left the recorder switched on, and went along to the armchairs by the lifts to await the guests.

Ian came first, by no means drunk but slightly rocking. It made no difference to his face, which was as white, calm, and expressionless as ever, or to his speech, which had no fuzzy edges. He told us with great lucidity that on Friday evenings and Saturdays, when there was no flap on, he embraced the great Russian leisure-time activity with the fervor of the converted. And where, he asked, did I keep the bottle?

We retracked down the corridor to my room. Ian

chose vodka and had tossed off his first before I had finished pouring Stephen's. I refilled his glass, and got myself some Scotch.

Without visible emotion, he regarded the tape recorder.

"If you play that up there much, my old son," he said, "you'll want to look around for a sticky stranger. If they think you've got something to hide, they'll plant another ear."

Stephen silently reached for the recorder and took it on a thorough journey around the room. Ian watched, absent-mindedly downed his drink, and poured himself a replacement with an almost steady hand.

The search results were fortunately nil. Back on its perch, still no whine. Stephen left the recorder there on sentry duty, and he and Ian sat down on the sofa.

Ian spent five minutes describing the extreme boredom of the diplomatic life as lived by the British in Moscow, and left me fervently wishing he were stone cold sober.

Malcolm arrived like a gale blowing in from the desert, hard, noisy, and dry.

"Extra," he said boisterously, picking up the vodka bottle and reading the label. "The Rolls-Royce of the domestic distilleries. I see you cotton on to the best pretty damn quick, sport."

"Stephen's choice," I said. "Help yourself."

For Malcolm, too, it appeared, Saturday night was to-hell-with-inhibitions night. He poured and tossed back in one draught enough to put an abstainer to sleep for a month. "You didn't tell me it was a party, sport," he said.

"Only the four of us."

"Could have brought a bottle."

At the present rate of consumption, we might need it. Stephen was looking as if that sort of party was low on his list of favorite hobbies, and I guessed that he was only staying out of a vague sense of not leaving the sinking ship before the rats.

"What've you got, there, sport?" Malcolm said, with half a tumblerful in his grasp. "What's all this about a page from my notebook?"

I fished it out of my pocket and gave it to him. He buried his nose in his glass and looked at the small page sideways, over the rim. Some loose drops of vodka trickled down his chin.

"Christ, sport," he said, removing the glass and wiping himself up with the back of his hand. "It's just a lot of doodles." He turned it over. "What's all this writing?"

"I don't know."

He looked at his watch and seemed to be coming to a fast decision. A fresh gulp brought him near to the bottom of the glass, and he put it down on the dressing shelf with a snap.

"Look, mate, got to run." He folded the page of notebook and began to put it in his jacket pocket.

"I'd like to keep that for a bit," I said mildly. "If you wouldn't mind."

"What on earth for?" He tucked it firmly away out of sight.

"To see if I can decipher the writing on the other side."

"But what's the point?"

"I'd just like to know who you gave it to in England . . . to see what he wrote on it."

Malcolm still hesitated. Ian clawed his way to his feet and helped himself to Extra.

"Oh, give it to him, Malcolm," he said irritably. "What the hell does it matter?"

Malcolm collected observant stares from three pairs of eyes and reluctantly put his hand in his pocket.

"It won't do you any bloody good, sport." His voice was sharp with the beginnings of malice.

"All the same," I said, taking back the note and stowing it away, "it's interesting, don't you think? You wrote that page at Burghley but you didn't tell me you were at that meeting. I was surprised that you didn't mention being there. I was surprised you *were* there, actually."

"So what? I went to write it up."

"For *The Watch?* I thought you were a foreign correspondent, not a sportswriter."

"Look, sport," he said, the muscles setting like rock in his solid neck. "Just what is the point of all this crap?"

"The point is," I said, "that you know—you've known all along—what I came here to find out, and you've been trying all along to make sure I ended up in a fog, if not in a mortuary."

Stephen and Ian had their mouths open.

"Balls," Malcolm said.

"Can you drive a horsecar?"

His only reply was a stare of intense animosity reinforced by some sort of inner decision.

"Dinner at the Aragvi," I said. "Your invitation, your dinner. There were two men there, sitting near us—they in my sight, I in theirs. Face to face for a couple of hours. After that they would always know me again. You took my glasses away and everyone could see I was lost without them. When we left the restaurant I was attacked in Gorky Street—by two men who tried first to knock my glasses off, and then to bundle me into a car. They wore balaclavas, but I saw their dark un-Russian eyes very clearly. And I asked myself who knew that I would be walking alone down Gorky Street at precisely that moment?"

"This is a load of horse shit. Look, sport, you'll end in a psychiatric hospital at the wrong end of a needle if you go on like this."

Malcolm was deeply angry, but his basic confidence was unshaken. He was still certain that I would not hit the absolute bull's-eye.

"The telex," I said, "and your little informer. I've no doubt that when a very long telex came for me, you were told. So I set off to the embassy by the shortest route, and on the way I was jumped on by the same two men, who were *waiting for me*. That time I was saved by some sort of ironic miracle, but when I got my senses back I asked myself who could possibly have known I would make that journey?''

"I knew," Ian said, sounding studiedly impartial.

"Of course," Malcolm said forcefully. "And Ian knew we were dining at the Aragvi. And Ian knew you were going to see Kropotkin at the Hippodrome, because you told us both in Oliver's office. . . . So why the hell aren't you accusing Ian of all this? You're off your bloody rocker, sport, and I'll have you for slander if you don't back down and apologize this immediate bloody instant. He looked at his watch again and revised this ultimatum. "I'm not staying here to listen to any more of this bloody junk."

"Ian helped me. You just told me to go home." I said.

"All for your own bloody good."

"It isn't enough," Ian said uneasily. "Randall . . . all this might be *possible,* but you've surely got it all wrong."

"I haven't got to prove anything to any court of law," I said. "All I do have to do is let Malcolm know what I think. That's enough. If a prying neighbor knew you were planning to rob a bank, you'd be a fool to go on with the plan. So call me a prying neighbor . . . but what Malcolm was planning was far worse than robbing banks."

"What, then?" Ian said.

"Killing people at the Olympics."

Malcolm's reaction went a long way to convincing Ian and Stephen. The shock turned his skin as white as the walls, leaving odd blotchy patches of broken thread veins on cheeks and nose. He literally lost his breath: his mouth opened, and no sound came out. There was sick disbelief in his eyes; and this time I

really had chopped into the self-confidence with a lethal ax.

"So you may never get to court," I told him. "But
if any of the Olympic riders die the same way Hans
Kramer died, the world will know where to look."

He was, in effect, stunned—almost as if losing consciousness on his feet. The room was still, with a silent
intensity you could almost touch. Ian and Stephen and
I watched him almost without breathing; and at this
impossibly fraught moment, someone knocked briskly
on the door.

It was Ian's bad luck that it was he who moved first
and went to open it.

Malcolm's friends attacked with their usual brutal
speed, bursting in through the opening door like bulls
and hitting out at whatever stood in their way. The
sheer animal fury swept into the room like an emotional volcano, and the half-concealing balaclavas only
seemed to intensify the horrendous impact.

The swinging riot stick wielded by the one in front
crunched solidly into Ian's head. He fell without a
sound and lay unmoving by the bathroom door.

The one behind kicked shut the door to the corridor
and strode forward purposefully, holding a small screw-
topped glass jar. On his hands he wore rubber gloves.
In the little jar, a pale golden liquid, like champagne.

Everything happened exceedingly fast.

Malcolm came to life with wide-staring eyes and
shouted, "Alyosha." Then he said, "No, no." Then,
as he saw the riot stick swinging at Stephen he said,
"No, not, that one," and pointed at me.

I leaped on the bed and picked up the tape recorder,
and threw it at the man who was attacking Stephen.
It hit him in the face and hurt him, and he turned my
way even more murderously than before.

The man with the little jar unscrewed the cap.

"That one," Malcolm screamed, pointing at me.
"That one."

The man with the jar stared with appalling ferocity at Malcolm, and drew back his arm.

Malcolm screamed.

Screamed.

"No. No. No."

I picked up the chair and lashed out at the man with the jar, but the one with the riot stick stood in the way.

The man with the jar threw the contents into Malcolm's face. Malcolm gave a high wailing cry like a seagull.

I crashed the chair down again and hit the wrist of the jar-carrier with a blow like chopping wood. He dropped the jar and jerked with agony. I jumped off the sofa and, with the chair, laid into both of them with a fury fed by theirs, while Stephen picked up the vodka bottle and slammed it at the eye slits of one of the balaclavas.

I had never in my life felt such a rage. I hated those men. Shook with hate. I swung the chair not to preserve my life, but to smash theirs. Sheer primitive blood-lusting vengeful hatred, not only for what they were doing to this city and this room, but for all their counterparts round the world. For all the helpless hostages, for all the ransom victims, I was bashing back.

It may have been reprehensible and uncivilized, but it was certainly effective. Stephen smashed his bottle against the wall and crowded into them with the broken ends thrusting forward sharply, and I simply belted them with chair and feet and fury, and we beat them back into the narrow passage by the bathroom, where Ian still lay unmoving.

With what looked like a joint and instantaneous decision, they suddenly turned their backs on us, dragged open the door to the corridor, and fled.

I turned back into the room, panting.

"After them," Stephen said, gasping.

"No . . . come back. . . ." I heaved for breath. "Shut the door. . . . Got to see to Malcolm."

"Malcolm?"

"Dying," I said. "Ninety seconds . . . Jesus Christ."

Malcolm had collapsed, half on the floor, half on the bed, and was whimpering.

"Open the matroshka," I said urgently. "Misha's matroshka. Quick. Get that tin with the naloxone."

I yanked open the drawer that contained my breathing things and snatched out the plastic box. My fingers wouldn't work properly. Serve him bloody right, I thought violently, if I couldn't save his life because they'd smashed my hand when he tried to have me killed.

Couldn't tear the strong plastic off the hypodermic syringe. Hurry. For God's sake hurry. . . . Did it with my teeth.

"This?" Stephen said, holding out the cough lozenge tin. I opened it and put it on the dressing shelf.

"Yes . . . Get his trousers down."

Ninety seconds. Jesus Christ.

My hands were trembling.

Malcolm was gasping audibly for air.

"He's turning blue," Stephen said with horror.

The needle was packed inside the syringe. I got it out and fitted it in place.

"He's hardly breathing," Stephen said. "And he's unconscious."

I snapped the neck of one of the ampules of naloxone. Stood it with shaking hands upright on the shelf. Mustn't . . . mustn't knock it over. Needed two good hands, two hands working properly and not shaking.

I picked up the syringe in my right hand and the ampule in my left. I was right-handed. I couldn't do it at all the other way round, though I would have done so, if I could. Lowered the needle into the precious teaspoonful of liquid. Hauled up the plunger of the syringe, sucking it in. My fingers hurt. So what, so what. Ninety seconds . . . all but gone.

I turned to Malcolm. Stephen had pulled the trousers down to expose a bit of rump. I shoved the needle into the muscle, and pressed the plunger—and God, I thought, could do the rest.

We lifted him onto the bed, which was no mean task, taking off his jacket and tie and ripping open the front of his shirt. His color and breathing were still dreadful, but no worse. He was conscious again, and terrified, and he said, "Bastards," between his teeth.

Along by the bathroom Ian began groaning. Stephen went over to him, and found him rapidly regaining consciousness and trying to rise to his feet. He helped him up and supported him, and got him as far as the sofa.

The little glass jar lay near the sofa on the carpet, and Stephen almost automatically bent down to pick it up.

"Don't touch it," I said, my voice going high with alarm. "Don't touch it, Stephen. It'll kill you."

"But it's empty."

"I doubt it," I said. "And I think a few drops would be enough." I picked up the fallen chair and planted it over the jar. "That'll have to do for now. . . . Don't let Ian touch it."

I turned back to Malcolm. His breathing seemed to be slightly stronger, but not by much.

"How do we get a doctor?" I said.

Stephen gave me a despairing look which I interpreted as dismay at getting ourselves enmeshed in any form of Soviet officialdom, but he picked up the telephone and dialed through to the reception desk.

"Tell them the doctor should bring naloxone."

He repeated the request twice and spelled it out once, but looked troubled as he replaced the receiver. "She said she would call a doctor, but about the naloxone . . . she said the doctor would know what to bring. Unhelpful. Obstructive. The more you insist, the more they just stick their toes in."

"Randall . . ."

Malcolm's lusty voice came out as a weak croak. "Yes?" I bent over him, to hear better.

"Get . . . the . . . bastards."

I took a deep breath. "Why did they throw the stuff at you, and not at me?"

He seemed to hear and understand, but he didn't answer. Sweat stood out suddenly in great beads all over his face, and he began gasping again for air.

I filled the syringe from the second ampule of naloxone, and pushed the needle into his haunch. The reaction came again, sluggish but definite, taking the labored edge off the breathing but leaving him in a dangerous state of exhaustion.

"The bastards . . . said . . . I . . . robbed them."

"How do you mean?"

"I sold them . . . the stuff. They said . . . it wasn't worth . . . the money."

"How much did they pay you?" I said.

"Fifty . . . thousand."

"Pounds?"

"Christ, sport . . . of course. They said . . . this afternoon . . . I'd robbed them. I told them . . . to come . . . here . . . finish . . . you . . . too clever by half. Didn't know Ian . . . would be here."

I reflected that when he had found Ian and Stephen with me, he had attempted to leave and intercept his friends before they reached my room. No one could tell whether the outcome would have been much different if he'd succeeded. The friends were about as predictable as forked lightning.

I took a tumbler to the bathroom, half filled it with water, and brought it back to hold to Malcolm's mouth. It did little more than wet his lips, but that seemed to be all he wanted.

I looked at my watch. It was two minutes since I'd given him the second injection; four since the first. It seemed a lifetime.

Ian was recovering fast and beginning to ask questions. It was extraordinary, I thought, that no one at all had heard the fracas and come running. No one had heard—or reacted to—Malcolm's scream, and I would have thought they could have heard Malcolm's scream in the Kremlin. When the bugs were switched off, the walls were deaf.

Malcolm went into another sudden and devastating collapse. I grimly filled the syringe from the last ampule and injected the teaspoonful into his muscles.

There was no more naloxone: no safety margin for any of us.

16

The upswing came again. He breathed a little more positively and regained consciousness, although his skin was still grayish blue and his pupils remained pinpoints.

"I feel . . . dizzy," he said.

I gave him a few sips of water and said casually, "Was it you or your friends who poured the stuff on Hans Kramer?"

"Christ, sport . . . not me. I'm no killer."

"What about the horsecar?"

"Only meant . . . to hurt you . . . frighten . . . send you home." He took another sip. "Reckoned you wouldn't stay."

"But your friends weren't fooling," I said. "Not in Gorky Street, and not by the river."

"They said . . . not safe . . . with Kropotkin helping. You might . . . find out . . . things."

"Mm," I said. "And that was after you told them

that I knew what Hans Kramer had said when he was dying?"

"Bloody boy . . . Misha."

"Was this deadly liquid your idea, or Hans Kramer's?" I said.

"I learned of it by chance. Got Hans . . . to steal it." He achieved a faint sneer. "Stupid bastard . . . conned him. He did it for nothing . . . for his ideals."

"He went to the Heidelberg clinic," I said.

"Christ." Even in his cooperative state, he was unpleasantly surprised. "In the telex . . . didn't think you'd spot that, but it was . . . risky. They wanted to prevent . . . you from seeing it."

"So why did they kill Hans? Why Hans, who had helped you?"

He was tiring visibly. His voice was faint, and his breathing was still slow and shallow.

"Cover . . . all . . . tracks."

Ian stood up restlessly and came over to the bed. It was the first close view he'd had of Malcolm since the attack, and the shock penetrated the inscrutability of his face.

"Look, Randall," he said, already horrified, "leave all these questions until he's better. Whatever he's done, it will keep."

He had no idea, I thought, of the sort of thing we were dealing with, and it was hardly the moment to tell him.

I gave Malcolm some more water, and because of Ian's intervention he began to reflect and regret that he had so willingly answered. Reactivated hostility sharpened visibly in his pinpoint eyes, and when I took the glass from his lips his whole face settled into the old stubborn mold.

"What are their names?" I said. "And their nationality?"

"Sod off."

"Randall!" Ian protested. "Not yet."

"One of them is Alyosha," Stephen said, steering a careful path round the chair, and crossing to join us. "Didn't you hear? Malcolm called one of the Alyosha."

There was almost a laugh from the bed. A large sardonic sneer twisted his mouth. His voice, although nearly a whisper, came out loaded with spite.

"Aloysha, sport," he said, "will kill you yet."

Stephen looked at him incredulously. "But your *friends* tried to kill *you*. It's Randall who saved you."

"Balls."

"He's confused," I said. "Just leave it."

"Christ," Malcolm said. "I feel sick."

Stephen looked rapidly around for a suitable receptacle, but there wasn't one, and it wasn't needed.

Malcolm's shallow breathing perceptibly lessened. I picked up his wrist and could feel no pulse. His eyes slowly closed.

"Do something," Ian said urgently.

"We can try artificial respiration," I said. "But not mouth to mouth."

"Why not?"

"That stuff was thrown at his face. You can't trust it."

"Do you mean he's dying?" Stephen asked. "After all?"

Ian energetically began pulling Malcolm's arms up and backward in the old Schafer method of respiration, refusing to let him go without having done everything possible.

Malcolm's neck and hands and bare chest turned from bluish gray to dark indigo. Only his face stayed pale.

Ian persevered, hauling the rib cage up and down, trying to get air into the lungs mechanically. Stephen and I watched in silence for what seemed a very long time.

I didn't try to stop Ian. Stopping had to be his own

decision. And I suppose some quality in Malcolm's total lack of response finally convinced him, because he reluctantly laid the arms down to rest, and turned to us a blank and Sphinx-like face.

"He's dead," he said faltly.

"Yes."

There was a long pause while no one could quite bring himself to say what was in all our minds, but Ian at length put it into words.

"The doctor's on his way. What do we tell him?"

"Heart attack?" I suggested.

The others nodded.

"Let's tidy up, then," I said, looking round at the aftermath of battle. "What we desperately need is some rubber gloves."

The small glass jar still lay on its side under the guarding chair. I reckoned it would have to be shoveled somehow into a tumbler, and was looking around for a suitable long spoon for supping with the devil when Stephen brought out his packet from the chemist.

"What about these?" he said. "They're supposed to be impermeable."

On any other occasion we'd have laughed too much to make it possible. Instead, I quite seriously dressed the thumb and fingers of my left hand in *preservativy*, keeping them in place with an elastic band round my knuckles.

Stephen had protested that as they were his *preservativy*, it should be he who used them, especially as I was proposing a left-handed operation. Shut up, I said, and let's get on. It was my job, I thought. It was where the buck stopped. A matter of the beginning and the end of responsibility.

He removed the chair. I knelt on the floor, and summoning up an act of faith in the baggy and improvised rubber glove, picked up the little jar and stood it upright in the tumbler.

My mouth, to be honest, was dry.

The jar had looked more or less empty when it lay on its side, but this had been deceptive. There was now clearly about a dessert-spoonful of pale golden liquid lying in the bottom. Pale gold . . . a pretty shade of death.

"The cap of the jar must be somewhere," I said. "But don't touch it."

Ian found it under the sofa. He shifted the end of the sofa, and I picked up the small screw top and put it in the glass alongside the jar.

"What will you do with it?" Stephen said, looking at the remnants with understandable awe.

"Dilute it."

I took the tumbler into the bathroom and stood it in the center of the bathtub. Then I put in the plug and turned on the taps. The water poured in in a tumbling cascade and the level quite soon rose to cover the glass. The little jar floated out like a bath toy, still holding its fearsome cargo. I pushed it with my covered fingertips, into the depths.

Turned off the taps. Stirred the jar around in the water briskly with the handle of my toothbrush, and then pulled out the plug to let the water run away. When it had gone, the washed jar, the cap, and the glass lay in harmless wet heaps on the clear white enamel. I picked them out of the tub and put them into the wash basin, and immersed them once again, to make doubly certain.

Then I stripped off the *preservativy* and flushed them appropriately down the loo; and took a great deep breath of relief.

In the room Stephen and Ian had restored everything to order. The syringe and the empty ampules were out of sight. The matroshka stood with her two halves joined. The broken vodka bottle and its scattered fragments had vanished. The chair stood quietly by the dressing shelf. The tape recorder stood upon it harmlessly. My suitcase was back in the wardrobe. All tidy. All calm. All innocent.

And Malcolm . . . Malcolm lay in his permanent silence with his trousers up and fastened, and his shirt buttoned to near the top. His jacket and tie lay on the sofa, but folded neatly, not in the heap into which we'd throw them. Malcolm dead looked a good deal more peaceful than Malcolm dying.

The Russian doctor came with an expressionless face and unemotionally began to roll out the red tape. Stephen and Ian gathered that he took a poor view of foreigners who keeled over on Saturday evenings, when all services were at a low ebb.

We drifted around as we were told, waiting mostly in the chairs by the lifts and not speaking much. The stumpy lady at the desk came and went several times, and Stephen asked her if she found her work boring.

She said stolidly that nothing much ever happened, but her job was her job. Stephen translated question and answer, and we nodded sympathetically and guessed she'd been away from her desk when Malcolm's friends had called.

The doctor was unsuspicious. In England, Hans Kramer's death had been adjudged a heart attack even after an autopsy, and with luck it would happen again here. The doctor had not mentioned having been asked to bring naloxone, and it appeared that the reception desk had not, in fact, passed on Stephen's request; fortunately, as it turned out.

Ian had developed a thundering headache from the effects of vodka and concussion, and sat moaning gently with his eyes shut.

Stephen bit a couple of fingernails.

I coughed.

There were a good many unsmiling faces coming and going, some of which finally said we could return to my room, for Stephen and Ian to retrieve their hats and coats, and me to pack to remove to another room in the hotel.

Ian groaned off home at that point, but Stephen helped to carry my belongings up in the lift to the fifteenth floor. The new room was identical in layout; slightly different in color; and there was no stiff shape lying under a white sheet on the bed.

Stephen cast his gaze round the walls and put two fingers to his mouth. I nodded. It didn't seem worthwhile fiddling about with the tape recorder. We made one or two suitable and shocked remarks about heart attacks, just in case, and left it at that.

I had found that in his fast tidying Stephen had rolled all the broken glass and ampules and the syringe in my dressing gown and stowed it in the suitcase. We had judged it sensible, in discussion while walking along the corridor, to get rid of them altogether, so we put them all in the outermost shell of the new matroshka, leaving a smaller mother beaming upon the shelf. We put the rubbish-filled doll into the string bag, and picked up the tape recorder, and very quietly let ourselves out of the room.

The lady at the fifteenth-floor desk gave us an uninterested stare. We smiled at her as we waited for the lifts, but smiling back wasn't her habit.

Made it to the ground floor. No trouble. Strolled unhurriedly around the longer route to the door, unaccosted. Walked outside under the watching eyes, which did nothing more than watch.

Climbed into a taxi. Traveled trustfully, and arrived safely at the university.

There was nowhere private to suffer from reaction. Stephen and I were both shaking after we'd taken off our hats and coats in his room, and we felt a great compulsive need to talk. I had seldom found anything so difficult as making asinine conversation with a mind stuffed with the evening's horrors, but the recorder had proved definitely again that we were not alone.

The unreleased tension made us both uncomfortable to the point of not being able to meet each other's eyes. In the end he said a shade violently that he would brew tea and empty the matroshka into the students' communal rubbish bin; and I went into the passage and made a long telephone call to Yuri Chulitsky.

17

Yuri picked me up outside the National Hotel in the wan light of nine o'clock on a Sunday morning in December.

There had been a fresh fall of snow during the night, and the roads had not yet been cleared, so that everything lay, like Malcolm, under a white shroud, and my spirits were as low as the air temperature.

The bright yellow car zoomed up like a golden cube, and I slid into the passenger seat beside Yuri, coughing violently.

"You have illness?" he said, letting in the clutch as if the cogs were made of titanium.

Death warmed up, I thought; but it wasn't the best of similes.

"You say," Yuri said, "you want very important comrade." The familiar accent rose above the engine noise. The bags under his eyes looked heavier and there was a slumped quality in his body. The upper lip rose convulsively two or three times, giving me the gleams of teeth. He lit a cigarette, one-handed, expert, dragging the smoke urgently into his lungs. There was a fine dampness on his forehead.

He had come dressed, as I had, in his neatest and most formal suit, with clean shirt, and tie. He was nervous, I thought; which made two of us.

"I get Major General," he said. "Is very high comrade."

I was impressed. I had asked him for a comrade of sufficient rank to be able to make decisions; although from what I'd known before and seen since I'd arrived, it had seemed that there was no one at all of that stature. The Soviet method seemed to be "action only after consultation," or "Until the committee's met, just keep saying *niet*." No official would make a decision on his own, for fear of its being wrong.

"Where are we going?" I asked.

"Architects' Circle."

So even the Major General wasn't sure enough to meet me upon official ground.

"He say," Yuri said, "you call him Major General. He not say his name."

"Very well."

We drove then without speaking. I coughed a bit and thought of the night gone past, much of which I had spent writing. It had been a laborious process physically, as I couldn't hold the pen properly. In the heat of battle I'd picked up a chair and gripped it hard to cut and thrust; but the anesthesia of hot blood was definitely missing in the cold hours after midnight. In the morning, when he had returned from Gudrun, I had given Stephen the explanatory sheets to read, while I put the telex, the formula, and the two pages of Malcolm's notebook into a large envelope.

He had read to the end, and looked at me speechlessly.

I smiled lopsidedly. "Ve have vays of taking out insurance."

I put the handwritten sheets into the envelope, and addressed it to the Prince, which raised Stephen's mobile eyebrows another notch. Then I looked at the walls and by common consent we went out and strolled down the passage.

"If the comrades should be so inhospitable as to cast me in the clink," I said, "you just beetle round to the embassy tomorrow morning and insist on seeing Oliver Waterman personally. Tell him the mountains will fall on his head if he doesn't send that envelope off pronto in the diplomatic bag."

Stephen said, "I know of a letter which was supposed to come to Moscow by diplomatic bag but ended up in Ulan Bator."

"So helpful."

"They say the Lubyanka goes down seven floors underground."

"Thanks very much."

"Don't go," he said.

"Come to lunch in the Intourist Hotel," I said. "They have pretty good ice cream."

Yuri drove round a white corner at speed and corrected the resultant skid with a practiced flick.

"Yuri," I said, "didn't you deliver a page of Malcolm's notebook to Mr. Kropotkin?"

The ash fell off his cigarette. His upper lip did a positive jig.

"I thought it must be you," I said. "You said you talked to him at Burghley, about buildings. If one could disentangle the writing on the back of that piece of paper with the help of blue filters, would it be notes about buildings?"

He was silent.

"I'll not speak of it," I said diffidently. "But I would like to know."

There was another of the long familiar pauses, and in the end he said, "I think paper not help," as if it excused his action in delivering it.

"It helped very much."

He moved his head in a way that I took to mean satisfaction, though I guessed that he still felt uneasy about allying himself with a foreigner. I wondered how I would feel if I were helping a Russian investigator and was not sure that anything he discovered might not be to the detriment of his own country. It made Yuri's dilemma most human, most understandable. And he was another, I thought, to whom I must do no harm.

Even at that hour of the day, there was a dragon on guard inside the door: short, dumpy, female, and stolid. She showed no pleasure at all in letting us through.

We shed our coats and hats. Everywhere in reception areas in Moscow there were acres of rails and hangers, and to every acre, a man in charge. We took our numbered disks and went through into the lofty ground-floor hall. Hall as in large meeting area, not as in entrance passage.

I had seen it two days earlier, passing through to the restaurant. Yellowish parquet floor, lightweight metal-and-plastic armchairs, and upright boards in loose groups, which divided the space like random screens. Pinned upon these with color-headed drawing pins were large mat-surfaced blown-up photographs of recent architectural activity.

Yuri led the way past one set of screens and arrived at an open central spot.

There were three of the light armchairs grouped round a low table; and on one of the chairs, a man.

He stood up as we approached.

He was of about my own height. Solid of body. Immensely well groomed. Dark hair sprinkled with gray, smoothly brushed back. About fifty, perhaps. Chin freshly shaved, everything immaculate. He wore understated spectacles and an elegantly cut business suit. The impression of power was instant and lasting.

"Major General," Yuri said deferentially, "this is Randall Drew."

We exchanged a few preliminary courtesies. He

spoke perfect English with only the ghost of an accent; and his voice was markedly urbane. Rudolph Hughes-Beckett, Soviet version, I thought.

"I would have asked you to come to my office," he said, "except that on Sundays it is not fully staffed, and perhaps here also we will be less interrupted."

He waved me to one of the chairs, and sat down again himself. Yuri delicately hovered. The major general suggested pleasantly, in English, that he should go and organize some coffee, and wait for it to be made.

He watched Yuri's obediently departing back view, and then turned to me.

"Please begin," he said.

"I was sent to Moscow," I said for openers, "by the British Foreign Office, and by the Prince." I gave the Prince his full title, because I guessed that even to a good son of the revolution the fact that I was on an errand for the monarch's cousin might pull some weight.

The Major General gave me a placid stare from uninformative gray eyes.

"Please continue."

"My brief was to find out if John Farringford—Lord Farringford, the Prince's brother-in-law—would be likely to be involved in a damaging scandal if he should come to ride in the Olympic Equestrian Games. There was some mention of a certain Alyosha. I was to find and interview this Alyosha, and see how the land lay. Er . . . am I making myself clear?"

"Perfectly," he said courteously. "Please go on."

"John Farringford had indiscreetly visited several rather perverted sexual entertainments in London with a German rider, Hans Kramer. This German subsequently died at the International Horse Trials, and people near him said that in his last few breaths he distinctly said, 'It is Alyosha.'" I paused. "For some reason that I cannot understand, a rumor arose that if Farringford came to Moscow, Alyosha would cause trouble. It was this rumor which led the Prince to ask me to look into things.''

"I follow,'' he said slowly.

"Well . . . I came,'' I said. A couple of coughs convulsively squeezed my chest. There was a well-known slow fever stoking up in there, but for that day at least it would be manageable. The next day, and the next and the next, would be a matter of luck. I girded up at least the mental loins.

I said, "I found I was not investigating a minor muck heap, but something a great deal different. I asked to see you today because what I discovered was a terrorist plot to disrupt the Olympic Games.''

He was not surprised, and Yuri, of course, must have told him that much in order to persuade him to meet me. Not surprised, but unconvinced.

"Not in the Soviet Socialist Republics,'' he said with flat disavowal. "We have no terrorists here. Terrorists would not come here.''

"I'm afraid they have.''

"It is impossible.''

I said, "If you encourage a plague, you must expect to catch it.''

His reaction to this unwise statement was an ominous stiffening of the spine and a raising of the chin, but at least we advanced into a territory in which he was prepared to face the possibility of pus on his own doorstep.

"I am telling you this so that you can avert a disaster in your capital,'' I said neutrally. "If you don't wish to hear me, I'll leave now.''

I didn't move, however, nor did he.

After a pause he said, "Please proceed.''

"The terrorists aren't Russians, I'll grant you that,'' I said. "And, so far as I know, you only have two here at present. But I think they live here all the time . . . and no doubt at the Games they would be reinforced.''

"Who are they?''

I took off my glasses, and squinted at them, and put them on again.

"If you keep a check on every foreigner who lives here in your city," I said, "you should seek out two men of between twenty and thirty years old, one of whom has today a badly bruised or broken wrist, and the other a damaged face. They may in addition have other bruises and cuts. They have sallow skins, dark eyes, and dark curling hair. I could if necessary identify them."

"Their names?"

I shook my head. "I don't know."

"And what could they hope to achieve?" he said, as if the whole idea was ridiculous. "It would be impossible for them to take hostages in this country."

"I don't think they mean to," I said. "The trouble with taking hostages is that it involves so much time. Time while the demands are delivered and discussed. Time, which means feeding the captors and the hostages, and sewage, and absolutely mundane things like that. The longer it goes on, the less chance there is of success. And the world has grown tired of these threats, and a great deal tougher. It's no longer seen as sense to release imprisoned terrorists to save innocent lives, when the released terrorists simply go out and kill a different lot of innocents. And I agree with you that a mass kidnapping here would be smartly stepped on by your comrades. But these men didn't mean to kidnap; they meant to kill."

He showed no emotion at all. "And how would they do this? And how would it help them?"

"Suppose," I said, "that they killed, for instance, Lord Farringford. Suppose they then said, If such and such a demand of ours is not met, a member of the French riding team will die, and a member of the German, and a member of the American. Or all the American team. Suppose they moved terrorism to a different level, where the hostages had no chance at all. No one would know who the hostages were until they were dead, and the supply of potential hostages would be the number of people at the Games."

He briefly thought it over and was not convinced.

"The theory is possible," he said. "But there is no suitable weapon. The murderers would quickly be caught."

"Their weapon is a liquid," I said. "A spoonful per person would be enough. It doesn't have to be drunk. It is deadly if it's just poured on the skin. And that's what makes the equestrian part of the Games so vulnerable, because it is there that the performers and the spectators mingle most freely."

A longer pause. I couldn't tell what he was thinking. I took a breath to go on, but he interrupted.

"Such liquids are extremely top secret and are kept in places of the utmost security," he said. "Are your supposed terrorists going to break into highly guarded laboratories to steal it?" The urbanity in his voice said that he thought this unlikely.

I pulled out of my pocket a copy I had made of the formula, and handed it to him.

"That liquid is neither top secret nor difficult to obtain," I said. "And it kills within ninety seconds. One of my supposed terrorists could tip a spoonful onto your bare hand without you thinking anything of it, and he'd be lost in the crowd before you could say you felt ill."

He unfolded the paper with the slightest of frowns, and read the list of words.

"What is it?" he said. "I am no chemist."

"Etorphine," I said, "That, I think is a morphine derivative. Etorphine, acepromazine and chlorocresol, those first three ingredients, would be an anesthetic. I am absolutely certain, though I haven't been able to check it in Moscow, as I could at home, that they make up a particularly useful anesthetic to use on animals.

"Anesthetic?" he said dubiously.

"It anesthetizes horses and farm animals," I said.

"But it is fatal for humans, in the tinest amounts."

"Why should anyone wish to use such a dangerous anesthetic?" he said.

"Because it is the best for the animals," I said. "I've seen it used twice. Once on one of my horses, and once on a bull. Both animals recovered quickly, with none of the complications we used to get."

"You've seen it. . . ."

"Yes. And each time, the vet prepared a syringe of a neutralizing agent for use on himself, if he should be so unfortunate as to scratch himself with the needle of the syringeful of anesthetic. He filled the neutralizing syringe before he even touched the vial with the anesthetic, and he wore rubber gloves. He told me that the excellence of the anesthetic for the animal's welfare was worth the precautions."

"But is this . . . rare?"

I shook my head. "More or less routine."

"You said . . ." He thought briefly. "You said 'scratch himself.' Does this mean this mixture would have to enter through a cut—a break in the skin? But you said it would be enough just to pour it."

"Yes," I said. "Well . . . most liquids don't penetrate the skin, and that doesn't either. Normally, all a vet does have to worry about is getting it into him through a cut or a scratch, except that if they do get a drop on them accidentally, even if there's no cut involved, they sluice it off with a bucket or so of water."

"Did your vet have the water ready also?"

"He did indeed."

"Please go on," he said.

"If you look at the formula again," I said, "you'll see that the next ingredient is dimethyl sulphoxide, and I actually do know what this is, because I've used it myself countless times on my horses."

"Another sort of anesthetic?"

"No. One uses it on sprains, bruises, sore shins—

on practically everything. It's a general-purpose embrocation.''

"But . . ."

"Well," I said, "its chief property is that it's a liquid which *does* penetrate the skin. It carries its active ingredients through to the tissues beneath.''

He gave me a grave comprehending stare.

I nodded. "So if one mixes the embrocation with the anesthetic, it will go clean through the skin into the bloodstream.''

He took a visibly deep breath, and said, "What happens exactly if this mixture invades the body?''

"Depressed breathing and cardiac arrest," I said. "Very quick. It looks like a heart attack.''

He looked pensively down at the paper.

"What does this last line mean?" he said. '' 'Antagonist naloxone.' ''

"An antagonist is a drug which works against another drug.''

"So naloxone is . . . an antidote?''

"I don't think it's the stuff they give animals to bring them back to consciousness," I said. "I think it's what the vet prepares as a precaution for himself.''

"Do you mean . . . you have to give the animal a second injection? The anesthetic does not simply wear off?''

"I don't know if it would in the end," I said, "but it's always reversed as soon as possible, as far as I know.''

"So naloxone is for humans.''

"Even terrorists wouldn't handle that stuff without protecting themselves," I said. "And I think," I went on tentatively, "that the amount of naloxone needed would depend on the amount of liquid one had absorbed. With animals, you see, the vet uses equal quantities of anesthetic and reviving agent. And sometimes a further injection of reviver is needed.''

For Malcolm, I thought, it had simply been a matter

of quantities. Too much killing liquid; not enough naloxone. His bad luck.

"All right," the Major General said, tucking the
formula away into an inner pocket. "Now please will
you tell me what led you to these conclusions."

I coughed because I couldn't help it, and took off
my glasses and put them on again because the outcome
of telling him might be not what I hoped.

"It started," I said, "at the International Horse
Trials which were held in England in September. At
that event, a British journalist, Malcolm Herrick, who
worked here in Moscow as a correspondent for *The
Watch,* persuaded Hans Kramer to steal a vet's case
of drugs when the vet came to attend some of the
horses. Malcolm Herrick received the anesthetic from
Kramer. He then mixed it with the embrocation,
which is easy to come by. And he then sold it to the
terrorists for fifty thousand dollars."

"For *what?*" The Major General showed the first
sign of uncontrolled surprise.

"Yes. It was not a matter of ideology, but of hard
cash. Someone, after all, sells weapons to the terrorists. They don't actually manufacture their own guns.
Fifty thousand, you are no doubt thinking, was a great
deal too much for an easily accessible commodity. The
thing was, of course, that Herrick didn't tell them
what it was. I daresay he made out that it was, in fact,
one of your top-secret things from maximum security
laboratories. Anyway, they paid for it, but not without
a demonstration. . . . A sort of trial run."

I waited for the Major General to comment, but
nothing came.

"They used a little of it on Hans Kramer," I said.
"Herrick no doubt suggested he should be the test
victim because if he was dead he couldn't tell anyone
he had given the stuff to Herrick."

"Given? Didn't he *sell* it to Herrick?"

"No. Kramer sympathized with terrorists. He did
it for the cause."

The Major General slightly compressed his lips. "Go on."

"Kramer's death was adjudged a heart attack. Herrick returned to Moscow, and so did the two terrorists. I think this may mean that he knew them here—met them here, perhaps—and that *because* he knew them, he thought up the scheme to sell them a compound he had at one time heard of by chance. And that is where everything would have stood until the Olympics; a nice little time bomb ticking away in the dark. Except that people started asking questions about Alyosha."

"At which point you came to Moscow."

I nodded. Coughed. Wished the coffee would come. Swallowed with a dry mouth, and continued with the dicey bits.

"Since then, Herrick has tried to persuade me to go home, both with words and trying to knock me over with a motorized horsecar. The two terrorists have also had a go, and I'm still here only because I've been lucky. But sometime yesterday they discovered that they'd paid a great deal of money for a very cheap product, and they became extremely angry."

I took a much needed deep breath. "Herrick had told them to come to my room at the Intourist Hotel and finish me off properly. I think he meant them to do it by mechanical means—bashing my head in, and so forth. But when they came, they brought a good deal of the liquid in a small jar, perhaps all they had, and whether they meant any of it for me or not, they threw nearly all of it at Herrick."

His mouth slowly opened and shut again.

I plowed on. "I had two friends with me, besides Herrick. We fought off the terrorists—which is why one of them has a damaged wrist and the other a damaged face, as well as other minor injuries—and they ran away."

"Malcolm Herrick . . . is dead?"

"We called a doctor," I said. "The doctor believes it was a heart attack. Unless someone does an extremely thorough autopsy, that's how it will stand."

The very faintest of smiles crossed his pale face. He rubbed a hand slowly round his jawline, and watched me with assessing eyes.

"How have you learned all this?" he said.

"I've listened."

"To Russian people? Or all to foreigners?"

"Everyone who has spoken to me has been concerned that Russia should not be shamed by terrorism at the Games."

"You speak like a diplomat," he said.

The chin rubbing went on for a bit. Then he said, "And Alyosha. Did you in the end find this Alyosha?"

"Mm," I said. "Hans Kramer and Malcolm Herrick both said 'Alyosha' in horror before they died. They both knew what they were dying of . . . and I think they had given it that name. A sort of code name, so that they could talk of it conveniently. I couldn't find Alyosha, because Alyosha is not a person. It's the liquid. Alyosha is the way of death."

18

Yuri Chulitsky drove me back to the Intourist and actually dropped me outside the door. He shook my left hand emotionally, and gave me several pats on the shoulder. And then, with a great air of having a burden well shed, he drove away.

He had been visibly pleased when the Major General had shaken his hand on parting, and on the way back to the hotel he had stopped the car abruptly by the curb and put the hand brake on with a jerk.

"He said is good I ask him to meet you," he said. "Was correct decision."

"Great," I said, and meant it.

"Now I keep bargain."

I looked at him in surprise.

"You help my country. I tell you about Alyosha."

I was puzzled. "Tell me what?"

"I tell peoples, many peoples, is not good Lord Farringford come to Moscow. I say, in Moscow, Alyosha is waiting. Alyosha is not good peoples."

"You told people . . . people in England?"

"*Da*. Peoples tell me, Hans Kramer die, it is Alyosha, Hans Kramer is a bad man, is friend of Lord Farringford. Is bad Lord Farringford come to Moscow. So I say to peoples . . . Alyosha is bad peoples. Alyosha is trouble if Lord Farringford come."

I shook my head slowly in amazement.

"But why, Yuri? Why didn't you want Lord Farringford to come to Moscow?"

He took a long time to answer. The longest pause of all. The lip went up and down six times. He lit a cigarette and took several deep drags. And at last he gave birth to his treason.

"Is not good . . . comrades use Lord Farringford. Not good we follow him . . . use him in bad things. I feel shame for comrades who do this. I feel shame . . . for my country."

Stephen and Ian were sitting in the foyer, waiting and looking glum.

"My God," Stephen said, seeing me standing before them. "They've let him go!" His face lit into instant good spirits. "Where are the handcuffs?"

"Being debated, I should think."

There was still nowhere private to talk, since we couldn't trust my new room, so we simply transferred to the end of the line of seats along the foyer wall, and fell silent if anyone came close.

"What's happening?" Ian said.

"With luck, nothing much. I don't think they'll want to advertise terrorist activity in Moscow, not if they can help it. From your knowledge of this place, would you think the comrades would hush up a murder? Would they be allowed to? I had to tell the big noise that Malcolm was bumped off."

Ian said, "Easier here than anywhere else, my old son. If it suits them to say our pal died of a heart attack, they'll say it."

"Let's hope it suits," I said fervently.

"Look . . ." Ian said. "Stephen has told me all you wrote last night. You must think me a poor dumb cluck not to have put all this together myself. But when I looked into it, I got nowhere."

"But then I had the password," I said, smiling slightly.

"Alyosha?" he said, puzzled.

"No. Horse."

"The brotherhood of the saddle," Stephen said sardonically. "It opens the most private doors all round the world."

"And don't you scoff," I said. "Because you're right."

"There's just one thing we want to know," Ian said, his calm, unchanging face showing no sign of the previous day's ravages. "And that is, why were you so utterly certain that Malcolm was at the heart of things? I mean . . . it was all so circumstantial, but you were quite sure."

"Um . . ." I said. "It was nothing conclusive in itself. It was really just one more circumstance—and there were already so many. It was the page from his notebook, which Yuri Chulitsky sent to Kropotkin. You remember what it looked like? All doodles. So when do you doodle? When you're listening, or waiting. When you're waiting for an answer on the telephone. If you remember, near the bottom of the page there were some letters and numbers, 'DEP PET 1855' and 'K's C 1950.' Well . . . they meant nothing much to me at first sight, but yesterday afternoon, while we were rolling around Moscow, I thought, suppose Malcolm doodled because he was *waiting* for those numbers . . . and then we passed a metro station and I thought of trains. And there it damn well was, staring me in the face. 'DEP PET 1855' meant 'Depart Peterborough 1855 hours,' and 'K's C 1950' meant arrive King's Cross at 1950.' He had been ringing up the timetable inquiries to find out."

"But what's so blinding about that?" Stephen said.

"Peterborough is the main-line station for Burghley."

"So," Ian said slowly, seeing the point, "when Boris overheard what he did on the train from Burghley to London, he was listening to Malcolm, who was selling his goods to his friends."

"It seemed possible," I said. "In fact, it seemed extremely likely. And on that same sheet of paper, probably while still waiting for the timetable people to answer, because they take ages sometimes, Malcolm penciled in Johnny Farringford as a star possibility for Alyosha. I don't know how well he knew Johnny, but he didn't like him. He referred to him as a shit."

"But why on earth should he give such an incriminating piece of paper to anyone else?" Stephen said. "He was really stupid."

I shook my head. "It was only by the merest chance that it reached me and meant anything. To him, it was only a doodle. He scrawled over it. It was just a piece of rubbish to be thrown away, or given to someone who wanted some scrap paper for making notes."

"How's your cough?" Stephen asked.

"Bloody awful. Let's have some lunch."

Because there were three of us, we sat at a different table, the next one along from the Wilkinsons and Frank.

Ian eyed Frank benignly and asked me quietly if the status in that area was still quo.

"Does he know I know?" I asked. "No, he doesn't. Does he know you know? Who can tell?"

"Does he know I know you know they know she knows you know?" Stephen asked.

Mrs. Wilkinson leaned across the gap. "Are you going home on Tuesday, like us?" she asked. "Dad and I won't be sorry to be back, will we, Dad?"

Dad looked as if he couldn't wait.

"I hope so," I said.

Natasha brought the soaring eyebrows and a fixed smile and said I hadn't kept my promise to tell her where I was going.

Nothing, it seemed, had changed; except that it was Stephen who ate my meat.

After lunch the three of us went up to my room for them to collect the coats and hats they had left there just before, and while we were debating when next to telephone and next to meet, there was a sharp knock on the door.

"Christ, not again," Ian said, instinctively putting a hand to his bruised head.

I went to the door and said, "Who is it?"

No reply.

Stephen came and said, "Who is it?" in Russian.

This time there was an answer, but to Stephen it seemed unwelcome.

"He said the major general sent him."

I let down the drawbridge. Outside in the corridor stood two large men with stolid faces, flat uniform caps, and long greatcoats. From the look on Stephen's face, I guessed that the posse had come for the outlaw.

One of them handed me a sealed envelope addressed to Randall Drew. Inside, there was an extremely brief handwritten note, saying simply, "Accompany my officers," and below that, "Major General."

Stephen, looking round-eyed and a little pale, said, "I'll wait here. We'll both wait here."

"No. You'd better go. I'll telephone."

"If you don't," he said, "first thing in the morning, I take the goods to Oliver Waterman. Is that right?"

"Uh-huh."

I pulled hat and coat from the wardrobe and put them on. The two large unsmiling men unsmilingly waited. We all walked along, in a cluster of five, and went down in the lift without saying very much.

During our progress through the foyer there was a certain amount of drawing aside of the skirts, and several frightened glances. The bulk and intent of my two escorts was unmistakable. No one wanted to be involved in my disaster.

They had come in a large black official car, with a uniformed driver. They gestured to me to sit in the back. I had a parting view of Ian's and Stephen's strained-looking faces as they stood side by side on the pavement, and then the car set off and made unerringly for Derzhinsky Square.

The long façade of the Lubyanka loomed along one side of it, looking like a friendly insurance company building if one didn't know better. The car, however, swept past its huge sides and pulled up in front of the big building next door, which was pale blue, with white painted scrolls, and would on any other day have looked rather pretty.

My escorts opened the car door for me to get out, and walked beside me into the building. Inside, Lubyanka or not, it was clearly no jolly children's home. We marched at a sturdy pace down wide institutional corridors, and came to a halt outside an unmarked door. One of my escorts knocked, opened the door, and stood aside for me to go in. With a dry mouth and galloping pulse, I went.

It was a comfortable, old-fashioned office, with a lot of dark polished wood and glass-fronted cupboards. A desk. A table. Three or four chairs. And by the window, holding back a dark curtain to look out at the snowy street, the Major General.

He turned, and walked toward me, and held out his hand. I was so relieved that I automatically gave him my right one in return, and tried not to wince when he grasped it. I wondered if he knew he'd just given me one of the most shaking half hours of my life.

"Come," he said. "I have something to show you."

He led me through a door in the back wall of the office, into a narrower secondary corridor. After a few yards we came to a door which opened onto a staircase, leading down. We descended to the next floor, and went along another, grittier corridor.

We stopped at a totally smooth metal door. The Major General pressed a button in the wall beside it, and the door swung open. He went into the room in front of me, and beckoned to me to follow.

I stepped into a square, bare room, brightly lit.

There were two armed policemen standing guard in there, and two other men, sitting on stools, with their arms fastened behind their backs.

If I was surprised to see them, it was nothing to their reaction on seeing me. One of them spat, and the other said something which seemed to shake even the KGB.

"These are the men?" the Major General said.

"Yes."

I looked into the faces remembered from the Aragvi restaurant. Into the eyes remembered from Gorky Street and under the bridge. Into the souls that had killed Hans Kramer and Malcolm Herrick.

One seemed slightly older, and had a drooping mustache. His lips were a little retracted, showing a gleam of teeth clenched in a travesty of a grin; and even in this place he exuded a bitter hostility.

The other had taut skin over sharp bones, and the large eye sockets of so many fanatics. Across the eyebrow and down the side of his face there was a scarlet cut, and there was a split swelling on his lower lip.

"Which of them killed Herrick?" said the Major General.

"The one with the mustache."

"He says his wrist is broken," the Major General remarked conversationally. "They were waiting at the airport. We had no trouble finding them. They speak very little English, by the way."

"Who are they?" I said.

"They are journalists." He sounded surprised at this discovery. "Tarek Zanetti"—pointing to the man with the mustache—"and Mehmet Sarai, with the cut."

Their names meant nothing to me, even if they were the ones they were given at birth, which might be doubtful.

"They have been living in the same compound as Herrick," the Major General said. "He could have seen them easily every day."

"Do they belong to something like the Red Brigades?" I asked.

"Something new, we think," he said. "A breakaway group. But we have yet to make more than the most preliminary interrogation. Immediately they arrived here, I sent for you. However, I will show you something. When we searched the bags they were attempting to leave with, we found this." He took a letter out of his pocket, and gave it to me. I unfolded it, but it was typewritten in a language I didn't know even by sight.

I shook my head and began to hand it back.

"Read lower down."

I did as he said, and came across the familiar words *etorphine . . . acepromazine . . . chlorocresol . . . dimethyl sulphoxide*.

"It's a copy of a report from a chemical company," he said, "sending an analysis asked for by your friend with the mustache. It seems to have been delivered to him yesterday."

"So they wanted to find out what they'd bought."

"It would seem so." He took back the letter and restored it in his pocket. "That is all," he said. "Your positive identification of these men was required, but nothing more. You are at liberty to go back to England when you wish." He hesitated slightly, then continued, "It is believed that you will be discreet."

"I will," I said, and hesitated in my turn. "But . . . these two will have colleagues . . . and that liquid does exist."

"It may be necessary," he said heavily, "to search every spectator at the entrances."

"There's a quicker way."

"What is that?"

"It will be summer. . . . Watch for anyone wearing gloves. If they have rubber gloves underneath, arrest them."

He gazed at me from behind his glasses and rubbed his chin, and slowly said, "I see why they sent you."

"And gallons of naloxone at every turn. . . ."

"We will work out many precautions."

I looked across for the last time at the naked hate-filled faces of international terrorism, and thought about alienation and the destructive steps which led there.

The intensifying to anger of the natural scorn of youth for the mess their elders had made of the world. The desire to punish violently the objects of scorn. The death of love for parents. The permanent sneer for all forms of authority. The frustration of not being able to scourge the despised majority. And after that, the deeper, malignant distortions. . . . The self-delusion that one's feelings of inadequacy were the fault of society, and that it was necessary to destroy society in order to feel adequate. The infliction of pain and fear, to feed the hungry ego. The total surrender of reason to raw emotion, in the illusion of being moved by a sort of divine rage. The choice of an unattainable end, so that the violent means could go on and on. The addictive orgasm of the act of laying waste.

"What are you thinking?" the Major General said.

"That they are self-indulgent." I turned away from them with a sense of release. "It is easier to smash than to build."

"They are pigs," he said, with disdain.

"What will you do with them?"

But that was one question he had no intention of answering directly. He simply said, with polished blandness, "Their newspapers must find other writers."

The Watch, I thought, would be facing the same problem; and an old irrelevant piece of information floated to the surface.

"Ulrike Meinhof was a journalist," I said.

19

The flight home was met at Heathrow at four in the afternoon by one of Hughes-Beckett's minions, who whisked me off to what he called a debriefing and I called a bloody nuisance.

I coughed my way into the mandarin's office and protested. I got an insincere apology and a small glass of sherry, when the only thing likely to bring me back to animation was a quadruple Scotch.

"Can't it wait until tomorrow?" I said, feeling feverish.

"The Prince wants you to meet him at Fontwell Park races in the morning."

"I thought of staying in bed."

"What's wrong with your arm?" he said, disregarding this frivolous statement and eyeing Stephen and Gudrun's farewell attempt at a restful sling for the journey.

"Fingers got hammered. But not sickled." I must be light-headed, I thought. Light-headed from the up-surge of relief at being back where liberty still poked up a few persistent tendrils. Light-headed at the sight of people smiling in the street. At Christmas trees and bright lights and cornucopias of shops. One could spurn the affluent society and seek the simple life if one wanted to; the luxury lay in being able to choose.

Hughes-Beckett eased himself in his comfortable office chair and studied the back of his hand.

"And how—ah—did it go?" he said.

I told him more or less exactly what I had told the major general. He stopped looking at his hands and came to mental life in a very positive and alert way, quite different from his habitual air of boredom.

I talked and coughed, and coughed and talked, and he gave me another and slightly larger sherry.

"So there you are," I said finally. "As far as I could tell, there will be a great deal of hush over the whole scene. And as for Johnny Farringford . . . well, I got no definite assurances, but I doubt if after this the comrades would consider him a suitable prospect. So from that point of view I think it would be safe for him to go . . . but it's of course up to you and the Prince."

I stood up. I really felt most unwell. Nothing new, however. The story of my life.

He came with me all the way to the front door and saw me off in an official car, which represented a radical rethink on his part of the usefulness of horses.

I found that meeting the Prince at Fontwell Park races involved lunch wih him, the Princess, Johnny Farringford, the chairman of the racecourse, sundry stewards and assorted ladies, all in the glass-walled corner box at the top of the stands, looking down over the green turf.

There was a lot of champagne and civilized chat, which on other days would have pleased me well enough; but the shadows of Moscow still sat close at my shoulder, and I thought of the fear of Boris and Evgeny and the doubts and caution of Yuri and Misha

and Kropotkin. I should be glad to hear in time from
Ian and Stephen that none of them had come to
harm.

I had spent a toss-and-turn night in a hotel and hired
a car and driver to take me to the races. Practically
every remedy in the plastic box had been pressed into
service, to only moderate avail. It was a bore to drag
around with lungs filling up like sumps and every
breath an effort, but I'd ridden in races in that state
once or twice in my foolish life, so why fret at some
gentle spectating. Bits of lines of the Scottish ballad
of the dying Lord Randal, with whom I'd identified
heavily as a child, ran from a long habit in my mind,
more as a sort of background music than as organized
thought, but now with an added new meaning.

. . . *make my bed soon,*
For I'm weary wi' hunting, and fain would lie doon.

"Randall," the Prince said, "we must talk."

We talked in short snatches through the afternoon,
standing alone on the stewards' balcony between the
races, using the times when everyone else went down
to look at the horses in the parade ring.

. . . *make my bed soon.* . . .

"There were two plots involving Johnny," I said.
"Two?"

"Mm. Being who he is, he's a natural target. He
always will be. It's something that needs to be faced."

I told him bit by bit about the terrorists, and about
the identity of Alyosha. It all shocked him a great deal
more deeply than it had those two wily games players
Hughes-Beckett and the Major General.

"Dreadful. Dreadful," he said.

"There was also," I said eventually, "some question of the KGB setting him up."

I explained about the pornography.

"Johnny?" The Prince looked surprised and most
displeased. "The bloody fool. Doesn't he realize that
is just what the press are always looking for?"

"If he was warned, sir—"

"Warned?" He looked grim. "You can safely leave that to me."

I'd like to be a fly on the wall, I thought.

A memory struck him. "But look here, Randall," he said. "What about those two men who attacked Johnny on the day he came to my house? The day he crashed into your car. Where did they come from? Were they . . . the terrorists?"

"No. Um . . . as a matter of fact, they didn't exist."

He gave me a right royal stare. "Are you meaning to say that Johnny was *lying?*"

Yes, I was. I said, however, more temperately, "I think he invented them, certainly."

"But he couldn't have done! He was badly beaten up."

I shook my head. "He was injured from crashing into my car."

"There you are, Randall," the Prince said with exasperation. "He only crashed because he was already hurt."

"Er . . ." I said, "I think, sir, that he crashed because he fainted at the sight of blood. I think . . . he cut his finger to make it bleed . . . to put some blood on his face to back up his story of being attacked . . . and when he got to the front of your house he simply passed out. He had his foot on the accelerator, and his car kept on going."

"You can't be right!"

"You could ask him, sir."

. . . *make my bed soon.* . . .

"But why, Randall? Why ever should he invent such a story?"

"He passionately wants to go to the Olympics. He didn't want people poking into his relationship with Hans Kramer, which was a little less innocent than he would have us believe, but not really so terrible. I would guess he was afraid all the same that if you found out, you might not buy him the new horse . . . so he invented two men and a beating up to persuade

you not to send me to look for Alyosha. I quite believe
that Johnny himself knew of no scandal, but he didn't
know what I might find out about Hans. He didn't
want me to look, that was all."

"But," he said, loking bewildered, "it had the opposite effect. After that I was more sure than ever that
the rumors must be looked into."

I watched Johnny weaving his way with the Princess through the crowds returning to the stands for
the next race. His crisp red curls gleamed like copper
in the December air.

I sighed. "He's a great rider, sir."

The Prince slid me a sideways glance. "We all do
dumb things from time to time, Randall. Is that it?"

"Yes, sir."

. . . *and fain would lie doon.*

"Why are you so sure they weren't your terrorists?"

"Because from Johnny's account they weren't at all
the same sort of people. Johnny said they spoke English and were ordinary British men, which the terrorists were not."

Johnny and the Princess climbed the steps and came
up onto the balcony. The Princess was untroubled,
but Johnny had been uncomfortable with me all day.

I said mildly, "Johnny, how well did you know
Malcolm Herrick?"

"Who?"

"Herrick. Journalist. Wrote for *The Watch.*"

"Oh, him." Johnny's face said it was an unwelcome
memory. "He was at Burghley. Always hanging
around Hans. Er . . . Hans Kramer." He hesitated,
shrugged, and went on. "I didn't like the fellow. Why?
What's he done? He called me 'sport' all the time.
Can't say I liked it, what? I told him to piss off.
Haven't seen him since."

It seemed a bit much to put a man at the top of the
death list for saying piss off, but Malcolm had done
it. "Sport" and "piss off" . . . Next stop. Alyosha.

For I'm weary wi' hunting, and fain . . .

"Cards on the table, Johnny," the Prince said. "Were you beaten up by those two chaps, or weren't you?"

The Farringford expression went through a lot of motions in very quick time. He started to nod and say yes, and then switched his gaze suddenly to my face. Correctly read my skepticism; realized I had told the Prince; changed his plea instantaneously to guilty, and finished with a sheepish little-boy grin.

The Prince compressed his lips and shook his head. "Grow up, Johnny," he said.

Emma came for the weekend, two days later, silver and brittle and ajangle with tensions.

"How boring of you to be in bed," she said. "I'm lousy at mopping fevered brows."

She moved restlessly round the room, getting rid of electric energy in purposeless fidgeting.

"You're wheezing like an old granny," she said. "And spitting. That's a really disgusting disease."

"I thought you liked facing life's nitty-gritties."

"Why did you want me to come?" she said, rearranging the brushes on my dressing chest. "You usually tell me to stay away when you're ill."

"I wanted your company."

"Oh." She seemed disconcerted, gave me a quick sharp glance like a startled bird, and went out of the room. Friday night, I thought ruefully, was too soon for truth.

She returned in an hour, bringing a tray; bringing supper. Soup, bread, fruit, cheese, and a bottle of wine.

"They seemed to be lying around," she said defensively. "So I thought I might as well lug them up here."

"Great."

We ate in reasonable peace, and she asked about Moscow.

"You might like it there," I said, peeling a tangerine. "Mind you, over there the life you chose to lead here wouldn't be an act of rebellion, but a necessity forced upon you."

"I hate you sometimes."

"If you ever get tired of your shop," I said, "I could give you another job here."

"What as?"

"Domestic servant. Nanny. Cook. Laundry maid. General all-purpose dogsbody. Farmhand. Wife."

"It wouldn't work."

I looked at the shining fall of platinum hair and at the finality in the delicate, well-loved, determined face. The patterns of youth couldn't be changed. One became a rebel, a romantic, a puritan, a bigot, a hypocrite, a saint, a crusader, a terrorist. . . . One became it young and stayed it forever. She could never return to the well-off, well-ordered country life she had kicked her way out of. She would revisit is uneasily for weekends as long as I pleased her, but one Monday morning she would drive off and not come back.

I might regret, might feel lost and lonely without her, but she was depressingly right.

As a long-term prospect, it wouldn't work.

In the New Year edition of *Horse and Hound* I read that the Germans had sold one of their best young horses to Lord Farringford, who would be training it in the hope of being considered for the Olympic Games.

73

Mystery, Christie Style

Starring
HERCULE POIROT,
*Agatha Christie's best-
loved, best-dressed,
bestselling detective.
No one handles bodies better.*

Get these Hercule Poirot murder mysteries—
find out what stylish sleuthing is all about!
From Pocket Books.

_____ 41492 ABC MURDERS $2.50
_____ 41888 CAT AMONG THE PIGEONS $2.50
_____ 42879 THE CLOCKS $2.50
_____ 43461 CURTAIN $2.50
_____ 82908 EVIL UNDER THE SUN $2.50
_____ 42512 FUNERALS ARE FATAL $2.50
_____ 41595 HALLOWE'EN PARTY $2.50
_____ 41594 HICKORY, DICKORY DEATH $2.50
_____ 43201 MRS. MCGINTY'S DEAD $2.50
_____ 42513 MURDER OF ROGER ACKROYD $2.50
_____ 42212 MURDER ON THE ORIENT EXPRESS $2.50
_____ 42853 PERIL AT END HOUSE $2.50
_____ 41854 THIRD GIRL $2.50

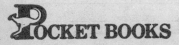

POCKET BOOKS